FriesenPress

One Printers Way
Altona, MB R0G 0B0
Canada

www.friesenpress.com

Copyright © 2022 by Kevin H Johnson
First Edition — 2022

Illustrated by Catherine Donnelly

All rights reserved.

No part of this publication may be reproduced in any form, or by any means, electronic or mechanical, including photocopying, recording, or any information browsing, storage, or retrieval system, without permission in writing from FriesenPress.

ISBN
978-1-03-913282-5 (Hardcover)
978-1-03-913281-8 (Paperback)
978-1-03-913283-2 (eBook)

1. FICTION, FAIRY TALES, FOLK TALES, LEGENDS & MYTHOLOGY

Distributed to the trade by The Ingram Book Company

THE TALES OF RITHANON

KEVIN H JOHNSON

Table of Contents

Prologue	9
Visvaldis the Dragon	13
The Sword Master	25
Gabby Gail and the Gadget Shop	33
The Adventure of Bluebell and Lily-Green	46
The King of Greed	60
Holy Warriors	65
Bangar and Grundel	69
The Winter Rose	87
The Jewel of Fortune	115
The Tragic Tale of Uthgrail, the Mad	124
The Gold and The Dragon	129
Clovis and the Village of Sword Makers	133
A Hero's Tale	146
In the Dark of Shadows	169
Brave Knights	175
The Wizard on the Hill	182
Epilogue	190
A Little Mythology	193
Special Thanks To…	196
Special Dedication	197
About the Author	198

Prologue

It was early one lovely morning that I awoke after a festive evening of playing music, dancing, and telling stories. I gathered my belongings and left the scenic and serene town of Ravenwood. Ravenwood sat right in the middle of the kingdom called Edingal and was a bustling place full of business and escapades. I would say, most folks there were relaxed and content. Nothing bad ever really happened in Ravenwood—most of the time!

I made my way west through the charming countryside, towards a friend whom I had not visited in some time. His home was settled between the villages of Cotter and Burow, on the Western Road. He lived near a small town called Willow Haven that belonged to the gentle halfling folk.

While sitting upon my horse, playing my lute, I enjoyed the warm gentle rays of the midmorning sun. The countryside was enchanting with its rolling hills, charming woodlands, and fields of farmland. There were low, smooth-peaked mountains all around, not rugged like the mountains in other parts of the world.

After travelling for not too long, I had arrived at my destination: a giant, knobby and hollow oak tree house. Well, the tree was more than just a big tree house; it was also a pub. The pub and home were owned by my friend, the dwarf Denmar Iron-Helm.

The sign above the pub's door read: "The Gnarly Oak." A halfling in a straw hat sat on the outside porch, smoking his pipe. His belly revealed, by my guess, his fondness for fine food and drink. He suddenly greeted me by raising his pipe without a word said. I greeted the halfling back, and politely asked, "Morning, my friend. Is Denmar in this fine day?"

"Why I believe he is. I just put in an order for my first mug of fresh ale," the halfling responded.

"Aaaah, drinking early I see," I said to him.

"Early? It's almost noon! I usually start much earlier. After my morning pint, I always kick back with my late morning tea just before lunch. But today I slept in and had to skip most of my morning pleasantries. So, my pint of ale will just have to do," he explained.

I chuckled to myself. "I see. Might that I join you if I knew your name, my fine fellow."

"My name is Gerald Wobble-Stick; and yes, you may join me if you wish," said the halfling.

"Pleased to meet you, Gerald. My name is…"

"His name is Valdevo Baudelaire, the travelling minstrel and storyteller," interrupted Denmar, who came out of the door. "Well met, my good friend; it is good to see you once again," Denmar added.

"Well met, Denmar. I am so glad I dropped by. I trust that you're well?"

"I'm well as always and well enough to hear one of your entertaining stories, Valdevo," chimed the dwarf.

"Well, of course, but first, I would like to partake in a cup of tea," I requested.

"Any particular brand or just regular tea?" asked Denmar.

"Oh, whatever Mr. Wobble-Stick usually has, since he has replaced his teatime with pint time," I replied.

"Well, then, orange pekoe it is, with a dash of cinnamon," said Denmar. "I will bring it out right away," he added.

"Splendid, my old friend. How kind of you."

Just as Denmar was getting my tea and another pint for Gerald, two farm kids, a boy and a girl, showed up rather winded from running. They seemed glad to greet me.

"Ahoy there, Mr. Bard," they said to me.

"Ahoy there, my young friends. It's a fine morning to exercise," I responded with amusement.

"No, no, we just saw you pass casually through Burow, strumming and singing along the way. We recognized you. You're the famous travelling minstrel and storyteller," said the boy, who appeared to be almost fully grown.

"We were trying to catch up to you," said the young lady, not far off in age from the young lad.

"Well, I see. I was unaware I was so well known," I said, flattered.

"I guess fame has its perks," Gerald chimed in, just as Denmar came out and handed him his second mug of ale.

"He is well known for telling good stories, my halfling friend. Maybe he will tell us one today," responded Denmar as he handed me my tea.

"Yes, yes, that's why we came," said the boy, all excited.

"We want to hear a few of your famous tales of the past," the girl added.

I settled down at one of the small tables nestled among the big roots of Denmar's giant, knobbly oak tree. "Well, since I have an audience before me and I'm in no great hurry, I could tell the odd tale," I said thoughtfully.

The two youths responded in excitement.

"But first I want to know who my audience is," I said.

"I'm Quinton," said the boy.

"And I'm Aveline," said the girl.

"Well, pleased to meet you both, my name is—"

"Your name is Valdevo Baudelaire, the most widely known bard in all of Rithanon," interrupted the girl.

I chuckled merrily and said to them, "Well, it's an honour to meet you both; and this is Mr. Denmar the dwarf, and my friend." The kids seemed to already know him despite my introduction.

"Hello to you, kids," said Denmar, smiling. "I've watched both of you grow up in the neighbourhood; and since you're going to be sticking around for a while, listening to adventurous stories and tales of old, I'm going to go prepare some lunch for everyone. And I might as well get Mr. Gerald Wobble-Stick his third pint," grumbled the dwarf.

So, we all settled in with some lunch, and I tuned my lute for the odd hymn that accompanies some of the tales I tell. I thought about where to start. "OK, where do I begin? What do you want to hear?"

Quinton and Aveline put in a list of requests before I even tuned my lute.

"Give the man a minute or two," interjected Gerald, who seemed to want to hear the odd story himself.

I laughed heartily and said to my attentive audience, "There are a great many tales on Rithanon—stories of adventure, of great battles, sword fighting, love and darkness. Tales of dragons, fairies, and mysterious things brought about by the gods. Kings contesting for rule, and powerful wizards of note. There are a great many events and myths of legend I could tell. But let us start with a simple hymn first before I indulge you in the tales of Rithanon."

I strummed my lute and began!

*Come listen to my stories told
of acts of valour and warriors bold,
with legends of heroes and villains dire,
the power of magic and dragon fire,
of mythical creatures that roam the land,
of artifacts, wealth, and treasures grand,
of shadows cold and lore of old—
the strength of light and nature's hand.*

Visvaldis the Dragon

A long time ago in a magical land, there lived a dragon, the largest of his kind. He was not a mean, nasty dragon, but had a good soul and a fair heart. This bronze-coloured dragon's name was Visvaldis.

Visvaldis liked doing what most dragons do, which was hunting for food, collecting treasure and magical things, along with lots of sleep time. and like most dragons, he preferred to be unbothered. He liked to be left to himself, just being a dragon.

One day, Visvaldis woke up from a nice, long slumber—longer than most denizens of the world. He stretched himself and yawned, then shook his head to wake himself. In the process, he hit his head on the ceiling of his lair. Visvaldis cursed but brushed it off quickly because he knew today was no ordinary day, but one of high activity.

"It's going to be a busy day," Visvaldis said to himself. "And moving to a new lair is no small task. This one is a little cramped, and I am tired of being stuffed in a hole. Too many times I have smashed my head on the ceiling," he grumbled.

Visvaldis looked back at his loot and treasure hoard as he left his cramped lair in search of a more accommodating space for a dragon of his size, which was large, exceptionally large!!!

My treasure pile will have to stay for now, he thought. "It will be safe. Nobody would dare steal from Visvaldis," he rumbled dangerously, then muttered, "It's magically warded anyway."

The dragon's pile of treasure was built from bands of thieves and goblins who had stolen from others and then passed through his territory. It was the price for passage, and Visvaldis was holding the wealth for safe keep—until the original owners of the loot had come back to claim it. Though he doubted they would, Visvaldis grew fond of his treasure hoard. He was a dragon after all, and he loved gold, gems, and magic.

After a couple days of scouting, Visvaldis found a rather cozy and promising lair situated in some mountains just east of the Kingdom of Toril. Toril was situated between the kingdoms of Edingal and Canora, not too far from his original lair, so moving to this new home would not be as difficult as he presumed. The lair was cozy for one of his size, and after transporting his treasure, Visvaldis happily and quickly settled in.

Not far off, in the Kingdom of Toril, King Esmour sat on his throne, stroking his greying beard in deep thought. His scouts had reported that a big dragon had settled in his kingdom, and this news troubled him.

"How long has the dragon been there?" Esmour asked Sir Palmer, his most skilled and experienced knight and captain-at-arms.

"Not long, Your Highness. The dragon has just settled in this week," Sir Palmer answered. "I have scouts and men-at-arms monitoring him as we speak, your majesty"

"Good!" said King Esmour. "Tell me, Palmer, what kind of dragon is it?"

Sir Palmer shifted nervously and responded in a slightly broken speech. "Um… um… a large dragon, my king, an exceptionally large dragon as far as dragons go." In his best efforts to hide his discomfort, he continued, "And its a male, I believe. He's a bronzy, brownish hue.".

Sensing Sir Palmer's unease, the king sternly looked at him. "Don't be so frightened," he commanded. "We've dealt with dragons before," he scoffed.

"Um, not like this one," Palmer said delicately with a half-smile. "His name is Visvaldis, and he's originally from the Sylthanian western mountains of South Rithanon. The dragon holds a fierce reputation," the knight warned.

"Fierce or not, we must deal with him!" insisted the king. "Keep monitoring the dragon," Esmour instructed. "I command that you convince him to move on out of my kingdom. He is a danger to my taxing enterprise and dragon's have a fierce love for gold and treasure."

"Yes, my king," Palmer obeyed. Then he bowed and took his leave.

King Esmour had a tax law that taxed his people every month, and any merchant or traveller that came through his kingdom had to pay a tax as well. It was unjustly unfair, as the amount he demanded was far too much. Most people could not pay the taxes the King of Toril had demanded and enforced. Those who couldn't pay were roughed up by the king's men-at-arms. Those who refused ended up in the dungeons under the king's Great Tower. Sir Palmer was not too enthusiastic about the king's greedy and inhumane taxing enterprise.

A nervous Sir Palmer made his way to the newly set-up dragon's lair. Visvaldis, the dragon, was quietly sleeping and did not want to be disturbed. As Palmer approached the lair's entrance, a few newly shed dragon scales were strewn about the area, which made the anxiety of the captain-at-arms expand greatly. As Sir Palmer peered into the dark gloom of the cave, he paused, paralyzed in fear. However, he quickly gathered his wits, and while wiping the sweat from his brow, he said to himself, "Well, there's nothing for it. Just go talk to the beast in a diplomatic manner and be done with it."

After his little pep talk to himself, Sir Palmer found his courage and strolled on into the dragon's lair. As quiet as he could, Palmer made his way along the rather large cavern filled with stalactites and stalagmites. The cavern soon opened into an enormous chamber. Right in the middle of the chamber, on top of a mountain of treasure, a very large, bronze dragon peacefully slept. Palmer froze when he saw the beast and let out a silent scream. Visvaldis opened one eye and then slowly lifted his giant head.

"Don't bother trying to run or hide, intruder. I can see you and smell your every move. I can sense your ability, motives, and nature," rumbled the dragon. "Who are you and what do you want?" But Visvaldis had already guessed.

As Sir Palmer stepped forward, Visvaldis stretched his head to meet him with a steely glare. At that moment, Palmer learned a new definition for the word fear. He gathered his wits and cleared his throat.

"Um, I am Sir Palmer from the Kingdom of Toril, captain of the king's guard," he squeaked.

"Yes, Sir Palmer, what is it you seek? Are you delivering a message?" Visvaldis calmly asked as he narrowed his eyes and moved a bit closer.

"You see Mr. Visvaldis the Mighty, I represent King Esmour, and he feels that your presence is a danger to his enterprise," Palmer explained with as much tact and charm he could muster.

Visvaldis moved a bit closer. "What do you mean?"

"Well," Palmer stuttered, "it's taxes, you see. King Esmour feels that people in the kingdom will move out due to your presence, and then the king will make less money in turn. It would benefit us greatly if you, um, well… moved on!" the guard captain explained diplomatically and apologetically.

"MOVED ON?" Visvaldis roared at Palmer, which made him stumble back and fall to the ground in horror. "I just moved in, and I'm not going anywhere!" the dragon sounded. "I have no quarrel with your people, but I am offended by this greedy king who could not benefit from unfairly overtaxing of his own people because of my presence. I'll teach this King Esmour about the wrongs of pillaging his own kingdom and disturbing Visvaldis the dragon," he proclaimed loudly. And with that, Visvaldis stood up and thundered passed Sir Palmer out of his lair. He then stretched his wings and took to the sky, leaving his lair and a speechless Palmer behind.

Visvaldis flew to the city of Toril and descended upon the king's castle. The king's guards, knights, lords, and ladies watched in horror as the dragon came out of the cloudy sky and shot a large ball of fire from its mouth. The fire engulfed a row of fancy wagons, incinerating them to smoldering ash. The people screamed and panicked, falling over each other from fear as Visvaldis came about for another run.

Doing his best not to engulf anyone in his storm of fire, Visvaldis did quick work in burning all the wagons and anything combustible. He even melted part of the castle towers with his volatile breath. Finally, the Dragon landed on a section of the castle wall and when he did, his powerful talons were so strong, the top of the wall crumbled apart. Viewing the dragon's might, everyone fled—except for King Esmour.

He came out onto the balcony of the castle's keep to face Visvaldis.

"Hail, mighty dragon and villain of the sky. By what right do you have to bring peril and doom to my keep?" the king roared.

"By the right of your unwelcome greeting to me and your greedy policy," Visvaldis calmly leveled with the king. "And I will take all the gold you have in your treasury and give it back to the people you so wrongly overtaxed," the dragon said while narrowing his eyes and showing a toothy grimace.

"You will not," the king roared in protest. "I have the best knights and dragonslayers in the realm. They will slay you by my command and my gold will be safe in my dungeon vault from you."

Visvaldis could sense the gold's location, and using a magical spell, he teleported all of it back to his lair. With a smirk, Visvaldis met the king, nose-to-nose. "Send your knights and so-called dragonslayers," the dragon mocked. "The day is wearing on and I haven't eaten yet." Visvaldis then stood up and spread his wings, preparing to take the sky. As he did, he yelled back to the king, "As for your gold, King Esmour, it's already mine!" With that, the dragon flew back to the comfort of his own lair.

Shortly there after, Sir Palmer made it back to Toril. He was in utter dismay to learn of the dragon's attack and devastation of the king's castle. He reported straight away to the king, who had just found out what the dragon had proclaimed was true: his vaults were indeed empty. The king was outraged. He quickly put together a force of his best knights and dragonslayers to go on a mission to slay the dragon Visvaldis and take back his gold. But, one dragonslayer was missing—his best!

Breathel had not gotten back yet from a mission of dealing with another dragon. He had the greatest tally of dragons slain over any other dragonslayer. In King Esmour's haste for vengeance, he did not wait for Breathel to arrive and decided to send the troop anyway.

"We must not be hurried," Sir Palmer protested to the king. "If you are so bent on slaying that dragon, we are going to need Breathel. We cannot do this without him. This is not just any dragon; this is Visvaldis the dragon."

"We can and we will do this deed," shouted the king. "And what's more, Captain Palmer, you will lead the troop. You are as fine a warrior as any."

Feeling slightly defeated, Palmer lowered his head. "Yes, my king." He headed out of the castle to gather the troops and lead them to the lair of Visvaldis. Palmer was not in the mood to face and try to slay a big dragon.

Fifty comprised the troop, and within it were ten dragonslayers. With Sir Palmer leading, they made their way up to the dragon's lair. They entered the lair and faced Visvaldis in open battle.

The ten dragonslayers tried every trick they knew or had against the beast, but Visvaldis unleashed a wrath of fire and magical power that engulfed most of them. He knew their tricks. The knights that survived he promptly devoured, as he was a bit hungry anyway.

Only one survived the terrible onslaught, and that one was Sir Palmer. Out of wit or speed, Palmer had dodged the dragon's fiery breath or managed to overcome his spells. Visvaldis had taken notice of this. There was something else the dragon noticed about this one warrior that survived: Visvaldis sensed that Palmer wasn't as wicked as the rest and was reluctant to fight him. The dragon also sensed that Palmer knew somehow that Visvaldis was not wicked as well. So once again, for the second time, Palmer and Visvaldis stood nose-to-nose. But this time, there was a calm and even vibe between them—an unspoken understanding and respect.

"Why do you serve that greedy vile king? Do you fear him?" asked Visvaldis curiously.

"No, not really," Palmer responded.

"Do you think yourself lesser than him?"

"Well, I-I don't really know," Palmer stuttered, confused.

"Oh, but you do fear him and you think yourself lesser than him," persisted Visvaldis. "And yet you are the greater warrior. You are also not as dark hearted as your master king is; I can sense it." The dragon moved around Palmer, never taking his eyes off him. "You are better than him in ways you don't even know, and I think we can benefit each other greatly," the dragon hinted.

Surprised at the sudden turn of events, Palmer regained his stature and asked, "What do you mean? What are you going to do now?"

"Not I, but we," the dragon expressed. "I have an idea that will free you and me from that bothersome King Esmour, that despot of a ruler," Visvaldis boomed.

With a sigh of resignation, Palmer realized the truth of how he felt—the dragon was right; he did not like King Esmour and his tyrannical rule. Resolved to this fact, Palmer met the dragon, face-to-face, and said, "OK, what must I do?"

Later that day, Palmer reported back to the king about all that had happened with a message from the dragon. "The dragon says to 'King Esmour the pig' that he demands a virgin maiden in sacrifice to him. In return, he will depart, leaving the Kingdom of Toril unharmed. She must be delivered to his lair by noon in two days' time."

King Esmour was a hot-tempered man and was growing tired of this beast haunting his doorstep. He flew into a rage and smashed everything in sight. All his best knights and all his dragonslayers were either roasted, torn apart, flattened or eaten alive, save for one—his best dragonslayer Breathel, who had just arrived back that morning from a separate mission. With that, Esmour hatched a secret plan.

The king hand picked the virgin maiden, that of a Lady Lavina. She was beautiful and fair, almost elf-like, with green eyes and long blonde hair.

Though Lady Lavina was chosen, she was sad but not afraid. She did not like the king, but she would do her duty for the kingdom and sacrifice her life to save the lives of many others. So, Lavina got ready to meet her fate!

During preparations, Breathel, the champion dragonslayer, approached the king and Lavina. His tall, large, stout, and muscular form was imposing indeed. Combined with his long black hair, strong jaw and steely grey eyes, he had a rather intimidating presence.

"I will save the Lady Lavina from this grisly fate," Breathel announced. "I will slay the beast with my enchanted great sword, which has slain many dragons before Visvaldis. Before the dragon has a chance to dine on Lady Lavina for lunch, I will end the beast's life," he boomed proudly.

"And I will stand beside our champion on this quest!" the king shouted.

The people cheered, and as they did, the king and Breathel stood proud and tall, basking in the people's attention. Off to the side, Palmer watched solemnly and noticed the king and Breathel glance at each other. They looked at one another as if they had some sort of plan. That was all right, though, because Palmer and Visvaldis the dragon had a plan of their own, and so far, it was all working just as the dragon had foreseen.

On the morning of the second day, Sir Palmer lead a company of soldiers that escorted Lady Lavina up to the entrance of the dragon's lair. The king and Breathel were nowhere to be seen. Upon arrival, Palmer ordered his soldiers to halt a fair distance away from the lair's entrance.

"Stop here and stay back," Palmer demanded. "The dragon demands that I alone must deliver our fair maiden. Visvaldis won't have it any other way."

"I am not afraid," Lavina said solemnly. "And I will make my sacrifice with honour."

Palmer looked into the eyes of Lavina, and with a little smirk, he said, "You shouldn't be afraid, my lady. And yes, you will be doing a great honour for our people."

When all was said, Sir Palmer lead Lavina up the steep scree slope of the barren mountain, to the giant cave that was the lair of Visvaldis the dragon. It was high noon, and entering the lair was ominous for Lavina. The pair made their way through the cavern. It soon opened into the big room that held a large treasure mound, with a massive bronze dragon resting on top. Lavina felt faint and breathless. Visvaldis lifted his head and moved it forward, and in a booming calm voice, he said, "Welcome!"

Lady Lavina fainted, and Palmer caught her as she fell, then laid her down comfortably. He managed to revive her. Visvaldis magically bestowed a sense of calmness over the lady before she would meet him face-to-face.

When Lady Lavina opened her eyes, she was looking into the face of a big dragon but, this time, without fear. "O mighty Visvaldis, I feel and sense that you are not wicked and are not going to eat me," Lavina stated in disbelief.

Visvaldis laughed heartedly, along with Palmer, and said, "No, my lady, not all dragons are wicked in such ways. You are merely my guest, is all. You must be hungry! Make yourself at home, my lady. I think you're the only one here deserving of a hearty lunch," the dragon added joyously.

As Palmer arranged the good meal he had brought for the lady and himself, Visvaldis told tales and legends about the origins of dragons, fairy folk, and magic; the folklore of fantastic beasts and the creation of the world by the high gods. Lavina was enchanted by it all and merely enjoyed the dragon's tales and company. Sir Palmer could not help but be swept up in the stories as well. Just when the party was in full swing, Visvaldis sensed something in his lair. Palmer noticed the dragon's change of attention and sudden silence.

"They are here!" Palmer said seriously.

"Who's here?" Lavina asked, suddenly looking worried.

"King Esmour and Breathel," Palmer flatly stated. "We knew they would come and try to save you and slay the dragon as well to make themselves look good. Then they would claim all of the treasure for themselves."

"Good luck sneaking up on a dragon in its own lair!" Visvaldis added.

Lavina was suddenly irritable and couldn't help but feel tricked. "You used me as bait?" the lady asked angrily. Lavina took a swing at Sir Palmer, which Palmer blocked easily.

Palmer calmly restrained her from attacking him. Then he said, trying to reason with her, "Well, it was the only way, my lady, and you were not going to be harmed in any way."

Suddenly, crossbow bolts flew into the room from the adjacent cavern. One struck Lady Lavina in her right leg. As she screeched, Palmer grabbed her and pulled her to cover behind a large rock. Visvaldis reacted by thrusting his head down the cavern and breathing a searing blast of flame that rocked the cavern and melted stone.

But, out of nowhere, wielding his big magical two-handed sword, Breathel dropped from the ceiling onto the back of the dragon. He struck Visvaldis a mighty blow and the dragon thrashed violently with a big roar. Breathel went flying from the back of the dragon and struck the stone wall. He then fell to the ground. Visvaldis felt a sting of pain, but he was tougher than most dragons and he shrugged it off quickly.

"Don't you know who I am?" roared the dragon. "I am Visvaldis, the mightiest, the chief of all dragons of this age, next to Belicose the Gold. You won't ever destroy me, dragonslayer," Visvaldis thundered. The dragon shook the cavern as he stomped around, looking for the suddenly missing Breathel. Visvaldis could sense and smell the source of this mysterious dragonslayer warrior; it was magic!

Sir Palmer gently grabbed Lavina, faced her squarely, and said, "Time to go!" Then he supported her as they began moving out of the lair's main cavern towards the entrance. As they moved through the cavern devasted by dragon fire, Lavina's leg hurt and buckled. While stumbling to help her up, Palmer came face-to-face with King Esmour.

"Traitor!" the king sneered, then said wickedly, "I'm disappointed in you, Palmer." Esmour slowly drew his sword.

Palmer said nothing, remaining stone-faced. While meeting Esmour's glare evenly, he gently put Lavina down behind him.

"It matters not anyway, Palmer," the king sneered again. "Your bodies won't ever be found. You were just a pawn to get what I really wanted—the dragon's treasure!" Esmour laughed.

Palmer grimaced at the king. "I guessed your little game a while ago," Palmer growled angrily. With his hand on the hilt of his sword, Palmer laid out the events of the last few days while he and the king measured each other up. Lavina, hearing the truth of it all, moved her anger towards the king. "You really do have a black heart," she spat at Esmour.

"You're smarter than I thought," Esmour remarked to Palmer. "But I'm afraid the lives of you and the lady must end here."

In a flash, Palmer drew his sword and, in a sudden clash of steel, crossed blades with King Esmour.

Visvaldis searched the cavern and honed in on Breathel through the magic he possessed. "I can smell you, dragonslayer," Visvaldis muttered. "You cannot hide from me."

Perched invisible on a low ledge, poised to strike, Breathel held his breath. Visvaldis snaked his head around close to the ledge and looked straight at

Breathel. Then he said with a devious grin, "There you are!"

In a sudden movement, Breathel leapt from the ledge onto the dragon's nose and swung his big sword. Blow after blow, he landed, but even with his great enchanted sword, he could barely penetrate the dragon's tough scales. Visvaldis was mighty indeed.

The dragon roared and thrashed his head wildly to shake off this dangerous warrior called Breathel. Just before Breathel was thrown off, he plunged his great sword into the dragon's right eye. Then he sailed through the air to land heavily on the ground of hard stone.

Visvaldis quickly extracted the sword from his right eye in pain. Luckily, the strike wasn't true, and it just barely missed his eye. But the wound was still quite severe. Visvaldis flung the sword away, then struck Breathel as he was getting up. The dragon sent him flying again into the cavern wall once more. Breathel gasped for air in pain and realized the game was up. Without his sword, there was no hope, and he feared the worst—that he would be lunch.

The dragon reached forth and grabbed Breathel in his large taloned hand. "I've got you!" the dragon grimly rumbled. Visvaldis brought the warrior up to his nose and then cast an enchantment on him. Breathel suddenly found that he could not speak, nor could he move.

Sir Palmer and King Esmour fought ferociously. The clash of sword against sword rung through the air with each blow and block as one desperately tried to find an opening or opportunity to slay the other. When they finally came together with locked swords, they pushed against one another.

"You disappoint me further, Palmer," the king goaded. "I thought you were a better swordfighter than this." He laughed evilly.

Palmer, locking glares with Esmour, clenched his teeth and calmly said, "I'm just getting warmed up."

They pushed a part and the clash of their swords resumed. Palmer stepped up his skill in swordplay and worked Esmour deeper into the dragon's lair. He outmatched the king, and the king was getting a bit worried about the eventual outcome—until there was a sudden change in events. When they locked blades for the second time, Sir Palmer stumbled. Esmour pushed Palmer back and Palmer stumbled again, this time to the ground. The king didn't hesitate to question his good fortune.

"Your mine, Palmer; say goodbye." The king laughed with an evil glare. King Esmour moved to run Palmer through with his sword. Just as the king was about to strike, the giant jaws of Visvaldis the dragon suddenly came out of nowhere and clamped onto King Esmour. The dragon engulfed him in one bite, swallowing him whole.

The dragon's sudden attack had startled Palmer and Lady Lavina, but they felt relieved when it was all over and Esmour was gone.

After pausing and taking a breather, Palmer helped the lady up and back into the lair. Visvaldis healed Lavina's leg wound using some magical enchantment. Then he dispelled the enchantment on Breathel and let him go, agreeing to never cross paths again. The dragon kept Breathel's big enchanted sword and gave it to Palmer in thanks.

"I hope you have the better judgment to use this on evil dragons and abominations as opposed to just anything," the dragon advised.

"Don't worry, I will," said Palmer while smiling warmly.

"As for you, Lady Lavina," the dragon said gently. "I have something special to give you for your brave service."

"You-you do?" the lady stuttered.

"Yes," said Visvaldis. "You may choose one enchanted item from my treasure hoard that you desire."

"Oh, I couldn't." Lavina smiled. "That is so generous of you, Visvaldis." She blushed. Lavina then searched the big pile of treasure and chose a diamond necklace of a bright star that held a communing gem and a fairy stone.

"Wise choice, my lady. With that, you can telepathically converse with me and any fey folk creatures or spirits of the Woodland Realm," Visvaldis said confidently. "But you cannot converse with anyone without meeting them in person first."

Lavina smiled with Palmer. "Thank you, Visvaldis," the two of them both said.

"We must now take our leave," expressed Palmer.

"Of course," said the dragon. "I don't want to keep you. But before you go, I have two other things to give you."

The dragon gave Palmer a healthy pile of gold to give back to the people. Then Visvaldis cast a spell that gave each of them a dragon sigil tattoo that magically warned of any danger. Then he escorted them out to the entrance of his lair and bid Palmer and Lady Lavina a friendly farewell. Visvaldis watched them go before returning into his lair to curl up on his treasure hoard for a nice little nap.

As he dozed off, he thought about how the Kingdom of Toril was free of that greedy, corrupt King Esmour; and how that king was nice enough to offer himself as a tasty little snack. Then, as an afterthought, he decided that Palmer and Lady Lavina would make a nice couple.

With all these nice thoughts going through his head, Visvaldis the dragon dozed off to a nice sleepy slumber.

Palmer and Lavina made their way down the mountain back home to Toril.

"So, what do you plan on doing now, Sir Palmer?" asked Lavina.

"Oh, I don't rightly know yet. I might travel the world and find some more adventure," Palmer responded, smiling. "But imagine what one could do if they were a great proud dragon like Visvaldis?" Palmer added in amusement.

Lavina laughed. "Adventure sounds like an attractive idea. I hope you don't mind if I tag along."

"Not at all, Lady Lavina, not at all. You're welcome to join me," Palmer responded.

"And I'm curious, Sir Palmer, what would you do if you were a great proud dragon like Visvaldis?"

Palmer laughed. "Well, let me see…" Palmer thought.

If I were a great proud dragon,
I'd scare all the lords and burn up their wagons,
I'd take all their gold and tamper their greed,
I would devour all the knights that were sent after me,
I'd demand a fair maiden and invite her for lunch,
I'd recite to her stories about legends and such,
I'd give her some magic and bid her farewell,
so, life as a dragon, would really be swell.

Palmer and Lavina both shared a good laugh. Soon, after taking care of some business, they departed from Toril back onto the trail. They embraced the road of adventure, exploring the wide, open world.

The Sword Master

Demetor Mandez grew up in the port city of Quilarus in the Kingdom of Sylvalla. Quilarus was situated on the southern coast of Rithanon, looking out over the South Seas. Demetor, a rather astute sailor, was captain of King Fernando's guard. He was an avid explorer of the South Seas and practised a little privateering on the side. This gained the Crown much wealth, and Demetor became quite popular with the king. But his real talents were not in how he sailed or commanded a ship; they lay in the art of swordplay.

Demetor practised swordplay with a passion unmatched by any. It was said that he was the best in the land, and arguably the best to have ever lived—a title that would attract stiff rival competition. But Demetor was not one to actively seek out rival duelists. He was humble, polite, and charming, and he harnessed a fair degree of honour. He felt that he had nothing to prove to anyone!

One day, Demetor was mentoring a class of aspiring students in the art of swordplay when one such rival competitor trotted up on horseback.

"Ahoy their, Mr. Demetor, for I have heard that you are the best in the land and I have come to show you different," the stranger boasted with bombastic confidence.

Demetor paused his instruction, then approached the arrogant challenger with a sense of curiosity and amusement. "Well then, you better come down off that horse and face me to prove your boast. And if you do not best me, then I would be happy to give you proper instruction," Demetor said with a grin while stroking his well-kept beard and moustache.

"How can I refuse such a challenge, sword master?" the man said as he dismounted. "This might be the day I make history by besting the great Demetor Mandez." He approached smugly.

"Perhaps," Demetor responded back. "May I have the name of the man who plans to claim such confident victory over me before I disappoint him?" Demetor asked this seemingly arrogant challenger.

"My name is Orville, high member of the Duelist Guild, and three times standing swordplay champion of Sylvalla—in a row, I might add," Orville bragged with a bow.

"Well, Orville, Mister Three-times-standing-sword-champ-of-Sylvalla, I believe I am going to enjoy this," Demetor stated as he drew his sabre and long dagger.

The pair squared off, then circled each other, measuring each other up. Orville was the first to act, thinking he could seize the initiative, but Demetor had already anticipated his first moves. Demetor was quick to respond with a calm an easy manner, which caught Orville by surprise. Steel rang upon steel as they exchanged the first set of parries and thrusts.

"You fight well," Demetor said as they paused. "But there is much you have yet to learn," he added while grinning.

"How dare you mock me," Orville responded, irritated. He then flung himself at Demetor with his sword and dagger. Demetor's guard was up instantly, and they renewed their little contest of swordplay.

"Watch how he gets angry and loses all self-discipline and focus," Demetor voiced to his pupils, who were watching the spectacle in fascination. "You see, he becomes overconfident and starts listening to his ego more than his instincts, thinking with his brain," Demetor explained, as if it were a demonstration of instruction.

Orville growled in frustration. He tried all the best moves in his entire repertoire in various creative ways but to no avail. Demetor was controlling the entire duel with ease.

"Don't get me wrong, Orville. You're good; I will give you that. But you're not that good," Demetor added with a grin. Then with a few quick moves, Demetor ended the duel. He sent Orville's dagger flying from his hands and his sword soaring through the air. Then Orville's pants fell around his ankles from his cut belt, just as Mr. Demetor Mandez caught his airborne sabre by the hilt. A stunned Orville quickly drew up his pants out of embarrassment.

"You're not human; there's magic at play," Orville accused.

"There is no magic here," Demetor assured the young duelist. "But I thank you for the bout," he said with a bow. Then Demetor politely handed Orville back his weapons and bid him a good farewell with no hard feelings. Demetor's students fought hard to hide their amusement as a speechless Orville left with droopy pants and a rather bruised ego.

Word got out about Orville's brutal humiliation by the blades of Mr. Demetor Mandez. Other sword masters in the kingdom sought out Demetor to prove their own worth for glory, but Demetor was never bested. His skill with swordplay had grown to legend in the land, which spread to every corner of Rithanon. In fact, he was growing tired of all the arrogant challengers. Then one day, no one could challenge him anymore; he had become feared by the skilled and mocked by the jealous. Some say he was a sham and had used magic, which eventually became belief in various circles.

Finally, Demetor grew tired of the unjustly banter. He was tired of all the mocking rhetoric he received every time he had to go out in public. After a while, it troubled him and he shut himself away.

"What crime have I committed to deserve such dishonorable chiding?" he grumbled to himself. Demetor found himself escaping but not by practising swordplay. He escaped by the practice of drinking a bottle of wine or two every day. For weeks, he would hang out in his cabin, talking to himself, trying to escape his own sorrow.

Finally, a day came when one of Demetor's best students found him. The student apprehensively knocked on the door.

"Who's there?" Demetor asked loudly.

"Um, it's me Raymond Lucio, one of your students," the young man said timidly.

"Go away, Raymond. I am not seeing anyone today," he commanded in a drunken state. Then Demetor went back to his drunken self dialogue of personal pity.

Raymond poked the door open slightly and peeked in. There lying on the floor with his back up against the wall, babbling away while hugging his treasured bottle of booze, was Demetor. He was a sorry sight indeed.

"Hey, I told you to go. Now leave me alone," Demetor yelled as he threw a boot at the door.

Raymond shut the door quickly. "But Mr. Demetor, you can't just waste your life away drowning in sorrow like this. You deserve much better," Raymond said through the door.

"Deserve better?" Demetor scoffed. "The only thing I deserve it seems is this bottle of wine in my hands, the only friend I got around here," he spat.

"Everyone hates Mr. Demetor Mandez, the sword master," he added with sarcastic drunken flair. "I have no friends, kid. Now be off," he ordered.

"You have me, Demetor. I'm your friend," Raymond responded.

"You're a nice kid, Raymond. You're smart and talented with a sword. But do yourself a favour and use that intelligence somewhere else. Don't waste your time trying to become the next champion of the Duelist Guild, which also seems to make you a member of the ego club," Demetor said, dripping with sarcasm.

Raymond rolled his eyes and shoved his way through the door. "Listen Mr. Demetor, you're being a big buffoon," he said while sighing. "I know you're not a sham. You should be proud of your skill and ability, even if others don't believe you. I don't care what anyone thinks, either the upper crust or otherwise, and neither should you," Raymond reasoned. "Don't escape from it all by boozing your days away. I say you should get back up and face them all," Raymond said aloud and angrily while gesturing out the door.

Demetor was shocked and a little taken aback by the brazen youth. He looked at his bottle and realized that the kid was right. After a few moments of contemplation, he chucked his bottle of hooch out the door. Then he picked himself up off the floor and looked intently at Raymond's serious, unmoving face. Demetor started to chuckle, which grew to hearty laughter. Demetor had realized he was acting a little immature and being a bit of a jerk. Slowly, Raymond softened his visage and joined in on the laughing session.

Demetor clasped Raymond on the shoulder while shaking his own head. "You are an intelligent young man and speak with wisdom beyond your youthful years," he said warmly. "You are so right. You cannot find happiness at the bottom of a bottle; you only find sorrow. It's time to face all the naysayers and critics," he added with a grin.

"That's right; it's time to show them what Demetor Mandez can really do," Raymond said with enthusiasm and a slightly wicked little grin.

Demetor sobered up and got himself back together with the help of his student Raymond. It took a few days, but before long, they headed back to the Royal Palace with a plan.

The throng of lords and ladies milled about in the courtyard, summoned by the king for a very important announcement. As the trumpets blared, the king arrived on the balcony. He held his hands up to signal silence and the crowd fell silent. "I have brought you all here for a little matter that must be dealt with. For the peace of mind of my personal guard captain, he has an announcement to make. I hand the balcony over to Mr. Demetor Mandez," the king announced.

The king stepped away and Demetor stepped forward confidently. The crowd was so silent, even the birds didn't know what to chirp. Demetor calmly cleared his throat. "I know you all think I'm fake and use magic to beat all the best sword masters at swordplay," Demetor said. "But I assure you that all my skill at swordsmanship and fighting is genuinely without falsehood. And to prove I'm the best, I send word out to all that I shall challenge any sword master in all of Rithanon to a duel," he announced. "I shall face them in three months time in the Royal Garden. The king and his court shell bear witness, and a wizard will be on hand to assure that no magic is involved in the contest," Demetor said seriously, then boomed, "Now spread the word, and this matter will be settled in three months hence. I bid you all a good day." Demetor bowed and stepped away while handing the crowd back to the king.

The crowd began murmuring, and the king held his hand up for silence once again. "So be it, in three months time, all sword masters in all the lands who come and accept the challenge shall duel against the sword master Demetor Mandez," the king announced. "Let it be known far and wide," he added. Then with a wave of his hand, the trumpets blared, dismissing the crowd.

Over the next three months, Demetor trained with Raymond's help. The fierce duelling practice against multiple opponents was gruelling. Raymond had become quite the sword master himself, who could best most of those who foolishly challenged Demetor in the past. Raymond Lucio was an astute pupil and worked hard at learning most of Demetor's sword fighting secrets. Demetor was proud of him, and he enjoyed the lengthy sword bouts with his young friend. Demetor had taught all his students well, and trying to fight all of them at once had proven to be quite the challenge for Demetor.

The three months went by fast. Soon, the day came for Demetor to test his skill against the best swordsmen in all of Rithanon. On the morning of the ninety-first day, thirteen of the most world-renowned swordsman had arrived at the Royal Palace. They met Demetor and his assistant, Raymond, in the Royal Garden. King Fernando was there with a respected archimage called Nasim. Several members of the Royal Court were also there to bear witness. The morning air was charged with excitement. The crowd murmured as each duelist warmed up for the coming contest, but Demetor was relaxed and just kept to his own private counsel with Raymond.

"What do you think?" Demetor asked Raymond as they both measured up the group of challengers.

"You face a lot of skilled talent, but I think some are overly confident. And by the way they look at you, I think they believe that this challenge of yours will not last the hour," Raymond answered with a smirk, then added, "It will be challenging but possible to accomplish, if approached tactfully."

Demetor smirked with his young friend while clasping him on the shoulder. "We think alike, my friend, and you are right, a tactful approach is needed. And, this challenge will not last the hour," he said with a grin. "I should let you take this lot on," Demetor added with a wink.

Raymond smiled at his mentor's confidence in him.

A horn blared, and the king held up his hand to silence the crowd. "By my rule do I decree this contest," the king declared. "The archimage Nasim has informed me and the court that there is no magic involved, and I declare these duels to begin. Let the first challenger step forward."

One of the thirteen sword masters stepped forward. "I will be the first," he declared. "Know that I will end this contest before it begins," he added with overblown confidence.

Demetor stepped forward to face him. "Bold words, my friend, but I'm not going to fight you," Demetor said bluntly.

All the onlookers and witnesses, plus all who were involved, looked confused and a little bit disappointed.

"I will take on all thirteen of you all at once," Demetor declared with a sweep of his hand.

Everyone gasped in shock, including the king himself—everyone except for Raymond.

"But that's impossible! Do you know the skill you face?" one of the challenging sword masters asked.

"I know perfectly well, friend. Now, shall we get on with this?" Demetor asked. "Teatime is soon, and I wish not to miss it. And oh, yes, um, just to be fair, I will let all of you go first," said Demetor with a sweeping bow. Then Demetor readied himself with his hands resting on the hilts of his sheathed weapons.

The thirteen sword masters circled Demetor, and the crowd whispered in amusement at the seemingly brazen Demetor Mandez. Some bets were made and most of them we're not in Demetor's favour. A few of those bets were made on Demetor not lasting the first ten seconds.

Suddenly, there was a clash of steel as the thirteen master swordsmen moved in on Demetor. Demetor's weapons were in his hands at lightning speed. He gave an immediate dazzling display of parries, faints, and thrusts with his sabre and long dagger. His moves were as fluid as water as he shared the first blows with his assailants. He beat them off easily it seemed, which made all the master swordsmen just a little uneasy. Everyone watching the display was caught a little bit off guard as well.

The world-class combatants circled Demetor more cautiously. Demetor was now focused and within his element. The thirteen swordsmen started working together and moved in towards Demetor, and then out from him a few at a time. They used measured tactics, but Demetor foiled them all. It was an impressive display of sword skill that had ever been witnessed by anyone before. They tried too tire Demetor out but found that they were the ones getting tired. At one point, it looked as if Demetor was going to lose, but then the duel turned quickly to Demetor's favour. His footwork and movements were so subtle and fluid it was like an intricate dance. His technique was flawless as he suddenly switched his defence into offence.

"This is impossible," one of Demetor's most mocking critics said in frustration. "Are you sure that there is no magic involved in this?" he asked Nasim the wizard.

"I'm quite sure," the wizard answered with a smile, enjoying the impressive duel. "Maybe you should have made a different bet," Nasim added with satisfaction to the angered courtier.

Demetor's thirteen challengers started to wear down and tire. Then with a dazzling display of swordsmanship and flair, Demetor ended the duel. He left his thirteen assailants disarmed, unconscious, or humiliated in various creative ways. The witnessing crowd was speechless at first; then the cheering came. The only ones who were picking their jaws up off the ground were the critics who had bet against Demetor. They had lost a great sum of money.

The thirteen sword masters picked themselves up and admitted defeat with honour. "You are the mightiest swordsman who has ever lived, without equal," one of the challengers declared with all others in agreement.

"Demetor is declared champion swordsman and grand master duelist in all of Rithanon," King Fernando declared. "I am also declaring that thirteen is a rather unlucky number," he added with amusement of those who did not bet in favour of his guard captain.

Demetor bowed to the crowd, who had belittled him in the past but now praised him. He was mocked no more and was looked up to with the highest respect. The king was proud of him, and Demetor shared a warm embrace with his most prized student, Raymond, who was also proud of him.

"You are done just in time for tea," Raymond said jokingly.

"Teatime? I want a drink!" responded Demetor with a chuckle.

Demetor and Raymond shared a hearty laugh, then went off to find a drink at a local pub. Demetor's victory was final, and no other man on Rithanon has ever come close to such a victory to this day.

> *He had these nerves of steel;*
> *his presence you could feel*
> *when calmly he'd arrive back into town.*
>
> *With a squint and smirk, he shown;*
> *with agenda that was unknown,*
> *he had this hardened toughness so profound.*
>
> *His jaw was solid rock;*
> *his scars seemed quite a lot;*
> *he had roughly been dragged through mud and grit.*
>
> *His speed could not be cached;*
> *he was stealthily unmatched;*
> *his skill for fighting was more then most admit.*
>
> *If you were a filthy lordly rat,*
> *or a corrupt aristocrat,*
> *it mattered not; he seemed to get his way.*
>
> *He beat thugs by many dozen,*
> *with the calm so icy frozen,*
> *searching for the one to make his day.*

Gabby Gail and the Gadget Shop

In the Kingdom of Abingale, there once was a very charming and handsome prince named Harold. Harold was the prince of Verlan, a very prominent and prosperous city in the kingdom. Harold was so charming and handsome, ladies flocked to him incessantly. He became known as "Handsome Harold," and every lady in the kingdom wanted to be courted by him. But this made Harold conceited, and he was never satisfied with any woman he courted.

Then one day, he heard about Lady Lorena Gail. It was said, she was so pretty and so gifted, all who saw her were instantly charmed. She had faerie blood, and word had it that she was blessed by Umitar, God of Crafts and Skill. Harold had to have her, and he set off at once to seek her out and seduce her.

Harold found Lorena in a nearby village at her craft store. He approached Lorena and introduced himself.

"Charmed, my lady," Harold said with a bow. "I am Prince Harold of Verlan, and I have travelled to meet you. I've heard tales of your beauty, and I must say the tales pale in comparison to who I see before me."

Lorena blushed and said, "Why, thank you. Yes, I am Lorena Gail, and this is my young daughter, Gabby Gail, not more than ten years old. I have been widowed for two years, and Gabby is the greatest of help to me."

"Sorry to hear," responded the prince. "She's a wonderful child, so blonde and fair and full of life," Harold said. "Will you walk with me this fine morning?"

"I guess so, for a short time, for I'm quite busy," she responded. Lorena and the prince walked all morning, and Harold was so charming, Lorena fell for him instantly. Harold could not help but notice how animals and birds loved Lorena and followed her. Having fey blood, Lorena could communicate with them and had such a strong connection to the natural world. She far exceeded any other lady that the prince had ever courted.

Handsome Harold invited Lorena to a ball he was going to have. All the upper class and well-to-do would attend, and Lorena was to be the guest of honour.

She was ecstatic and under a trance. She left Gabby with the household and went too the prince's ball. Gabby waited and waited for her mom to return before finally falling asleep. The next morning, Gabby woke up to a silent household; her mother had not returned.

Gabby was concerned, so she packed a few necessary things in her backpack and set off at once to Prince Harold's palace in Verlan. When she arrived, she sought an audience with the prince, and she was granted it right away. When Gabby entered the throne room, she was greeted by her mother, who looked incredibly happy to see her.

"Welcome, Gabby, welcome to my palace," said the prince.

"It's very lovely, Your Highness," responded Gabby. She could not help but notice how grandiose, and overly snobby it was. "I travelled here to find my mother, for she did not come home as she always does," Gabby explained.

"Your mother had an enchanting time, and I now court her," the prince told Gabby. "She has amazing singing talents and enchanting skills at crafting things. I realize that I have made my choice," Harold added.

"The prince is so wonderful and charming; I am happy to be courted by him," Lorena said to her daughter.

"That's all very nice, but I was hoping my mother would come home with me," Gabby said. "You can see her again another time your highness," she offered.

"I'm afraid not. She will be staying here with me from now on. I plan on marrying your mother next season," Harold told Gabby.

"But I will miss her, and I want her back." Gabby sniffed and tears began to run down her cheeks. Gabby pleaded for the prince to hand her mother back; she could see that her mom was under his spell. The prince was not what he seemed, and Gabby would not leave without her mom.

Determined to keep her mother at the palace, the prince thought of something that would get Gabby to go away. Prince Harold said to Gabby in his most charming voice, "Bring me three magical gifts that can do wonderous things, and you can have your mother back."

Gabby nodded and agreed; then she walked out of the big palace with her head down. Even though she agreed to the prince's offer, she did not trust him, but she set off right away to find three magical gifts.

That night, the prince was visited by a thrush that landed outside his bed chamber window. Harold heard the bird say, "Greetings, Handsome Harold. I am a friend of Lorena Gail, and I have come to warn you!"

"Warn me of what?" Harold responded, shocked he was in conversation with a bird.

"I come to warn you to not be vain, greedy, or malicious in what you see, say, or hear. And if you do not honour your word to Gabby truthfully, it will be the end of you," the bird said.

"Be off, you damn bird," Harold yelled, and he waved it away. He had much on his mind. Lorena was fulfilling his desires with making wondrous things and being the most beautiful lady in the land. As far as Harold was concerned, he owned her!

Gabby searched high and low and far and wide for three magical gifts. After a while, frustration set in. She did find a few magical items, but they were of minor magical effect that just would not do for a grandiose prince like Harold. Finally, one old lady told her about a great wizard by the name of Dell-Shander who lived in the great citadel of the famous Knights of Carnebour.

The old lady said, "They ride great dragons, as well as horses, and they are the watchers and protectors of all the lands."

Gabby was intrigued by this. She thanked the old lady, who gave her directions, and Gabby set off at once.

Gabby travelled for a week before she arrived outside the gates of Carnebour Castle. Gabby was mesmerized by the enormity of the citadel, with its high walls over one hundred and thirty feet high and its large towers that jut up into the sky several hundred feet. The enormous castle was perched on a high pinnacle of rock. A hidden causeway bridge connected the adjacent mountain to the citadel's perch. At first, Gabby didn't see the bridge; it just appeared as she approached it. A few dragons were perched on the walls, snoozing in the midday sun, and a big silvery one greeted Gabby warmly.

"Why, hello, little one. Where did you come from?" asked the dragon.

"Hi, Mr. Dragon. I'm Gabby Gail and I have come to get help from Mr.

Dell-Shander," said Gabby nervously. "What's your name?"

"Don't be troubled, Gabby. My name is Sterling, and I am female," Sterling said gently. "Yes, Mr. Dell-Shander can help you, depending on what help is needed. You can find him at the top of the wizard's tower."

"Thank you, Mr. Dragon, I mean, Mrs. Sterling," Gabby responded. And then she preceded to tell the dragon all about her problem. Sterling listened intently. After her friendly conversation with Sterling, Gabby made her way through the gates and into the bustling citadel.

Inside, she saw various shops with a couple of pubs and people going about doing various things. Gabby was in awe of the place. She followed Sterling's directions up to the wizard's chambers.

When Gabby knocked on the door, it opened by itself and a voice said to her, "Gabby Gail, I've been expecting you." She was then met by an older gentleman with long grey hair and a long beard. He was all dressed in brown, save for his greenish blue robe, and wore a tall brown pointy hat.

"Hello, Gabby. I am Dell-Shander," he said warmly. "Sterling told me about your little problem, and I think I can help you."

"But how did you know I was coming and the reason for my visit so quickly?" Gabby said a bit flustered.

The wizard laughed heartily. He leaned over and grinned at her, all rosy cheeked. "We have our ways around here, Gabby. I am after all a wizard, you know," Dell said, with a wink. "Now, let's find you some help." Dell grabbed his funky looking staff. "This way, Gabby. Follow me."

Gabby followed Dell-Shander back down into one of the courtyards of the citadel that was laden with shops and pubs. She saw knights and folk everywhere working, doing business, or just socializing. The place was enchanting. Dell led Gabby to one interesting shop that had a peculiar way about it. Strange and curious objects all stacked up could be seen through the window.

"This is Giblet Gadget's gadget shop. Don't touch anything until we talk to Giblet," Dell warned Gabby before they entered the shop.

A bell rang as they did so. Gabby looked around the shop to see a room lined with shelves and tables full of interesting things. Piled high and unkempt were all sorts of machines, or objects, made from all matters of springs, gears, pulleys, and pistons. Some things were not recognizable at all; they were what you might call doohickeys, doodads, gimmicks, contraptions, thingamajigs, and whatchamacallits. One apparatus just looked like a bunch of constructed and combined gizmos. Some things were recognizable, though, such as clocks, boxes, steam pumps, wind chimes and spinners, crossbow pistols, and a phonograph. Gabby even spotted an electric hand pump. There was what Dell called a "vending machine" and some sort of weird printing press. A top hat with goggles and a weird book or two were just a few more items Giblet had in his shop.

"Most of these things Giblet made," Dell said. "The only thing is, half of Giblet's gadgets and gizmos don't even work, while the other half work either most of the time or just… some of the time," Dell explained further, with serious concern.

"And this is going to help me?" Gabby said sarcastically, and worried.

"Well, yeah, some of Giblet's things are special," Del sheepishly said. "Some are really special and have a magical quality about them."

When Gabby moved to touch one peculiar object, Giblet the gnome came bursting out of the backroom. "Don't touch that! It's very delicate," Giblet blurted out. "Dell, you're tarnishing my good reputation," Giblet lectured Dell while wagging his stubby finger at him. "Some of my things are very special, I'll have you know. And gnomes are quite good at making things," Giblet expressed.

"Relax, Giblet, that's why we're here. Don't worry, I didn't tell her about the time you invented a rocket to explore the cosmos, and you tried using Mrs. Rosie's corgi as a test subject," Dell confessed.

"Hey, that was better than the time you almost sunk the South Tower from a failed magical experiment," Giblet retorted back.

"Ah, well, yes, let's not talk about that shall we," responded Dell, avoiding the subject. "Anyway, we're here to help Gabby; that's our focus. Gabby, meet Giblet Gadget the gnome; he's very talented in so many ways."

"Hello, Gabby, I'm charmed to meet you. Why are we helping you?" asked Giblet.

"I'm pleased to meet you also, Giblet," Gabby replied, and then proceeded to explain the story about her mother, Lorena, and Prince Harold, and that if she ever wanted her mom back, she would have to bring three magical gifts to Harold. That was Harold's condition!

"Well, let us start with just one gift item, shall we? Two at once is a bit much, let alone three," said Giblet. "Let's see what we can dig up," the gnome muttered as he rummaged around in his endless pile of items and contraptions. He finally pulled out a fancy mirror. "This will do. Give this mirror to the conceited Prince Harold."

"Is it magical? What does it do?" asked Gabby curiously.

Even Dell was curious as he leaned in to analyze the mirror.

"This is a very special magic mirror," Giblet explained. "It makes one beautiful and stay young upon viewing deeply into its depths. But handle it with care and heed its pull, Gabby, for it is more charming than the prince," Giblet warned warmly. The gnome was growing fond of the young girl and felt he needed to help her.

"I will handle it carefully, and thank you, Giblet," Gabby said while giving him a hug. Then Gabby and Dell-Shander left Giblet's gadget shop.

Before Gabby left the citadel, Dell gave Gabby a gift of his own. "Here, Gabby, take this ruby pendant. It is also magical, but it's not for the prince. It's for you."

"What does it do?" asked Gabby.

"It is a truth gem. It can see through lies and fake actions, and will reveal to your eyes anything hidden from view," Dell explained.

"Thank you, Mr. Dell-Shander, and farewell," said Gabby. Then Gabby prepared for her trip back to Verlan.

Before Gabby left, the Knights of Carnebour set her up with a pony and then she went on her way. Gabby Gail travelled back down through the mountains to Verlan. She gave the magnificent mirror to Prince Harold, and he was pleased beyond all doubt.

"What an enchanting mirror." Harold beamed. The handsome Prince Harold viewed its reflecting surface as Gabby explained its power to him, which pleased the prince even more.

When interacting with the prince, Gabby's ruby pendant grew warm; and then she noticed something about Prince Harold. For Handsome Harold was not so handsome. He appeared handsome on the outside, but on the inside, well, he was something else. He had a cruel and dark interior. He was really an ugly malicious and greedy monster who coveted power and wealth. He felt entitled to dominate and exploit the less fortunate and weak, who could not defend themselves. He wanted it all.

Without so much as a thank-you, the prince said coldly, "Go and fetch my second gift for me, will you." Then he dismissed Gabby with a wave of his hand, lost in viewing his shiny new mirror. Gabby left with her head down, feeling a heavy heart. She really wanted to hug her mother.

That night, Harold continued to view his self-absorbed self in his new mirror. While admiring the self proclaimed beauty before him, a familiar bird landed on the windowsill. It was the talking thrush.

"Do not be vain, greedy, or malicious in what you see, say, or hear. If you do not honour your word to Gabby, it will be the ending of you," said the bird.

"Away with you, bird, or I'll catch you for my cat. Do not ever bother me again. Don't you dare disturb me," the prince roared.

The bird flapped away, not the least bit concerned.

Gabby made her week-long northern trek through the mountains back to Giblet's gadget shop at Castle Carnebour. The journey seemed not as scary as the first time but no less perilous. There were always lurking dangers along the way. There were always rouge highway men and goblins lurking about in the wilds.

Back at the citadel, Gabby was greeted warmly again, and this time, though, she took some well needed rest for a few days. In that time, Dell taught Gabby some magic, which she showed a bit of a talent for. He also gave Gabby a grand tour of the citadel before ending up at Giblet's gadget shop. Giblet showed Gabby all sorts of new and used weird, wonderful inventions until Gabby rested her eyes on a particular box sitting on the counter.

"What matter of box is that?" asked Gabby.

"As a matter of fact, that box is your second gift to Handsome Harold," Giblet answered with a chuckle.

"What does it do? How does it work?" asked Gabby, intrigued and curious.

"It's a magic gadget box that makes wondrous things. You open the lid and ask the box to make anything you wish," said Giblet, smiling. "But there is a limit of course; a limit to size and volume. Don't get too greedy, or it will shut down on you and everything it made will turn to dust," Giblet warned in a serious tone.

Gabby was fascinated by the box and ready to travel back to Verlan with the second gift for Prince Harold. "Thank you, Giblet, I will return soon for the third and final gift," Gabby said.

Dell-Shander saw Gabby off at the main gate. After she hopped on her pony, Dell handed her a book of spells as a gift. "I noticed you have a natural talent for magic," Dell said. "Farewell, Gabby, until we meet again. Have courage and trust in yourself. You are stronger than you may think." Dell gave her his customary rosy grin and a wink.

"Thank you, Mr. Dell-Shander. I will return," Gabby responded, smiling. And then she set off across the hidden causeway that was not so hidden from Gabby anymore.

In four days, time, Gabby arrived back in Verlan. She brought the gadget box to Handsome Harold, who was not so handsome. This time, Gabby was not as timid; she felt a little surer of herself. Dell's tutelage had given her confidence.

Harold was intrigued by the interesting box. "What in the world is this and whatever does it do?" asked Harold, puzzled by its unique design.

"It's a magic gadget box. All you do is open it up and ask for what you want," explained Gabby.

"Anything I want or desire?" asked the prince excitedly.

"Well, not anything. It's limited to size, of course, and it must be an item, not an effect. But don't get too greedy," Gabby warned.

Prince Harold opened the box and asked for a crystal singing canary, and that was exactly what the box materialized within it. Harold was giddy and pleased as punch. He loved his new magic box.

Gabby asked to see her mother before departing, but the prince was so enthralled with his new box, he barely even heard her.

"You can go now and fetch me my third gift," the prince said with a dismissive wave of his hand. "Then you can see your mother again," he lied.

Gabby knew he was untruthful, and she could sense it. But she took her leave anyway and started making her way back to Giblet's shop at Carnebour Castle. Gabby had grown stronger; she became set on bringing the vile, handsome prince down.

That night, Prince Harold was having fun asking his new box to make stuff for him. Then that familiar irritating bird landed on his windowsill again.

tThe bird said, "Prince Harold, don't be vain, greedy, and malicious in what you see, say, or hear. And if you do not honour your word to Gabby, it will be the ending of you."

Prince Harold blew his lid. He flew into a rage and yelled at the bird with all kinds of nasty rhetoric. Then he picked up a heavy random object and threw it at the bird. The item missed the agile bird, and it flew off unharmed.

"You have been warned, Prince Harold. You have been warned," responded the bird as it flew away.

Gabby slowly made her way back to Giblet's gadget shop at the citadel of the Carnebour knights. Gabby's frequent trips had attracted unwanted attention; however, studying Dell's book was a big help on her travels. She managed to avoid or keep at bay those who had a notion to rob or harm her. The new spells she learned from her book had come in handy for dealing with trouble. Gabby had a natural knack for magic of the arcane, as if it spoke to her. Her heart lifted, and she felt relieved when she once again finally arrived back at the big castle. The familiar sights and sounds of the welcoming place filled her soul with joy. Gabby realized she loved coming here and grew fond of the community of the Carnebour Citadel. Everyone was so friendly to her.

Gabby had a couple days of rest. In that time, Dell showed Gabby more magic, and Giblet did his best to explain how all his inventions worked, or didn't work. She got to know many knights and more of Sterling the dragon. She met a few other dragons as well. When the time came to go, Gabby stopped by Giblet's shop to pick up the third gift for Prince Harold. There were a good number of clocks of all kinds, sitting on the counter.

"Is that the third and last gift? A clock?" Gabby asked Giblet.

"Yes, but not just any clock; it's a special clock," Giblet responded, smiling.

"But which of the clocks will I be taking back to Prince Harold?" asked Gabby.

"Well, Gabby, you must choose. But choose well," Giblet said.

Gabby examined the clocks. She thought of Harold's grandiose tastes, and her eyes settled on a very fancy and fine silver clock with gold trim and garnished with gems.

"That one," Gabby said while pointing her finger at it. "As long as it works," she added jokingly.

"Not funny," Giblet responded, half-wounded. "But a very good and wise choice. This clock stops one from aging, as long as they can hear the sound of it ticking and toking. But be warned." Giblet's tone turned grave. "The bearer of the clock must be honest and truthful, or it will work against them."

"I will treat it well," said Gabby as she took the clock.

"And it will treat you well," Giblet responded, smiling.

Soon Gabby was all set and ready to head back to Verlan. Giblet and

Dell-Shander saw her off but not alone. On her third and final trip, Gabby was given a protective escort of three knights: Sir Quillen, Sir Ramous, and Sir Monti. They were also sent to ensure that handsome Prince Harold honoured his word to Gabby.

For Gabby, the return trip to Verlan felt a bit safer, thanks to her companions. Any unsavoury, unwanted visitors were dealt with quickly. Gabby had plenty of time to study Dell's book. Before long, they were at the gates of the prince's palace. But the gates were closed.

"For whom comes to the palace of Prince Harold with such an armed escort?" yelled the guard above the gate.

"It is I, Gabby Gail. I have come to deliver to Prince Harold his third and final gift. My escorts are none other than three of the famed Knights of Carnebour, seeing my safe return," Gabby explained.

After a long pause, the gate opened, and they were allowed in.

"Better be on our guard," said Sir Ramous as they passed through the gates.

Gabby and her friends entered Prince Harold's throne room, which was lined with guards. Her escort remained behind her, staying alert.

"Your third and final gift, my prince," said Gabby. Then as she bowed, she sat the clock down at Harold's feet.

The prince was pleased at the magnificence of the clock. "What does it do?" he asked.

"It stops one from aging, as long as they listen to it," Gabby responded. But that was all she said about the clock

Prince Harold set the clock on the wall above the throne over his head. Now he had all the time in the world. He felt complete. With his clock, he could outlive all while staying handsome and young from his mirror and getting all the things he wanted from his magical box. And, he had the most beautiful maiden in the land.

Gabby looked at the prince squarely. "Now that you have your three gifts and have it all, and you can have any pretty lady in the kingdom, can I have my mother back?" asked Gabby.

The handsome prince laughed. "Do you honestly think I'd give up the prettiest flower of a lady in all the land? I do have it all now, and you delivered. I thank you, young Gabby," the prince mocked. "Now be gone, all of you," he demanded.

Gabby's ruby pendant started warming and glowing, matching her heating temper. "You promised to give my mom back to me if I gave you three magical gifts. You gave your word," Gabby yelled, now visibly upset.

Gabby's knight escort felt tense as unease washed over the room; they grasped their sword handles and measured up the prince's guard, which would not match their prowess in battle. But there were many of them.

"Well, you foolish child, I lied," said the prince, shrugging. Then in a serious tone, the evil, handsome prince warned, "But if you don't leave, I'll be forced to arrest the lot of you and shut you away in the deepest and darkest dungeon that I have.".

Gabby turned to look at her three knight friends, who were ready to do whatever it took to rescue Gabby's mother. They gave her a subtle nod. Gabby felt her newly attained arcane power start to gather within her. She turned back to the prince and said through clenching teeth in a serious and threatening tone, "We are not leaving without my MOM!"

"ARREST THEM!" said the evil prince with a wave of his hand.

The room exploded into action, as the three Carnebour knights drew their swords and engaged the prince's guards. Gabby shut her eyes for a second and started muttering strange arcane words. When she opened her eyes, they were glowing white. She saw her mother, Lorena, and the room she was kept in and how to get there. Her knight friends were outnumbered eight to one, but they were handling themselves quite well with an impressive display of fighting skill. However, three times as many guards were on their way.

The prince moved to grab Gabby. When he laid his hands on her, his hands burned and he lurched back, yelping in pain. Gabby could see the reinforcement of guards approaching the throne room. In her mind, she shut the doors—and the throne room doors slammed shut in the faces of the newly arriving guards. The battle was still on, though. The prince drew his sword and took a slash at Gabby, who had just come back to herself. Gabby had just enough time to leap back and avoid being cut in half. Prince Harold tried a few more times, slashing his sword wildly, but Gabby outmanoeuvered him.

"Stay still," the prince yelled in frustration.

With a simple incantation, Gabby made him trip, then slip and fall, his sword clattering to the ground. Then in pure determination, Prince Harold managed to grab her.

"Ha, ha, I got you now, you little runt," the prince shouted with glee. "I think I will take care of you right now," he said in fury while reaching for his dagger.

Gabby's three knight friends were still too engaged to come to her rescue.

As the prince fumbled for his dagger, the clock stopped! Harold knew something was wrong, horribly wrong. In Harold's hesitation, Gabby pulled herself away from him. The knights had finished with the guards, but more guards were trying to break down the door to get into the throne room.

The prince started aging. His mirror on the wall cracked and he started becoming ugly and hideous to match his nature. Then the gadget box broke down and everything made from it started to fall apart.

"I know the way to my mother. This way!" Gabby yelled to the knights, who followed Gabby out the back door of the throne room.

One of the knights, Sir Monti, had to be helped due to a slash in his leg, while Sir Quillen had been hit in his arm. They made their way down a maze of hallways till they came to Lorena's room. It was being guarded, but even wounded, the knights subdued the guards quickly. Gabby opened the locked door with a handy little spell she learned. Inside the room stood Lorena, and Gabby rushed in to hug her mom.

Back in the throne room, the guards burst through the doors to witness their aging, hideous prince growing more and more older and uglier.

In a rasping voice, the prince ordered, "Find them and kill them!" It was the last command he ever gave.

After Gabby's happy little reunion with her mom, Sir Ramous said, "OK, we've got to get out of here."

"I know a way out," said Lorena. "I was planning an escape and found a secret passage to the courtyard." Lorena moved the bed and exposed the passage in the floor. Without hesitation, they made their way down.

In the throne room, a familiar bird flew in and landed not far from handsome Prince Harold, who was not so handsome anymore.

"You damn bird," Harold rasped while clutching himself and stumbling towards it. "That girl ruined me."

"You ruined yourself," the bird said. "I warned you, Prince Harold, to not be vain, greedy, or malicious in what you see, say, or hear. And you were to honour your word to Gabby, or it would be the end of you. Alas, it has been so and has come to pass. Farewell, Harold, may the gods forgive you in your afterlife." Then the thrush flew away.

The prince responded with no more than a croak, muttering, "Gabby tricked me." It was the last thing he said. And the last thing he heard was what the bird had said. And the last thing he saw was the bird flying away. Then Prince Harold exploded into dust beyond the grave.

The palace was in full alert, looking for Gabby, Lorena, and the three knights. Gabby, with her mother and their three knight friends, had reached the courtyard unnoticed, and very stealthily, they stole four horses. The guards did not notice until Gabby and company quickly rode out the front gate. The guards could not close the gate in time, but they fired arrows at them. When that didn't stop them, the guards tried giving chase. But it was to no avail. Lorena's connection with animals had made their horses the swifter.

Gabby Gail, Lorena Gail, and the three knights made their way back to Carnebour Castle. It was a joyful trip. Gabby had her mother back. Lorena was impressed at Gabby's ability to wield arcane magic and supported Gabby's wishes to learn from Dell-Shander.

Before beginning her training in arcane magic with Dell-Shander, Gabby visited Giblet at his gadget shop.

"So how did it go?" asked Giblet the gnome.

"Not as I expected," said Gabby. "Everything you gave me to give to the prince just broke apart," she explained.

Giblet shrugged. "Almost everything I make seems to either stop working or fall apart." He sighed. With a warm smile and a mischievous wink, he added, "But sometimes that can be a blessing."

> *The strangest things that people see*
> *are usually not foretold,*
> *and lots of things some people say*
> *come right from their soul.*
> *But wise old sayings most people hear*
> *are thought to be absurd,*
> *so think about pain you can avoid*
> *Bbefore you break your word.*

The Adventure of Bluebell and Lily-Green

In the magical land of Rithanon, there lived two pixies who were the best of friends: Bluebell, a blue fairy from the Bluebell Forest, and Lily-Green, a green fairy from the Greenwood. One fine morning, sometime ago, they were out for a wander and decided to go on a bit of an adventure.

"Let's go east," said Bluebell. "We rarely go east."

"Yes, let's go east," responded Lily-Green. "But not too far east. Swampwood is east; it's smelly, murky, and nasty. Swampwood is inhabited by trolls and goblins and is the home of a nasty old witch." She wrinkled her nose in disgust.

Bluebell grimaced with Lily-Green and said, "OK, we won't go too far east. Let's make it a safe adventure," she responded while smiling joyfully.

So, the two pixie friends nodded in agreement and happily sped off, flying through the forest, heading east. Amid their fancy flying, dancing, laughing, and having fun, Bluebell noticed a big dragon fly by not too far away. The dragon dropped something as it passed, and it did not seem to notice.

"Lily-Green, did you see that?" asked Bluebell.

"See what?" responded Lily-Green.

"A big orangey green dragon flew over there and dropped something without seeming to notice," explained Bluebell. "Let's go see what it is."

"OK, let's go see. I love dragons," responded Lily-Green. "I like the dragons that are the golden colour of my hair the most, but not the red ones that are the colour of your hair, Bluebell."

"What's wrong with my hair? I like my red hair," responded Bluebell, a little wounded.

"No, no silly, I meant that I don't like red dragons. They are nasty and mean. Your hair is fine, Bluebell. It works with your blue outfit, like my yellow hair works with my green outfit," explained Lily-Green.

"Oh, what a relief! I was worried you didn't like my hair," said Bluebell.

So, after the two fairies sorted out hair colours and outfits, they flew off through the woods to see what the dragon had dropped. It wasn't long until they came to a small clearing on the edge of Swampwood. And in the clearing sat a large, round object about four feet across in diameter that was speckled and light brown.

"What is it?" asked Lily-Green in wonder as they approached the object.

"It appears to be some kind of egg," Bluebell said, then added in disgust, "And it appears to be at the edge of Swampwood."

"Oh no, Swampwood?" Lily-Green gasped. "It appears we went too far east," Lily-Green said in concern.

Suddenly, the sound of big splashing footsteps, mixed with cackling laughter, came from the edge of Swampwood. Splash, splat, sploosh! "MEEEE, HA-HA-HA-HAAAA! There it is. I have been waiting a long time for this," a cackling voice said, then shouted, "It's just over here!"

Bluebell and Lily-Green quickly disappeared to a safe place so they could observe who was coming. A wizened, old-looking woman with scraggly long hair, grey torn robes, and a hooked nose appeared. Two big ogres stood at her side.

Lily-Green gasped. "It's Furious Nerges, the evil witch from Swampwood," she whispered to Bluebell.

"SHHHH! Quiet, not so loud! Or she will put a spell on us and turn us into sour jellybeans," Bluebell responded.

The hag Nerges approached the big object in the clearing with glee, then stroked its smooth surface victoriously. "Finally, I have one," the hag said excitedly. "My very own dragon egg."

The two hiding pixies gasped as they looked at each other. "Dragon egg?" they both said at the same time.

"Isn't it a little small to be a dragon egg?" one of the big ogres said, observing the egg.

"It's the right size, you big dumb buffoon," the witch snapped at the ogre. "You can load it into my boat. And stop asking stupid questions," Nerges scolded her two oversized, ugly servants.

One of the big ogres picked up the dragon egg and loaded it into a small boat not far from the clearing.

"Why do we's need the egg?" the second ogre asked.

"No dumb questions stump face," said the first ogre. "Didn't you hear master? She the boss!" he added.

"Listen, you big, oversized wart-headed gorilla, I'll explain it again since your memory can't recall what I said on the way here," Nerges said sarcastically. "We need it for a spell of powerful nature. Once the egg hatches, the baby dragon's blood is an important component that will help bring to bear a powerful enchantment—a powerful dweomer that will expand Swampwood. It will engulf all of the Greenwood and Bluebell Forest," she said while laughing wickedly. "And, to think, I knew the dragon was coming with what she carried. I cast a spell on her as she flew overhead. That is how she dropped the egg unnoticed, and this is no ordinary dragon egg. It is the offspring of Glifoless Glaze, a powerful Paragon dragon of a rare bloodline." Nerges cackled gleefully.

Bluebell and Lily-Green gasped in horror at what they heard and looked on from their hiding place in the nearby bushes.

"ARRG, a crack," the hag yelled. "Quick, we got to get this egg back to the hut before the baby dragon hatches," she said, panicking. So, the trio set off without any further delay.

"Oh no, we have to do something," said Bluebell.

"That nasty old hag means to put our world into swampy ruin," Lily-Green said in fear while diving into a thicker bush out of sight.

"Not if we stop her first," said Bluebell. "And we've got to save the baby dragon too."

"But she's got powerful dark magic," Lily-Green said still hidden in the thick bushes.

"Stop being such a wimp, Lily-Green, and get out of those bushes," said Bluebell, fed up. "We have magic too, silly," she pointed out. "If we put both our magic powers together, we can save the baby dragon and ruin her evil plans."

Lily-Green's head popped out of the bush. "I didn't think of that." She gasped. "What are we waiting for? Let's go," Lily-Green blurted out with excitement. "Nasty, evil old hag, we will show her what we're made of," she boasted. Lily-Green found her bravery.

"I'm going to turn her into a swamp root or a toad," declared Bluebell.

"Maybe even a pile of worms," added Lily-Green to which Bluebell nodded in agreement.

And with that, the two pixies turned into tiny glowing, floating lights and sped off after the witch, keeping a safe distance.

The hag of Swampwood, known as Furious Nerges, paddled along in her boat through the murky swamp. Her two big ogre minions walked with her, one on each side of the boat, slopping through the marsh. The dragon egg sat at the front of the boat and started to gain more cracks.

"We must hurry," demanded the witch. "Times running out!"

So, they quickened their pace and made their way through dingy, knobbly, knotty trees and thick choker vines, which were common in Swampwood. Mist and fog started to appear on the water, and the hoots of owls and the caws of crows could be heard as they headed deeper and deeper into the dank murkiness of the forested swamp.

Bluebell and Lily-Green followed diligently, staying behind in the trees and vines, out of sight. They used the fog to aid their elusiveness.

"I don't like this place, Bluebell," Lily-Green said nervously, not feeling as brave as she felt before entering the swamp. "It's full of goblins and trolls, and some of the trees are malevolent in nature," she expressed in a disgusted manner. "I have heard stories that they devour anyone who ventures in here unsuspecting."

"I know; it's dingy, gloomy, and spooky. We must be cautious," Bluebell added, who felt just as nervous as Lily-Green.

The two pixies followed the villainous trio all morning. Suddenly, the trees parted into a clearing. At the centre of the clearing was a rickety, old-looking hut perched up upon a tall, wide tree stump. It appeared that the tree had been hacked off part way up. A staircase zigzagged up the side of the hut, and there appeared to be a hoist out front. The witch and her ogre goons pulled up to a platform dock next to the hoist lift. Then they transported the egg into the hoist to lift it up.

"Careful with that," the witch said. "Once it's up there, put the egg in the back room," she instructed. "I must prepare the spell I will cast on the morrow's eve." She cackled evilly.

Bluebell and Lily-Green observed and listened from their hiding place behind a big knobbly tree.

"I think this is the centre of Swampwood; there are icky black oak trees growing here," Lily-Green observed nervously.

"Yes, black oaks usually grow at the centre of dark, haunting woods,"

Bluebell added. "But how are we going to save the baby dragon?" Bluebell was at a bit of a loss!

The two pixies sat in the misty, murky swamp of Swampwood all afternoon and into the evening. They looked on as the witch cackled away and went about her tasks for her evil spell. And so, they just sat there in the gloom of Swampwood, wondering how to save the dragon egg.

Finally, Bluebell had an idea.

"I know," said Bluebell suddenly. "We will push the boat around back under the window there and carry the egg down while flying."

"We will have to be our big selves to do that," Lily-Green put in.

"Yes, and the ogres have gone back to their big tree root caves, so nobody's watching," Bluebell added.

"Brilliant, let's do it!" Lily-Green said excitedly.

So, the two pixies looked at each other, wiggled their noses, and turned into little pebbles of light darting towards the witch hut. They got to the boat quickly. Using pixie muscle power, which can be rather substantial, they pushed the boat around back and flew into the back window and found the dragon egg in the backroom. It was looking very cracked indeed. The two pixies snapped their fingers in unison and turned into their big selves of five feet tall.

"It's nice to be big for once," Lily-Green said while smiling joyfully.

"Yes, it is but SHHHH! That nasty old hag may hear us," responded Bluebell, concerned. "So, let's be quick," she added, her focus centring on the egg.

The pixies picked up the cracked egg and started moving it out the window. As they were doing so, the egg moved and cracked even more. Startled, they dropped the egg, and when it hit the floor, the egg shattered, revealing a little coppery-coloured baby dragon covered in silvery-green speckles. It had a sharp pointy horn on its nose. The little dragon blinked its big eyes at its first view of the world, which was Bluebell and Lily-Green blinking and looking right back.

Then the two pixies looked at each other, and they both said in Unison, "Oh nooooooo!"

"It's a baby dragon," said Lily-Green, shocked.

"Yes, I know it's a baby dragon," Bluebell replied. "But the plan kind of required the baby dragon to be still in the egg, not outside the egg."

"It's a boy," Lily-Green observed, from knowing dragons.

"He's a colourful little boy dragon, too, but what are we going to do now?" Bluebell said in distress.

"We will think of something," declared Lily-Green.

Suddenly, they heard the clumps of footsteps coming up the stairs outside the door. The pixies stopped their chatter. "She's coming," they both said, gasping. Then turning invisible, they both disappeared.

"What's going on up here?" the hag croaked out loud when she reached the door. She opened it suddenly and stood there, staring into the big eyes of the baby dragon. "Ha-ha, it's hatched," the witch said with glee. Then Nerges grew suspicious. "You're not alone." Nerges stepped into the room. She squinted her eyes and said, "I sense... PIXIES!"

The hag then cast a quick spell and the two pixies dropped to the floor out of nowhere, back into their regular six-inch size.

"Ahaaaaa! I discovered you, meddlesome pixies," the witch screeched. "And now I'm going to do something with you two," the hag declared. Before Bluebell or Lily-Green could do anything, Nerges cast another spell that locked them into a magical pixie cage.

"Ha-ha-haaaaaa, I'm going to have pixie stew, or some kind of delicacy I've never tried before." The witch cackled. "Maybe some magical experiment?" the hag wondered out loud. Nerges just picked up the cage and scooped up the baby dragon in her other arm, then headed downstairs. She hung the cage from the ceiling and shackled the baby dragon to the floor, then retired and went to bed for the rest of the evening.

The two pixies hung there, unable to weave magical spells or magic tricks of any kind, as the pixie cage prevented them from doing so. They sat there in a funk wondering what to do. "So much for a safe adventure," Lily-Green muttered.

The gloomy night wore on. Then suddenly, in the early morning hours, Bluebell spotted a nail on the floor. It once held up a picture on the wall, which had fallen to the floor. The nail was only two inches long to a regular-size person but was about two feet in size in the scale of the pixies.

"Hey, Lily-Green, there's a nail on the floor. I have an idea," Bluebell whispered. "Give me some of your hair."

"My hair?" responded Lily-Green, perplexed. "What in the witch's brew for?"

"To make a rope, silly." She sighed in exasperation, as if it were obvious. "My hair is too short and wavy; yours is long and straight."

"OK, Bluebell, but you can't have all of it. Have you ever seen a bald pixie before?" Lily-Green responded back in exasperation as well.

Bluebell explained her plan to Lily-Green as they got busy stringing some of Lily-Green's long golden-blonde hair into a rope with a noose at the end of it. Once complete, they lowered the rope line down to the nail directly below. Then very carefully, they attempted to snag the nail. The first couple tense failed attempts resulted in the nail falling to the floor with a clatter and the pixies wincing and quietly arguing in the process. They didn't want to wake up nasty old Nerges. Finally on their third attempt, they managed to snag it. Being carefully diligent, they calmly pulled up the nail into the cage.

"Yaaay, success," the Pixies celebrated and marvelled in the strength of pixie hair. Then they set to work, using the nail to pick the lock of their prison cage. Before long, the lock clicked and the door swung open. Happy with their newly attained freedom, the pixies gained their magical powers back. Then they fluttered their wings and flew down to the floor to rescue the baby dragon. Bluebell pulled out a little wand and touched the baby dragon's shackles with the wand. They clicked open and the dragon was set free.

"We have to get out of here," Lily-Green whispered aloud.

"Can you fly, baby dragon?" Bluebell asked the little dragon, who only sat there and stared at her, blinking.

"He doesn't know how to fly yet; he was just born," Lily-Green said, then added, "I think he needs a name."

"You're so right. I didn't think about that," Bluebell agreed.

So, the two pixies went over a bunch of ridiculous names and argued over them before settling on a simple one they both agreed on. Because of the sharp horn on the end of the baby dragon's nose, they called him Spike!

Suddenly, the door from the hag's room burst open. "What do we have here?" Nerges bellowed in outrage. "I'm going to cook the lot of you up for a good meal once I'm done with my plans," she yelled. Then Nerges started chanting a spell.

The two pixies were shocked in surprise, but when the hag started casting her spell, Bluebell was the quicker. Before the hag got her spell off, Bluebell snapped her finger and the hag's spell fizzled. Then Lily-Green stamped her feet and the hag turned into a warty toad.

"We sure fixed you, nasty old witch," the pixies celebrated gleefully.

"You're not going to hurt us anymore," said Bluebell.

"We did turn her into a toad. Good idea, Bluebell!" said Lily-Green. "But we should go; the spell will wear off in a couple of hours, and we have a long way to go," advised Lily-Green.

"Yes, you're quite right. We must go," replied Bluebell in agreement.

Then they heard big footsteps as the hag's ogre goons came to investigate. "What's all dis noise den?" the first ogre said when he lumbered into the room, brandishing a big club. When the ogre viewed the scene of the pixies' handiwork, he realized the pixies were up to no good and moved in to deal with them.

"Hey, yous hurt the master," the ogre blurted out as he swung his big club at the pixies. The club smashed a chair into splinters, but the pixies easily avoided the attack.

Seeing the second ogre coming in the door, Bluebell didn't hesitate on her retaliation. She flew at the first ogre and knocked him in the face and he tumbled back into the second ogre. Both ogres went stumbling and sprawling out of the door and fell to the deck in a big heap.

"Take that, you big ugly nasties," Bluebell yelled. "Your smelly hag master should have told you how strong pixies can be!"

As Bluebell was rumbling with two big ogres, Lily-Green got a notion to sprinkle pixie dust over the baby dragon. He started floating in the air. Then Lily-Green gently pushed him out the window. "There you go, Spike. I will be along with you soon," said Lily-Green.

Little Spike was perplexed about what was going on around him. Loud crashing and banging he could hear from inside the hut. The loud noises and shouts combined with himself floating through the air—he understood none of it but enjoyed the new sensation. He was only just a little fellow and newly born, after all. So, he just floated in the air, enjoying the feeling.

Back in the hut, the ogres collected themselves and went charging back in through the door in a rage. "Yous pixie demons, we's gonna hammer yous flat like little bugs," the ogres yelled. And they proceeded to swing wildly at the pixies, who could avoid their big lumbering swings with ease. But the ogres were wrecking the place in the process. A wild swing from one of the ogres' clubs smashed into the door, narrowly missing the toad, which was still the nasty old hag. The toad only let out a couple of frog croaks, then jumped out of the window and into the swampy water.

"I have an idea. Let's lure those two big dumb buffoons outside," Bluebell said to Lily-Green.

Lily-Green nodded in agreement and the two pixies quickly flew past the ogres and out the door.

"Come and get us, you big ugly sillies," taunted Bluebell.

"We're over here, you big smelly wart heads," added Lily-Green.

When the ogres came out in renewed rage, Bluebell went left and Lily-Green went right. The first ogre went left after Bluebell, swinging his club and fist wildly. Bluebell made him lose his balance and then pushed him into the water.

The second ogre went right after Lily-Green, where she led him to the hoist winch. When she flew over it, she sprinkled fairy dust on the rope, making it float. The ogre caught his legs in the rope and got his feet all tangled up. Then Lily-Green pushed him over and winched the ogre up, leaving him dangling in the air by his tangled feet.

"You can hang around here for a while, blockhead!" commented Lily-Green with a giggle.

Bluebell then swiftly cast a spell that turned both ogres' clubs into butterflies.

"That was a great idea, Bluebell. I love butterflies," said Lily-Green merrily.

But the fight wasn't over. The first ogre who went swimming came bursting out of the water, swinging his fists wildly. The ogre blurted out all kinds of obscenities while trying to squash himself a pixie or two. Bluebell and Lily-Green weaved in and out of his wild swings without much effort.

"My, my he's mad. It's as if some crazy fairies pissed him off," said Lily-Green, giggling.

"Yes, and it's time for him to go for another swim," Bluebell responded.

The two pixies attacked the ogre's head and face with a series of various slamming hits. The ogre teetered and tottered on the brink of collapsing. Then Bluebell took out her wand and tapped the ogre on the forehead. The ogre's eyes rolled up into the back of his head, and he fell backwards into the murky water.

"He will be out for a while, and he won't remember a thing," Bluebell said confidently while smiling, her hands casually resting on her hips.

"No, he won't; nothing at all," Lily-Green agreed. "And we better get Spike out of here before that polymorph spell on the hag wears out. She's much too powerful for the spell to effect her permanently; it won't hold her for long," she added.

"Quite right," said Bluebell as she quickly flew up to get a hold of Spike, who was still floating in the air and enjoying himself. But in that moment, Spike had a feeling to stretch, and he tried flapping his wings.

Bluebell pulled Spike along as her and Lily-Green started on their way out of Swampwood. Even though they escaped and got away, they had a problem. They could only go as fast as Spike could go, and little Spike couldn't go very fast. He needed the aid of the pixies, and they had a long way to go.

"Going slow is one problem, but we have another," said Lily-Green.

"What's the other problem?" asked Bluebell.

"We don't have enough flying dust between us to keep Spike floating like this," explained Lily-Green.

"I didn't think of that," said Bluebell. Then Bluebell had a notion—an idea to help on their escape. "Hey, Spike," she said, getting his attention. "Watch me." Bluebell floated in the air and gently flapped her wings.

Spike started copying her motions. Being a dragon, it was in his nature to fly, and he caught on quickly. After a few miss-tries, Spike was flapping his wings merrily without the aid of the pixies.

"Yaaaayyyyyy, Spike, you're doing it! You're flying!" the two Pixies celebrated, excitedly flying around in a frenzy.

"The pixie dust will help you go faster, Spike, so let's go," Bluebell said, fired up to get out of Swampwood.

The two Pixies and Spike set off at Spike's speed while the pixies gave Spike simple pointers and advice as they went.

Back at the hag's hut, the spell cast on Nerges wore off and she turned back from toad form to her former self. She was still in the murky water of the swamp and was not the least bit happy. In raging anger, she crawled out of the swamp and onto the dock of her hut. Viewing the scene of her ogre guards and the destroyed state of her hut, she didn't take long to realize what had happened. Nerges entered her broken hut in a frenzy, throwing stuff around in anger. Her fear was confirmed: the two pixies and the little dragon were all gone.

The witch pulled a big book of powerful magical spells off the shelf and through it on the ground. She muttered a magical word, and the book flipped its own pages, falling on the one Nerges desired. She started casting a rare and powerful magic.

"By the power of the dark dominion, I beckon to all in Swampwood to come unto me and do as I command," the hag growled in a deep chant. The room grew gloomy, and a low rumble rippled through Swampwood.

"What was that?" Lily-Green wondered out loud.

Bluebell stopped and took note of the rumble that came past them. "It's the hag's power; we must hurry."

The two pixies and Spike started off faster than before. As they went, the swampy woods got murkier and foggier. Trees came alive and tried to grab them or get in their way. Swamp trolls crawled out of the water before them to block their path. Large bats started to chase them as well. It was as if Swampwood was preventing their escape.

Being guided by Bluebell, Spike flapped his wings vigorously. Lily-Green acted as interference up front. One troll rose to meet them before being dispatched by Lily-Green's wand.

"Not today, you big smelly nasties," Lily-Green yelled as she smacked the ugly troll with her wand, turning it into a beetle.

The two pixies took turns in guiding Spike and zapping trolls. But in all the chaos of their escape, their sense of direction turned around and the trio started to lose their way.

At the witch's hut, all matter of trolls, goblins, and ogres came to the hag's command. Nerges cackled wickedly at the sight of her newly summoned force. "You all know what I'm after, so let's go get them!" The hag's horde of Swampwood set out with their master to hunt down the two pixies and the baby dragon.

Little Spike and the two pixies were a bit lost. Everything seemed the same in every direction.

"Where are we? We should be out of Swampwood by now," remarked Lily-Green.

"I don't know," said Bluebell. "I think we have lost our wits and our way."

"It's this stinky, dingy, menacing wood," said Lily-Green in disgust.

Every turn they took, they were running into the same dangers and obstacles. More swamp trolls and creeper vines, amongst other nasty things. It wasn't until they went up above the trees to look around that they found their direction again.

"Look over there! I can see the Bluebell Forest beyond the fog," said Bluebell in excitement.

"Now we know which direction we need to go," Lily-Green added.

Big, oversized bats suddenly hounded them from underneath the trees, which the pixies handled easily by tapping each one with their wands and turning them into various sorts of harmless tiny bugs.

"We got to keep moving," Bluebell snapped quickly.

When they dipped down further under the tree canopy, they heard the rumblings of the hag's summoned army approaching them—and they were not too far behind. Bluebell and Lily-Green looked at each other in Unison and blurted out, "GOTTA GO!"

They grabbed Spike and blasted off as fast as their wings could carry them.

Furious Nerges and her swampy horde travelled at a determined pace and with dark intent.

"Let's ravage the Bluebell Forest and destroy all within," Nerges bellowed out to her army, who were armed with nasty thorny weapons of all kinds: spiky swords, thorny spears, and evil-looking hacking weapons, all black and foul as if they had been resting in swamp for years.

The pixies and Spike flew like they had never flown before, but the hag's dark horde kept pace.

"We must reach the Bluebell Forest. Our magic will be stronger there," Blue Bell yelled out to Lily-Green. "Don't stop!"

Lily-Green turned her head around to view the approaching horde of abominations. "I don't think stopping is really in the plan," Lily-Green replied and sped up to emphasize the point. Just as the Swampwood's efforts to keep the trio from escaping grew stronger, Spike and the pixies came out of the foulest part of forest—but they were not home free yet.

The hag and her mad horde were hot on their trail. Bluebell saw something out of the corner of her eye that caught her attention—a large coppery-coloured dragon off in the distance that seemed to be looking for something. Bluebell had a sudden notion and turned Spike's full attention to the searching dragon.

Spike spotted the flying dragon above. The dragon seemed strangely familiar to him, and so he cried out a small sound.

Before long, the forest changed from murky, swampy woods to majestic trees, and the ground became solid, all covered with green grass. After a while, as they kept going, the trees eventually became more enchanting and the forest floor turned into a carpet of bluebell flowers. Bluebell and Lily-Green stopped, with little Spike positioned behind them. They could see the hag's army approaching.

"This is it; we are on the edge of the Bluebell Forest," Bluebell shouted out loud. "Let's show that nasty hag our fairy magic."

Lily-Green nodded in response and drew out her wand. Meanwhile, Spike started to cry out more, getting louder. Bluebell and Lily-Green waved their wands, producing a sparkly mist that weaved about them. Giant thorny plants and vines rapidly grew out of the ground in front of them. The growth stretched out far and wide, out of sight on each side, cutting off the hag's horde from them. The thorny wall of vines was thick and impassable. The hag's army horde ran into the thorny mass in a heap, getting all tangled up. The pixies then cast their second spell, which rendered the horde confused and disillusioned. Half of the witch's horde was running back in all directions.

"Ha-ha, you ugly, smelly swamp crawlers! We fixed you good," Lily-Green yelled out. Bluebell added a few taunts of her own, but the pixies celebration was short lived.

Nerges cast out a spell from her book, dispelling it all! "The game is not over, my meddling little pixies," the hag spat in anger. Then she stretched her hands out and sent a sudden wave of magical energy, blasting the pixies and Spike. The force knocked them back and to the ground, leaving them dazed.

"Now you will suffer my full wrath, pixies," the hag boasted. Nerges ordered her horde, who had regathered, to move forward to spoil and ruin the Bluebell Forest. Then she started to weave a spell.

Spike and the pixies were far too dazed and could not collect themselves in time to escape the hag's spell.

Suddenly without warning, a thunderous ball of fire fell from the sky, raking the ground in front of the hag's horde, blocking the way. A very large coppery-green dragon landed between the pixies and the hag. The dragon landed with such a slam, it shook the very ground beneath them. The hag's spell fizzled out.

The hag was fighting her fear and tried to cast a spell on the dragon, but to no avail. "I-I-I am Nerges of Swampwood, and I will get what's mine," she said, stumbling over her words.

"I know who you are, hag," the dragon rumbled in a dangerous tone. "And I know what you stole from me. It is lucky for you that I'm not very hungry. Now be gone from sight, back to your dank dark forest, and never return. If you do, I'll burn your stinking swampy woods to smoldering ash," the dragon threatened with a roar.

The hag and her army turned and fled in wild abandon. The dragon breathed out a horrific fire storm just to drive the point home. When the hag and her horde were gone and things turned calm again, the dragon turned its attention to the two pixies and, of course, Spike.

"Wow, you're a big dragon. I'm Bluebell," Bluebell introduced herself while smiling her best meeting-a-big-dragon smile.

"And I am Lily-Green, and this is Spike," Lily-Green innocently said, joining in on the introductions. "What's your name?"

The dragon chuckled in amusement. "My name is Glifoless Glaze, and I am also Spike's mother."

"Spike's mother?" Lily-Green responded and then looked over to Bluebell, who was smiling from ear to ear, knowingly.

"Spike is a very unusual name, but it seems to fit him," the dragon acknowledged. "I will give him an official dragon name later, but I think the name Spike will be with him for all his days."

Spike flew to his mother for a happy reunion. Glifoless Glaze thanked the pixies for saving her little son from the nasty old hag, Furious Nerges. She said Spike could play in the Bluebell Forest or the Greenwood with the pixies whenever he wanted. But before the mother dragon and her son departed, Bluebell invited them into the Bluebell Forest for a little celebration, pixie style!

Lily-Green told the story to the mother dragon on how they rescued Spike. She reassured her that the next time they go somewhere with Spike, it would be a safe adventure.

Under trees and around the stones
and through the duff of forest loam,
a place for those who call it home,
a home for pixies and forest gnomes.

A magical dance that's rarely seen
performed throughout the forest green;
rarely understood that there has been
what the fairies dance can truly mean.

The King of Greed

In the heartlands of Rithanon, long, long ago, there once ruled a cruel, greedy, and vile king. He ruled in the mighty Age of Empires before the Second Darkness. He was so vain he had the most and best of everything—so he had thought! This king's name was King Teadren and he ruled of the Kingdom of Croilair. King Teadren had the biggest, fanciest castle, the biggest army, and the biggest country, which was the entire expanse of the Heartlands. He also had the most gold and jewels of all and the biggest chamber to fill them with. But what he did not have was the most beautiful wife and queen of any kingdom. This he wanted most of all, even more than anything he had over anyone.

One day, King Teadren set out to search all the surrounding kingdoms for the most beautiful of possible maidens he could betroth to be his queen. Eventually in one kingdom in the west known as Guskony, he found the Princess Evelina and she was the fairest of all.

Teadren said to Evelina's father, the king, "Give me your daughter's hand in marriage and I will not invade and take your kingdom from you."

Evelina's father could not contest King Teadren's large army, so he had no choice and reluctantly agreed. Though horrified, Evelina went back to King Teadren's Kingdom of Croilair to become his wife and queen. Evelina was so fair and so beautiful that any man who looked upon her fell instantly in love. King Teadren instantly grew jealous and possessive, and he guarded her feverishly from his own company on the way back to his kingdom.

Upon arrival at his court, he decreed, "No man shall speak to Evelina nor look upon her with interest, or I will behead them."

Though he flaunted Princess Evelina like a trophy, King Teadren wanted all of her in a way that only he could look upon her in such fashion. Due to his possessiveness, many men and lords lost their heads from viewing her in any way that displeased him.

On the day of the wedding, all the kings, queens, and princely lords of the surrounding kingdoms were in attendance. For if they were not, King Teadren would threaten to claim their kingdoms for his own as he had threatened to Evelina's father.

In attendance was one such prince by the name of Afflon. Afflon was a charming and handsome prince from a southern kingdom called Palosa (now Bethinia), and Evelina became instantly smitten with him. Afflon was also smitten with Evelina, and they secretly fell in love with each other.

The wedding was grand—the most grandiose wedding that there ever was. The Princess Evelina, now Queen Evelina, was showered with gifts from every kingdom. But the only gift Afflon gave her was that of love and potential freedom. Even though Evelina was now queen of King Teadren's grand Kingdom of Croilair, she did not love him.

On the night after the wedding and grand celebration, Queen Evelina and Prince Afflon eloped so they could be together. They travelled far in the night to not be found.

At dawn, after discovering Evelina and Prince Afflon's treachery, King Teadren became furious, unleashing an uncontrollable anger.

"How dare she betray me! I have the best of everything and gave her the best wedding that all the kingdoms have ever seen in all of Rithanon! And this is how she repays me?" the king raged.

But there was one thing the king did not give her, and that was love and freedom. He was far too lost in his own importance and greed for material wealth. He was blinded by the desire to own all!

"I will search far and wide, high and low, and put Prince Afflon's kingdom to the sword," the king declared. "I will chop and burn down every forest, and I will search every castle and every cottage to find them. They can never hide from me." With that, the king gathered his massive army and set out in search of Evelina and Afflon.

In his search, he laid both Evelina's and Afflon's kingdoms in ruins by sword and fire. He searched every dwelling, town, and forest. Evelina and Afflon could not hide anywhere, for King Teadren's army was too vast. King Teadren even cut down every forest he could access to find them—except for one woodland, forbidden to outsiders.

Evelina and Afflon eventually entered that particular and peculiar enchanted woodland after running from King Teadren's soldiers, day and night. For days, they avoided his wrath before they risked entering the forbidden forest.

"This place is forbidden and haunted! Some call it the Dark Forest, or Dark Woods, and it's right on the doorstep of Croilair," Queen Evelina said with concern.

"It's only forbidden but not haunted. It's the realm of the dryads, and there is someone who may be able to help us: the dryad queen," Prince Afflon reassured her. Evelina was intrigued.

The prince and the queen cautiously entered the forest of the dryads and the realm of the fairy folk.

"At the centre of the mossy damp forest of knobby giant oak trees, lived the queen of the dryads. Her name was Sylvantia, and Sylvantia lived in a grand silver oak tree," Afflon explained. Afflon knew of her through legend, and he took the chance to seek her out.

For three days, they travelled through the murky woods. All matter of unseen eyes were upon them. It felt like even the trees seemed to be watching them. Then they finally came upon a grand silver oak tree at the centre of the forest, which was the home of the dryad queen.

Suddenly, they were surrounded by dryads. A beautiful silvery-green-haired girl slowly glided down from the tree to stand before them. Evelina and Afflon felt a little overwhelmed.

"Welcome Prince Afflon and Queen Evelina. Welcome to my kingdom. I am Sylvantia, the dryad queen," she said with a singing voice.

"We are in search of refuge, O Queen of the Forest, and look to not trouble you. King Teadren has chopped down every forest in all the land, save for this one," the prince explained.

"I know," said the dryad queen. "My kin and I have noticed. Some of my kin have moved from other woods into my wood because of the king's actions, and for that, I will help you." Sylvantia reached out and opened her hand, revealing an acorn in her palm before continuing. "I will give you a gift to help replenish the forest land. Swallow this silver acorn I give to you; it will give you the power to enact a great enchantment. Then you must face and defeat King Teadren to release the magic bestowed upon you."

Prince Afflon agreed and then he took the silver acorn and swallowed it. A second acorn was given to Queen Evelina to plant in a location of her choosing.

Meanwhile, King Teadren had pillaged and searched in vain. He was wary and growing mad with frustration. He had nowhere left to look that was accessible to him, except for one: the forbidden enchanted woodland of the dryads. It grew on the southern side of his kingdom, up the mountains. Though his council advised against it, Teadren chose his very best men for the task of searching the forbidden woodland. But it mattered little to Teadren; he wanted his revenge.

Blind to the danger, King Teadren and his men entered the forbidden dark woods. He did not attempt to cut these trees down, for all who dared to do so would be cursed. The forest was vast, and they searched for days through the unsettling, gloomy forest until they came upon a great silver oak tree.

Standing under that tree, waiting for the king and his men was Prince Afflon and Queen Evelina.

"At last, I have found you I will show you what folly it is to betray me," King Teadren raged. "Take them away!" he ordered his men.

Suddenly, as they moved to apprehend the prince and queen, the king's guards were swarmed and blocked by a mob of dryads.

Prince Afflon laughed. "I have made some friends." The prince drew his sword and pointed it at King Teadren, saying very calmly, "That one is mine!"

The battle was on. The dryads overcame the king's soldiers quickly. Teadren and Afflon fought, steel against steel, crossing blades in a ferocious contest. Finally, Afflon overpowered King Teadren and defeated him. In his grief of losing, the king begged the prince to kill him, but Prince Afflon would not. The prince just casually stepped away.

"There is another fate in store for you, King Teadren," Prince Afflon said to him.

As the king looked puzzled by this, he was suddenly entangled by roots from the forest floor and swallowed into the earth. The enchantment had been released, and every soldier in King Teadren's army grew roots and became a tree. His army had replenished the woodlands he had cut down. The enchantment also healed the kingdoms stricken by King Teadren's wrath. His army and his rule were no more.

Prince Afflon and Queen Evelina emerged from the forest of the dryads. The surrounding kingdoms rejoiced in their victory, and the kingdom of Croilair accepted Afflon and Evelina as their rulers.

Queen Evelina, the fairest of all queens, planted her silver acorn where it would grow to be a strong and vibrant silver oak tree and be viewed from afar. So, from that time forth, the only thing that was the best in all the land was the Silver Oak, which was shared by all its subjects, who were free to visit it. And new friendships blossomed between the surrounding kingdoms and Croilair. King Afflon and Queen Evelina also shared the tranquil forests provided by King Teadren's soldiers. The forests were open for all to enjoy, with the freedom to come and walk through them and enjoy them as they were.

Be aware it's good to share
and give to those who need.
In return, be kind and fair;
don't bite the hand that feeds.

Be grateful for what you have in life
in loving what you do.
With open generosity,
rewards come back to you.

Holy Warriors

Long, long ago, before the coming of the Second Darkness, in a faraway land across the Eastern Sea from the continent of Rithanon was a land called Rilendore, on the continent of Vastania. There, a great evil had risen from the darkness of the abyss of the underworld. A strange horde had been travelling around the lands of Rilendore, plundering, pillaging, and slaying all before it.

The horde consisted of all matter of abominations: goblin kin of all kinds mixed with ogres, trolls, and big giants that came out of the vast mountains from the East to join the horde. The horde grew and followed the rule of a man named Haumdrel, who wielded a mighty black sword. Haumdrel's black sword was darker than the darkest night. It had a thirst for feeding on life and souls, and with hunger, it fed.

Those from the holy house of the high god Halios had heard of such a dark black sword from a distant time. The clerics pondered and researched the possibilities as to the true identification of this sword. Some said it was one of the demon swords, but they were only subservient to a specific dark lord line of evil and vile men who lived unnaturally long lives. It did not fit the profile.

The horde kept growing and growing, and it kept raiding by the will of Haumdrel. Word had spread, that whole kingdoms were fleeing the massive horde. Mysteriously, even some of the people were joining it. Then just before winter, the horde suddenly headed north to unoccupied lands and the raiding stopped. All went quiet as winter set in.

The House of Halios did not hesitate to unite the now free kingdoms of Rilendore and combine all their forces. When winter broke, they planned to meet Haumdrel and his evil horde. During the winter preparations, three brothers of the House of Halios stepped forward. They offered to lead the armies of the free kingdoms against the horde. Their names were Andrin, Gondrin, and Sundrin. Each brother wielded a holy sword of great power and had the blessings of the high gods. They had come to meet the dark storm that was the horde led by Haumdrel with his vile sword.

The kings and high clerics of the free kingdoms of Rilendore saw and recognized the three brothers' power. Combined with their will to face Haumdrel, the clerics accepted the offer by the three brothers.

Winter gave way to spring and the horde poured out of the Northern Mountains of Rilendore. Dark thunderous clouds grew and followed the horde as it went. Lightning flashed periodically, but unlike a regular storm, this one had an ominous presence to it. Driving this storm was Haumdrel at the horde's head, wielding his mysterious black sword. Dark mist poured off it as he held it high so his horde could view it. They were screaming, destroying, and slaying all in their wake, like a dark storm without end.

The three brothers rallied the free kingdoms' forces to meet Haumdrel's horde on the plains of the central Kingdom of Goutha. There, the allied kingdoms planned to stop the mysterious storm.

The two armies met in a titanic clash of arms. The titanic, violent battle went on for three days and three nights, without any end in sight. It was the largest clash of mortals to date. There were hundreds of thousands on both sides. The horror of the battle was never seen or heard of before in the history of the world. The horde would not break, and it was all controlled and driven by Haumdrel and his vile, mysterious black sword. As Haumdrel slew, the sword fed; and as it fed, he gained power.

As the battle wore on, the free kingdoms' combined armies grew weary with fatigue. It looked hopeless as the horde drove on as if by an unseen power. The three holy brothers met up, and together they prayed to the high gods for an answer. At first, no response was given.—then all the brothers blessed swords started to ring.

As the battle raged, nobody could face Haumdrel and survive. Whole waves of clerics and units of holy warriors would perish from the dark blade of Haumdrel. Time was running out for the allied armies of the free kingdoms. Haumdrel was gaining the upper hand, and he pressed on, eating souls, and feeding the bloodlust of himself and his great vile sword.

The three holy brothers, Andrin, Gondrin, and Sundrin, looked up to the heavens of the high gods with wonder. The ringing of their swords reached a crescendo and then suddenly stopped. Each brother's sword shined bright and warm. It felt as if they were keeping the darkness at bay. There was a renewed feeling of empowerment and hope. The three holy warriors raised their empowered, enchanted holy swords and charged forth to meet the horde's dark master.

As the brothers charged in, they felt compelled to combine their blades and they crossed them. When they did, all the three holy swords became one mighty great-sword, and Sundrin, the eldest brother of the three, held it aloft. Andrin and Gondrin backed off, and only Sundrin, with his mighty divine sword, moved forward to meet Haumdrel. With renewed strength, the free kingdoms' armies pressed back into the battle, and they cheered the brothers on.

At the very centre of the battle, Sundrin met Haumdrel who challenged him to single combat. They clashed with a force of which the gods would take notice. It was a duel of epic proportions, and it, too, seemed to go on without end. Both combatants had wounded each other greatly.

Finally, luck had run out for Haumdrel and his big vile sword. The two combatants were matched, but Sundrin had finally got the upper hand, and he ran his sword through the chest of Haumdrel. Haumdrel fell and the horde wavered as his black sword dropped from his hands.

Haumdrel was vanquished, and morale rose in the armies of the free kingdoms. They pressed the attack, and soon, they overran the horde of Haumdrel.

Haumdrel and his horde were defeated. The Battle of Goutha was over. When the dark war was finished, Sundrin later died from his wounds. And so, Sundrin became a saint. The mighty holy sword that Sundrin faced

Haumdrel with had turned back to the three respective and separate holy swords that they once were. They were named after the three brothers who wielded them.

Andrin and Gondrin laid the sword of Sundrin on Sundrin's monument, and a big celebration was held in his honour.

Haumdrel's mysterious black sword was never found after the battle. And much debate had risen as to the blade's true origin. Nevertheless, the brothers Andrin and Gondrin carried on the torch against evil and started a new brotherhood order of holy warriors. In honour of Sundrin, the slayer of Haumdrel, the first nights of the holy order had risen to protect the free kingdoms of Rilendore from such evil again.

Was made by divine immortal hands,
not meant for use by mortal man;
its shadow calls to make balance fall
and corrupt immortals created lands.

The power unseen in which it holds
is feeding on mortal moral souls;
it drives its darkness relentlessly
to destroy and engulf the world whole.

Bangar and Grundel

Far west, just outside the dwarven lands of Cambria, stood a formidable citadel high atop a craggy mountain. This citadel was the home of Grundel, the giant cyclops goblin king. Grundel was a giant strong cave goblin. He stood twelve feet high and had one central eye in his forehead. He sported a menacing jaw with sharp teeth and jutting tusks that added to his fierce presence. He was menacing and cruel, and he took what he wanted without mercy.

Grundel was always raiding, but he grew tired of raiding the surrounding area, so he looked east to the dwarven lands of Cambria. He had heard their riches were untold, and their crafting and mining skills were legendary. Grundel needed skilled slaves for his rich gold and jewel mines, and dwarves were the best miners. He grew tired of goblins and humans. They just simply would not do anymore.

Grundel gathered all the local goblin tribes and ogre clans to his call. He combined them with some mountain trolls and his elite cyclops goblin force. With his mountain horde, he raided all the communities in the dwarven western mountain lands of Cambria. Grundel's horde rounded up all the dwarves, then marched them back to Grundel's mountain citadel, east in the Mountains of Malice. Before sending them all to his mines, he gathered them together to announce what was to become of them.

"You shall work my mines until all your lives are spent, and if your work does not satisfy my hunger for gold and jewels, your life will be spent faster," Grundel informed them loudly. "Now go and make my kingdom more wealthy and stronger, then the kingdom of your own kin." Grundel then shuffled his new dwarven slave force down into his deep mines, to a world of hardship and misery.

The dwarven slaves worked hard in chains under whips and forceful threats. They delved deeper and deeper yielding untold wealth. But Grundel's greed was unsatiable, and he worked them harder when the volume of wealth slowed down. He laughed callously as his mountain of treasure grew. As the dwarves suffered through the many months of forced slave labour, Grundel was growing ever so richer.

Deep resentment grew among the dwarven slaves. One tough, brown-haired dwarf by the name of Bangar was the strongest among his folk, who worked in Grundel's mines. His resentment was the greatest. From the moment he arrived, Bangar had been forming an escape plan. It had been months, and the conditions of his folk were worsening. Many started dying in great numbers, and he knew he had to escape soon if he was to come back and free his people.

During a rare moment of rest, one old dwarf named Tagrin looked at Bangar and said, "How do you plan to escape? What will you do? Is it even possible?"

Bangar scratched his beard in thought. "I have been watching the guard change on the ore tram schedule. There's a pattern I've figured out, with one change to act on," he replied in a serious tone. "I have to stay vigilant and be ready to act on that change."

"But it's an impossible feat; you will never make it," the old dwarf whined.

Bangar looked at old Tagrin hard with his steely blue eyes. "I can make it, and you must stay ready when I do and be quiet about it when I go, understand!" he sternly expressed.

The old dwarf nodded in surprise of Bangar's gumption and determination, so he wisely left it at that. He knew that Bangar was agile and quick for a dwarf and probably had the better chance of escaping than most. So, he decided not to argue with him.

The chance that Bangar was waiting for came a couple days later, and Bangar seized it. There was a change of guard at the same time a shipment was ready to go. Bangar had previously rigged one of the ore buckets on the tramline with a false bottom so he could get inside it and be hidden under the ore. Then he would just ride it up to the surface. Without hesitation, Bangar got into that ore bucket. The old dwarf looked on with skepticism as Bangar got into the bucket and some dwarves filled it with ore. Bangar's escape attempt was set up just in time before the guard change was completed.

The daily ore haul was taken to the surface later that day. When the ore bucket Bangar was hidden in emptied its load on the big pile of ore, the false bottom gave way and a very dirty Bangar tumbled out, down the ore pile between two big giant cave goblins standing ten feet high. Bangar was so filthy, he just looked like another grungy chunk of ore to the goblins, and they seemed not to notice him. Bangar thanked his luck and gingerly sneaked away. It was getting dark, and the gloom helped greatly since the giant cave goblins' infra-vision had not set in yet.

After a sneaky escape, Bangar made his way back to the mountains of Cambria and the great city of Rack-Hagen, under the silver Spire Mountain. It took him days, but he arrived in a feeble state, both hungry and fatigued. He was in rough shape but alive due to his sheer will to get back to his homeland and his determination to free his kin from Grundel and destroy the cyclops king.

Upon arrival, Bangar collapsed just outside the mighty front gate of the great dwarven city. The dwarven guards looked on in shock as he said, "I have finally arrived! I am Bangar Cairnegorm, son of Doron and I have come to seek aid. I have purpose beyond measure!" Then he fell unconscious.

An old high priest by the name of Gwillom took Bangar in. Gwillom nursed Bangar back to full health and listened to the tale Bangar had to tell and the mission he wanted to fulfill.

"It is a foolish quest," Gwillom said, not impressed at all with Bangar's plan. "Sieging a mountain citadel of that magnitude has never been accomplished without high magic in the history of our kin, maybe even in all of Rithanon," he reasoned. "The king would not allow it. It's far too much to risk."

"If I spoke to him about the captured condition of our people and my motive of freeing our kin, maybe he'd send an army. And we do have some high magic—you!" Bangar pointed out hopefully.

"I do not have the high magic required to accomplish such a feat. It takes much more than what I have to be effective," Gwillom said seriously. "I cast divine magic that is granted to me by the gods, not arcane magic of the greater path, which is required for an offence of that scale," Gwillom explained.

"I am going to speak to the king anyway, and I'm sure he will see reason," Bangar insisted. Then he left to go talk to the king.

And so, Bangar had his audience with dwarven King Moarin, and he was not granted his wishes. Gwillom was right all along about what the king would decide. Bangar stormed out, vowing to take matters into his own hands and find a way to free their kin from the mines of Grundel the cyclops king.

"I did tell you he'd not allow such a campaign that would only lay in failure," Gwillom said to a really angry Bangar. "We just simply do not have the immediate means or resources to take on Grundel's mountain citadel," he added.

"But there must be a way. And I am determined to find it," Bangar roared.

Gwillom and Bangar didn't say anymore for a period. At length, Gwillom sat there, stroking his long white beard in thought, weighing the risk and morality of Bangar's quest. After a rather long uncomfortable silence, Gwillom gave in to the brooding Bangar. Bangar was right; something had to be done. Doing nothing would only anger the gods and future dwarven generations, he thought. "OK, I will help you," Gwillom said with a sigh.

Bangar's mood brightened up a little bit. "Really, you'd help me?" he asked Gwillom hopefully.

"Yes, but you're going to have to listen to me and trust me," the old priest told Bangar sternly and seriously. "And it's not going to be easy," he added.

Bangar got all excited and embraced the priest in a thankful hug. "I will do whatever you tutor or tell me, and I will be in your debt," Bangar said to the old priest.

"All right, all right." Gwillom laughed. "Now get some rest; there is a lot we have to do," the priest said suddenly growing serious again.

Several days passed since Bangar had escaped Grundel's mines. The goblins didn't miss just one dwarf, since dwarven slaves died daily from either being worked too hard or by being buried in collapsing tunnels. Tagrin, the old dwarf, was anxious to hear word from Bangar because conditions grew bleaker. He swore to stay quiet about things, but his kin needed morale. Some glimmer of hope to hang onto before the escape. He struggled internally whether to say something or not.

One dwarf noticed Tagrin's irritation. "You've been acting a bit suspicious the last while Tagrin; what's on your mind?" the dwarf asked him.

"Nothings on my mind," the old dwarf grumbled. "I've just been thinking is all," he added, trying to not seem suspicious.

"We know you know something; all of us do," pressed the dwarf.

"I told you, I don't know anything," Tagrin responded angrily.

"Cut the crap, Tagrin. Something's going on that you're aware of," the dwarf spat at Tagrin. "Now let us in on it!"

Other dwarves began to join in, which added to the pressure. Finally, the old dwarf gave in to the relentless insistence.

"All right, all right, I'll tell you," Tagrin said in exasperation. "Young Bangar Cairngorm has escaped to get help," he confessed. Then the old dwarf related the whole story to a very attentive audience.

Nearby, two dwarves who helped Bangar escape looked on in disappointment. "You're a fool," they said to Tagrin after he finished his story about Bangar's escape. "Grundel's going to eventually find out, and then we will all be in for it." Their tone turned defeated.

Tagrin did not know what to say. "I'm so very sorry," he said, and then walked away.

Word quickly spread in whispers throughout the dwarven slaves, and there was a fresh spring in their step. Poor Tagrin didn't know whether to feel guilty or satisfied. But he finally resolved to himself, what did it really matter?

Bangar and Gwillom woke up the next morning, all fresh and ready to do important tasks. Gwillom lead Bangar to the temple of the dwarven gods. The old priest showed him a ritual to communicate with the gods and use their power to enhance his progress. There were two things Bangar was talented at before he and his kin were captured by Grundel: fighting and weapon forging. Bangar understood those things well and was instructed by Gwillom to embrace these—and embrace them he did. In the dwarven cities great forge, he learned new lessons and greater skill.

Weeks went by, and Gwillom told Bangar stories and secrets from the gods that had been withheld from dwarven ears for many centuries. Then, one night before Bangar retired for the evening, he had an intuitive thought to pray to the gods. For some reason, he felt that this was important to him; after which, he went to bed and fell asleep.

In the middle of the night, Bangar woke up sweating from an intense dream. The vision of this dream was locked in his head. He envisioned the halls of the lost and forgotten dwarven city of Ratulga. He saw Ratulga's great forge, the crafting hammer, and the anvil of spirits. Then he saw the gods and his forbearers using them. The dwarven gods turned to him and spoke as if directly to him.

"Mighty Bangar, hero of your kin, you must forge a hammer that will be worthy to free your people," the gods told him. Then the gods gave him instruction and direction. "Take this knowledge and hand it down your family line, but only one smith may know these secrets. Only in your clan's line can these secrets be known—the line of Cairnegorm," the gods concluded.

Bangar tried to get back to sleep but was too restless. The vision was strong, and the gods' instructions were swimming in his head. "This is dumb," grumbled Bangar as he finally gave up trying to sleep. He hopped out of bed early. "I have a lot to do," he said to himself.

Bangar got all geared up with tools and supplies in preparation to begin his task to construct a mighty war hammer. He travelled to the deepest mine in all of Cambria and climbed down to its lowest pits. There he gathered twenty pounds of pure blue silver steel.

Bangar took the rare, coveted metal to a powerful Paragon dragon in North Cambria known as Tailen. With Tailen's given blessing, Bangar set up his anvil and forge in the dragon's lair. Once he was set up, he began forging his hammer one week prior to a full moon. With the strength and heat of dragon fire, Bangar laboured, only stopping to eat or sleep. In those seven days, he never wavered. Finally, on the seventh and last day, his hammer was complete, but all was not done. The last task was to be completed by the light of a full moon.

There are two moons in the skies of Rithanon. Though Mosk, the smaller of two moons that hung in the sky, glowed a reddish colour, it was the day of the silver moon Syltella. Syltella shone full and bright. Bangar was very anxious. This was a critical time for the hammer to be completed. He climbed to the summit of the silver Spire Mountain and made it just in time for the height of the full moon.

Bangar raised his hammer over his head. He felt his connection to the mountain and said the words of prayer the gods had given him. He felt the feelings of strength and power, and they grew stronger within him. Then, a flood of power came from somewhere. The power passed through him and into the hammer. Bangar suddenly felt weak, and he could feel himself falling. When he hit the ground, Bangar passed out unconscious.

Grundel sat on his jewel-encrusted throne made of solid gold. He was bored and a little annoyed that the production of the mining had slowed down a bit. He was considering new painful and evil ways to motivate his slaves to work harder. Without warning, a very nervous goblin came into the throne room, right past Grundel's giant guards.

"Who is so bold that they disturb my contemplation?" Grundel growled at the little goblin.

"I-I, um, have urgent word from the mines your eminence," the little goblin stammered.

"Then approach and speak your words. Even if they hold little value, I am in need of some stimulation of any kind," Grundel confessed.

The little goblin approached the throne, terribly scared. "One-one of the dwarven slaves has escaped, O mighty one," he said.

"How does one missing dwarf concern me," Grundel balked. "He was probably crushed in a tunnel collapse. It happens every day," the giant cyclops king reasoned with a shrug.

"It's not just any missing dwarf," the goblin said. "His name is Bangar Cairnegorm, and he is strong willed and held in high regard by his kin. Guards from the mines overheard the dwarven slaves' whispers and low talk," the goblin explained.

"What!" Grundel said, his attention now stimulated but not alarmed. "A troublemaker, huh? It's of little consequence; he could not have gotten far. The country is rough and vast. We will hunt him down, catch him, and make an example of him," Grundel concluded confidently.

"There's more, O great powerful king," the little goblin said while visibly shaking.

"More what? More dwarves? You don't keep information from me, do you?" Grundel rumbled, eyeing the goblin. "Flattery won't help you if you are."

"No, Your majestic Majesty, it's only one dwarf. But that one dwarf apparently plans to return with an army to free his kin and to crush your kingdom," the goblin explained further, which did not help his survival.

"WHAAAAAAAAT!" Grundel yelled, his eyes bulging out of his head. He pounded the throne with his great fists and let out a roar that shook the entire hall. The little goblin backed up, shaking, and the guards left the room. Containing his rage, he got off his throne and leaned forward, nose-to-nose, with the little goblin, his eyes narrowing. "How long has this Bangar been gone?" Grundel calmly asked, danger in his glint.

"Over a month," the little goblin squeaked while cowering.

Grundel lost absolute control of his rage. Before he stormed out of his throne room, he scooped up the little goblin and ate him whole. Grundel the cyclops king had to prepare for Bangar's return. He had to prepare for war!

Bangar woke up freezing. It was snowing, and a fresh layer of snow had covered him. He suddenly remembered the hammer, still clutched in his frozen hands. He groaned while he collected himself up and began his slow trod back down the mountain. The hammer spoke to him in whispers, and he realized he had created something special, something powerful. He would learn to wield that power.

Grundel prepared his horde of various goblins, trolls, and ogres to defend the citadel. He worked the dwarven slaves harder for two solid weeks in the Adamantite mines. He needed the mineral Adamantite in order to make stronger weapons and armour and more of them. Many dwarves died, which resulted in Grundel unable to attain what he wanted: more weapons. So Grundel prepared another raiding party to capture more dwarven slaves. And why not? He would take the fight to the dwarves first, which would eliminate fewer potential soldiers that Bangar could recruit against him.

With an evil grin, Grundel approached his most trusted cyclops cave-goblin captain and champion of his forces—Brezig! Brezig was a monster of a goblin. He was even bigger than Grundel, but no less fierce. And he was loyal.

"Most trusted champion of arms," Grundel said to him.

"Mighty King Grundel," Brezig replied while bowing his head.

"Lead my raiding war party and capture as many of those dwarven scum as you can. Take the strong, slay the weak, and burn everything," Grundel ordered Brezig.

"I will do what you ask with pleasure, my king," Brezig obeyed willingly.

That same night, Brezig lead a sizable force out of the cyclops king's mountain citadel, to bring war and ruin to the dwarves of Cambria for the second time.

Cold and wet, Bangar collapsed in front of Gwillom's door. Gwillom opened the door and found Bangar in a bedraggled mess. Bangar had a mighty-looking war hammer clutched in his hands.

"This is starting to be a habit of yours, Bangar," Gwillom said with a sigh. "Come on, let's get you better."

While Gwillom was helping Bangar in, he could not help but examine the magnificent hammer Bangar had constructed. It had a strong, divine power radiating from it, and Gwillom was pleased. The hammer was sentient, and it spoke to him. Being a priest, Gwillom understood its power.

When Bangar was fit again, once more, he began training to unlock the power within the hammer. In doing so, Gwillom and the hammer guided him. For fourteen days and fourteen nights, Bangar trained, practised, and meditated the warrior's path. Finally on the fourteenth day, Bangar trusted his inner strength and connection to the earth, and just let go of all his anxieties. Everything came together in a flood that heightened his battle skill. He felt invincible and unstoppable. The hammer unlocked all its secrets, except for one. The last one was to be discovered in battle.

On the first day, after his fourteen-day warrior's journey, Bangar and Gwillom sat in contemplation on a big flat rock high on the mountainside. A young dwarf came running up the trail. He seemed excited to speak with them but was too winded to talk.

"Catch your breath, lad. What important news do you bring?" old Gwillom asked.

"Dwarven towns in the West burn from the hordes of Grundel," the dwarf revealed in horror.

"Does the king send warriors to handle the raids?" asked Gwillom.

"The king stands down. He does nothing, in the fear of infuriating Grundel. He still feels it's too much of a risk," the messenger concluded in disappointment.

Bangar looked at Gwillom with an ignited flame in his eyes and jumped off the rock, clutching his hammer.

"Where do you think you're going?" Gwillom asked Bangar, already knowing the answer.

"I want to test my hammer. It's time to pick it a fight!" Bangar stated flatly. "Are you coming or are you going to let me smash Grundel and his horrid horde on my own? Either way, it's game on."

Gwillom sighed and got up off the rock. He looked at the messenger and said, "Well, I guess we didn't get all prepared for nothing." Then Gwillom followed Bangar down the mountain.

Grundel's horde, led by Brezig, attacked dwarven towns without mercy! They smashed and burned everything in sight. All able-bodied dwarves, both male and female, were loaded into cage wagons. Those who fought back were either slain or captured.

One of Brezig's captains approached him and asked, "What do we do with the elderly and child dwarves, my lord?"

"Slay them, slay them all!" answered Brezig without remorse. Then he walked away, looking for new victims to satisfy his bloodlust.

"Yes, my lord," responded the captain unremorseful and obediently.

An armed crowd gathered outside near the main gates of the great dwarven city of Rack-Hagen. At the centre of that crowd, Bangar stood on a large, six-foot-high boulder, his hammer resting easily on his shoulder. The crowd was agitated and divided to the news of Grundel's latest attacks. Bangar was failing to make his kin see reason and fight. Many of them were too indoctrinated by the king's passive values. King Moarin was the softest and most passive king that ever sat on the Cambrian throne of Rack-Hagen, and Bangar did not like it. He felt that he needed to act dramatically or make a grand statement to get their attention. Maybe even both!

"We must face them and destroy them," cried one dwarf.

"We can't. The king won't muster the army," cried another dwarf.

"Grundel is far too strong. We can't fight his giant cave goblins," said a third.

"QUIET!" Bangar yelled. "Listen to yourselves. You quibble as if you were worthless and weak. Grundel is strong, but he underestimates us—so does our very own king. We are mountain dwarves, tougher than the hardest mountain stone. We are warriors, every single one of us, and you scurry away like mice," Bangar yelled out, building his speech. "We can destroy Grundel, and I have found a way."

"And what way might that be?" one dwarf asked sarcastically, which drew the odd chuckle from the crowd.

Calmly, Bangar looked at the dwarf and said, "This way!" He held up his mighty war hammer and slammed it into the big rock he was standing on. There was a thunderous crack and a flash. The big boulder Bangar stood upon was pulverized on the front side. The rock was also split in two, with Bangar straddling the great crack.

The crowd gasped, then started talking low to each other. Bangar had made the impression he was looking for.

Bangar looked at his hammer. "And now I shall give you a name," Bangar said to it. "I shall call you... Slammer!" He grinned, as if he and the hammer knew it all along; it seemed so fitting a name. Bangar raised the mighty war hammer called Slammer over his head and yelled, "Follow me to destroy Grundel and his evil, vile horde, or we all shall fall into oblivion."

Bangar jumped off his pulverized rock and sprinted through the crowd. The crowd yelled in triumph and made way for him. Then they fell in behind Bangar, with arms in hand, and followed him west, towards Grundel, the cyclops king.

Brezig and his goblinoid horde had raided many towns; their caged carts were full of new dwarven slaves. Many of the dwarves who could not be useful were slain without mercy. Many dwarven warriors resisted, and Brezig had lost a fair amount of his force in the process. But Brezig had routed them at a great cost. The dwarves had proven strong, much stronger than the first raid conducted many months ago.

"Take these newly filled cages back to the citadel and report to Grundel," Brezig ordered one of his cave-goblin captains.

"At once, mighty war leader," the giant goblin obeyed. "What do we do from here?" the captain asked Brezig.

"Now, I will go to see what lays beyond," replied Brezig in his blood-lust tone.

Brezig moved on a day's march further east to a vale that was occupied by a large known community of dwarves. When he crested a slight hill before the dwarven town, a sizable, armed dwarven force stood silently between him and the town. One brown-haired dwarf with a short beard stood out front, clutching a rather large and fancy-looking hammer. He was apparently the leader.

"Who stands before Brezig?" Brezig bellowed menacingly.

"What stands before you are death and ruin," Bangar bellowed back.

"That death and ruin shall be yours," Brezig retorted.

"We shall settle this in blood, you giant freakshow. Come and taste my hammer," Bangar challenged, lifting his hammer, Slammer, over his head.

The dwarves cheered a great roaring cheer while banging their shields and weapons together. Bangar smiled and winked at Gwillom, who stood beside him. Gwillom nodded back as they set their plan into motion.

Brezig looked at Bangar with utter hatred and the intent to rip him apart.

Gwillom closed his eyes and raised his arms. He started to mutter strange words and the clouds above gathered in a dark mass over Brezig's force.

Brezig bellowed out a command, and the menacing mixed goblinoid, troll, and ogre force charged the dwarves. The dwarves set into a strong shield wall as lightning strikes from the clouds overhead started to pummel Brezig's horde, who then slammed into the dwarven shield wall with such force, they were knocked back. But the dwarves held strong, and they did not buckle.

Further to the west, the slave caravan moved slowly back to the Grundel's citadel. The cave-goblin captain observed the rather out-of-place storm to the east. He pondered it curiously. The others were also distracted by the same strange occurrence. "Keep it moving," the captain yelled. He looked on at the storm and concluded to himself, "Magic! But, to what end?"

As the caravan moved on through a rocky pass, they heard a roaring cheer. A force of dwarves had been waiting up above on both sides of the slope, flanking the caravan.

"AMBUSH!" The cave-goblin captain bellowed out.

The dwarves furiously charged down the sides of the pass and caught the disoriented goblinoid war band off guard. Crossbow quarrels and explosive pot bombs rained down on them before the goblins could engage the charging dwarves. The big cave-goblin captain had no time to yell out any tactical orders before one tough and menacing dwarven warrior cut him down with a great axe.

Back at the main battle, Gwillom's lightning storm took its toll on Brezig's force. The goblinoid horde could not break the dwarven line. The dwarven shield wall was two strong. The dwarves began to regain ground and push back. They also began cutting down Brezig's horde systematically. Bangar and his great Slammer swept goblins, ogres, and trolls, big or small, aside like a sweeping broom.

Brezig moved to meet Bangar, and with a roar, he charged the seemingly unstoppable dwarf. Bangar noticed the big menacing Brezig charging towards him. He felt the surge of energy ignite within his war hammer, then felt compelled to throw it. With a great heave, Bangar threw Slammer. There was a mighty crack of thunder as Slammer turned into a titanic lightning bolt. That lightning bolt blasted Brezig to scattered bits and pieces of burnt cyclops before it immediately returned to Bangar's hands. Bangar was in awe as he realized the hidden power within his war hammer.

All goblins and dwarves alike were surprised at the sudden display of power by the hammer. But the dwarves didn't waste anytime cheering. The goblin force was leaderless and quickly grew weaker. The horde's force soon fell apart as the dwarves pressed the attack. Then the dwarves routed the goblins, and the battle soon ended. Brezig and his horde did not stand a chance!

Bangar's army met up with the dwarven force that freed the slave caravan. After consolidating forces in a big wooded area, they made some preparations that evening for the final approach on Grundel's citadel. To their surprise, they were also joined by the dwarven king's army, who had marched up behind Bangar's forces. Out of a made decision, King Moarin decided to finally help.

"Your Majesty, you finally made it," said Bangar, while dropping to his knee with a bow. Everyone else followed suit.

"Yes, Bangar, I have finally seen reason. What kind of dwarven king in the history of our kin would I be if I did not move to help my own people?" the king confessed with a bit of shame. "Forgive me!"

"You are forgiven, my king," Gwillom said, approaching him. "We're just all glad you could join us." Gwillom smiled as he clasped the king's shoulder.

King Moarin smiled back at Gwillom and said with a sigh, "Right, let's get it done!"

So, united once again, the king, Bangar, and Gwillom went over strategies for the upcoming assault on the big goblin citadel. The next morning, together as one mighty force, they set out west, into the craggy mountains. The final approach to the citadel of Grundel, the cyclops king.

Grundel impatiently sat on his jewel-encrusted throne. He had no word from Brezig. It had been far too long, and he should have heard from his champion by now.

"What's taking him so long?" Grundel bellowed. "I should be dining on dwarf by now. Not a single word from him in the last several days. Fetch me my best shaman. I demand answers," Grundel yelled at a passing goblin servant.

The goblin servant obeyed and left quickly. He did not want to be eaten, which was Grundel's favourite punishment.

While Grundel waited for his shaman to arrive, he heard a horn sound from the wall. That sound meant one of two things: Brezig's return or trouble.

Grundel rushed to his outside balcony to view what could have sounded the horn. Off in the distance moving into the valley dale, hundreds of spear points glistened in the sun, reflecting its light.

"Brezig!" Grundel assumed. But those hundreds of glinting spear points soon turned into thousands. As they got closer into view, Grundel discovered it was not Brezig's raiding war party coming back with spoils, but a large army of dwarves—an army of many thousands. For the first time, Grundel was speechless. Only one thing came to his mind, and it was the only word that escaped his mouth. "Bangar!" he muttered.

The dwarven army halted in the valley dale a few hundred yards out from the gates of Grundel's citadel. His imposing walls stood one hundred feet high, constructed of thick, hewn granite stone. Grundel's cyclops goblin captains scoffed at the dwarves.

"They don't even have a single piece of siege equipment with them. There is no way they can stage any sort of siege," said one of the captains with amusement.

They all laughed heartedly with mockery, including Grundel.

"This is going to be easier than I thought. Prepare for battle," the cyclops king ordered casually while grinning. "We will all be feasting on dwarf before the day is out." Grundel chuckled.

When the dwarves arrived, they were astounded at the size of Grundel's citadel. "It's a mighty and big fortress," commented King Moarin, his words reflected on the face of every dwarf in the army.

"Well, Bangar, it's your show," said Gwillom

Bangar nodded, then stepped out a little way in front of the dwarven army. He clutched his hammer Slammer in his hands with purpose on his stoic face. "GRUNDEL, come out and face me!" Bangar roared.

"So, this is the mighty Bangar. He doesn't look like much to me," the huge cyclops cave-goblin said mockingly with a chuckle.

"Come out and see how much I am," Bangar retorted back.

"I think I will stay right here, little dwarf. With no sieging equipment or engines, you are useless and weak," thundered Grundel.

"Let me display to you how useless and weak I can be," Bangar yelled back.

Bangar motioned to have something brought forth. Two dwarven warriors trotted a heavy sack closer to the citadel walls. Then they emptied its contents. A big cyclops goblin head rolled out.

"Remember your champion? Since you might have been missing him, I thought it would be gracious of me to return his head to you," Bangar yelled.

All the dwarves roared with laughter while Bangar did a sweeping bow to Grundel in mocking fashion.

It was the head of Brezig, and Grundel was not laughing anymore. "Fire the bombards," Grundel commanded in a serious tone.

The mixed goblinoid, troll, and ogre army waited in anticipation of battle as Grundel's bombards fired at the dwarven army. However, the bombard salvo fell short of the dwarves, who deliberately placed their forces just out of range. The dwarves were quite skilled on the use of bombards themselves and knew them well.

"Is that all you've got, you giant one-eyed mountain of ugly," Bangar shouted. "I challenge you to single combat, you coward, hiding behind your big thick high walls. C'mon, let's play!" Bangar taunted.

Grundel responded with more bombard salvos. "He is mine when we meet the dwarves on the field of battle," Grundel declared.

"Maybe you didn't quite get the message," Bangar yelled while grinning. "Let me help you understand a little better. My turn!" He sounded while raising his hammer above his head.

Bangar felt a great surge of power well up in him as he wound up to throw his hammer. As he let go, a thunderous crack of lightning flew from Bangar's hands, and in an instantaneous explosion, the hammer hit Grundel's citadel walls. The area of wall where the mighty war hammer hit crumbled to rubble. A host of various goblins fell with the wall. The dwarfs roared and cheered, then started chanting, "Bangar, Bangar, Bangar!"

In stunned silence, Grundel and his horde looked on. Rage welled up within the cyclops king. "Very well, dwarf, so be it!" Grundel muttered to himself. Armed with his big war axe called Splitter, Grundel strolled out to meet Bangar for a contest of single combat.

"I knew you'd get the point. I see you've come out to surrender," Bangar taunted with a smirk.

"Not quite, dwarf, I have a few tricks of my own," Grundel replied. Grundel brought his great axe to bare and with a mighty blow, he chopped the ground and split it. It caused a big rift between Bangar's feet, but Bangar quickly rolled out of the way and back to his feet again.

"That's a nice little trick. Shall we throw legendary powers around or settle this with honour?" Bangar said stoically.

"I think honour will do. I look forward to making an example of you and displaying your head on my main gate," Grundel responded.

Bangar bowed, and without a word, he positioned himself for combat with Grundel. Grundel did the same, and they measured each other up. As they moved around each other, Grundel seized the initiative. He moved in with a great sweep of his axe, meant to split Bangar in two, but Bangar jumped over it. He then blocked Grundel's backswing with stunning force and rolled between Grundel's legs with intent to knock out his knee. But Grundel quickly evaded it, and as he did, Grundel brought his axe down with intent to split the dwarf down the middle. Bangar was also quick to evade the earth-splitting axe that quaked the ground, and again, it left a rather large crack.

And so, it went on between Bangar and Grundel. Attacking, evading, blocking, tumbling, and taunting. They were both talented warriors with mighty weapons. The outcome was very much in doubt. Finally, Bangar was caught off balance and received a blow from the flat of Grundel's big axe. He went bowling over, his hammer flying from his hands. Bangar's companions gasped in shock. Grundel's warriors from the citadel wall cheered!

"HA-HAAAAA, FIRST BLOOD!" Grundel yelled with satisfaction. "Let me tell you how I will mount your head as my greatest victory, mighty dwarf," Grundel said as he moved in to finish Bangar off.

Meanwhile, in the mines, word had trickled down from the surface that an army of dwarves had shown up, and apparently, Bangar was facing Grundel alone. A mixed feeling of relief and anxiousness was felt among the dwarven slaves. During the distracting spectacle of Bangar's one-on-one battle with Grundel, Tagrin seized the moment to quickly rally a revolt.

Bangar was hurt, but he was not down. Bangar was tougher than the hardest mountain stone, and he feigned injury. As Grundel was yammering on and raising his big axe for the final blow, Bangar's hammer reappeared back into his hands. Then Bangar brought Slammer down onto Grundel's toes. A big crunch and a mighty yelp from the giant cyclops king was heard as he hopped in pain. Bangar casually got back up, ready to continue his little quarrel with Grundel.

"Hurts, don't it? That's blow for blow," Bangar said as he squared off with the big cyclops king once more.

Grundel growled in rage and re-engaged with the dangerous dwarf. He pulled out all his tricks of combat. The two combatants swung and blocked, parried and out-manoeuvred each others feints and attacks. Finally, Grundel landed his second blow, and Bangar went flying. He brought his axe down and chopped the earth. In a great thunderous quake, the earth split open under Bangar. Bangar was wounded, but he still had the sense to roll away before almost falling into the big crack. Grundel knew he had to finish off Bangar quickly, so he moved in fast to finish the job.

"Hear now, my axe is the last thing you'll ever see descending on your neck, dwarf, and it will be the last thing you ever feel. You are the best I've ever fought," Grundel declared.

As Grundel moved in for his final blow, Bangar clutched his hammer. Bangar was barely standing when Grundel moved in on him. When Grundel wound up for his killing blow, Bangar let fly his war hammer Slammer with a mighty throw. There was a thunderous crack as the hammer slammed into Grundel's head, and Grundel the cyclops King fell dead.

There was a great cheer from the dwarven ranks and gasps of horror from the citadel walls. Grundel laid on the broken ground without his head. Gwillom came forward to tend to Bangar while the dwarven king rallied the army for the final assault. They charged into the citadel, pouring through the broken wall from Bangar's hammer. As the dwarves moved into the citadel after Bangar's victory over Grundel, the dwarves that rallied under Tagrin in Grundel's mines attacked the goblin guards.

"Follow me my fellow dwarves and let us show the hordes of Grundel our vengeance and the tenacity to overthrow tyranny," Tagrin said. And follow Tagrin they did.

A great battle was fought! The casualties were many on both sides, but the dwarves prevailed and were victorious. They sacked the citadel and soon met up with Tagrin's revolt in the mines. The dwarven kin that were once slaves in Grundel's mines were now free. The wealth of Grundel was eventually transferred to the dwarven city treasury of Rack-Hagen. But a good portion of it was shared amongst all the dwarves.

Bangar was forever hailed as the hero of the dwarves. Him and his war hammer Slammer would pass down into legend. He became known as the dwarven hero who saved the dwarves from slavery and who had single handily defeated Grundel, the cyclops king.

*There he stood, with big war hammer,
the weapon known as mighty Slammer.
Grundel's walls stood thick and tall;
by Bangar's hammer, did they fall.*

*Grundel, the cyclops king, was raged;
to battle Bangar, he engaged.
Grundel and Bangar, faced and fought;
the head of Bangar, Grundel sought.*

*Bangar the dwarf, he did not quail
to battle Grundel, tooth and nail.
They fought like legend, and fought like storm.
By Bangar, Grundel's plans were torn.*

*Bangar's hammer slammed Grundel's head;
then Grundel, the cyclops king, fell dead.*

The Winter Rose

Vicinia Takauri was a dark elf of noble blood. She was skilled in magic, astute with sword, and strong in connection to the dark entities of the lower underworld. At the will of Ushativa, Queen of Shadows, in the underworld, Vicinia rose from the belly of Rithanon known as the deep earth lands. She rose as Ushativa's vessel, to deceive and dominate Rithanon's surface elves and fairy folk and to enslave them under the will of Dokalfar, father of all dark elves.

After one hundred years of domination, Vicinia was promised immortality in the dark underworld at Ushativa's side. The collective life force of the enslaved elven population would sustain her power, but to achieve this, she needed what was known as the Winter Rose.

Vicinia travelled to Elendar, home of the wood elves, to charm and join in marriage with Thandwin, King-Priest of Elendar. As she embarked to the surface world, Ushativa's voice entered her mind with a message.

"Vicinia, champion of dark elves, an important message I have for you. From under what is known as the Silver Oak Tree of Life grows the lavender rose, also known as the flower of life. When the first roses grew under the first Silver Oak, the Earth Mother blessed the weakest rose to become the strongest. It would bloom once per year on the winter solstice and was forbidden to be touched by all, for it was sacred. But the Rose was secretly tainted and cursed from the shadows. Anyone picking the Rose would gain control over the lands, and they would have eternal life at the cost of eternal winter. The lands life force is tied to the bearer of the Rose. Though anyone good at heart would never pick the Rose without reason, they could, however, sustain the lands. But if they are wicked at heart, the lands energy would drain to the Rose bearer, and as a result, they would gain control and create despair. But be warned, Vicinia, the Earth Mother saw the curse for what it was; so, she decreed that a blood relative, and only a blood relative, of the rose's bearer must slay them to end the eternal winter."

Ushativa left Vicinia's mind. Vicinia pondered the words of Ushativa and formulated a grand and wicked plan.

Vicinia arrived at Elendar, home of the elves of the Woodland Realm. Her entrance was grand, and the King Thandwin was charmed by her, for Vicinia was beautiful, even by elven standards. Vicinia approached King Thandwin and said, "I am Vicinia Takauri, and I come to aid your kingdom, for I am from Armon-Anzerbon, realm of all good dark elves." Then Vicinia bowed to Thandwin in respect of his kingdom and his people.

Thandwin was so enchanted with Vicinia, he beckoned her to stay. And soon he married Vicinia to be his queen—even against the wishes of his court and people, for they dared not trust her. Vicinia was a dark elf, and most dark elves meant ill will, even if she claimed to be from Armon-Anzerbon.

Soon after their union, they had a child called Ellen-Row. And after nine years had passed since Vicinia's joining with Thandwin, on that winter solstice, she went to Elendar's sacred Silver Oak and picked the Winter Rose. Then, Vicinia quietly murdered Thandwin by draining his life force. Vicinia was going to drain the life of her daughter, Ellen-Row, as well so she could not potentially undo the spell of the Winter Rose, but Ellen-Row escaped.

Ellen-Row had witnessed her father's death, and she ran as far away as she could to the South.

The elven Kingdom of Elendar and the surrounding elven Woodland Realm fell into eternal winter. Vicinia made herself ruler of Elendar, Queen of Winter. Then, Vicinia hunted for her daughter, Ellen-Row.

After seventy years, the elves of Elendar were in strife. Ellen-Row was living hidden in Absania, a human kingdom to the south that bordered the elven lands. There, in exile, she had a child with a commoner elf named Thallus, who accepted her half-dark elf heritage. They named their daughter, Mirial. Ten years after Mirial was born, Vicinia finally found Ellen-Row and murdered her. Mirial barely escaped with her life.

Mirial lived in exile, as her mother did, shunned for her being part dark elf, but Mirial knew of her mother's history and of her grandmother deceiving her elven home. While surviving in the wild's, Mirial swore an oath to herself to save her kingdom and avenge the deaths of her mother and grandfather, and to regain her lost family's honour. She moved far north of Elendar's lands and survived in the wilds. Mirial learned the ways of hunting and survival for the next fifteen years. And in that time, she became super connected to all woodland folk, who became her friends.

It was now almost one hundred years since Vicinia took the throne of Elendar, and soon, Vicinia would gain the power of Ushativa.

Mirial was grown up and strong now. She was rather stalky, with long brown hair and deep green eyes. She was slightly tanned and dressed in green and brown to match the woodlands she tromped around in. And she had a little brownie friend to keep her company.

One day, Mirial and Flix Dazzle-Dew, the brownie, were out doing what they always did best: tracking and spying on nefarious creatures that plagued the land, even slaying them if necessary. It was winter; it was always winter in the Elendar lands, and the days seemed to be darker lately as winter went on. Mirial looked down at an incredibly large set of tracks in the fresh snow. They were familiar but also different than what she had ever seen or encountered before.

"What is it, Mirial?" asked Flix.

"Dragon landed here, but no dragon I've ever seen before," responded Mirial.

"Dragon?" said Flix, a little concerned.

"Yes, dragon, a very large dragon. And not more than two hours ago. But what kind of dragon and to what purpose?" wondered Mirial out loud.

"Maybe it is just passing through," Flix said hopefully.

"You would hope so, but I feel it is not," Mirial said wryly. There was another thing that stood out to Mirial besides the tracks: all the surrounding trees and plants were withered; plus, all the animals and birds in those trees appeared to be sick and unwell. "I'm not an expert on dragon lore, but I suspect that whatever dragon landed here was not of the good variety. And it's awfully close to Elendar city," Mirial explained.

"Maybe we should investigate," Flix suggested, always looking for excitement and adventure.

"Yes, I think we need answers. Vicinia's power has been growing, and foul creatures have been entering the area more and more," Mirial concluded. "They seem to centre around the city of Elendar."

So, Flix and Mirial went around speaking with forest animals in search of some answers. The animals talked of a huge dark dragon that had recently arrived in the area. Anything or anyone caught within its shadow would be put into deep despair. Living things withered and were drained of life if they were exposed to the dragon's shadow for long enough.

"It comes and goes from Elendar city," explained a hawk to Mirial.

"I would like to learn more of this dragon's connection to Vicinia," said Mirial, concerned.

"It sounds very nasty indeed. I want to see this big nasty beast. Should I go look?" Flix offered. "He will never see me. I'm way too fast," he boasted.

"Well, OK, Flix, but don't get caught," Mirial said after some thought to the potential risks.

"Get caught? Pffffaw, when has Flix Dazzle-Dew ever been caught? I'm so fast, even lightning can't catch me," Flix bragged while puffing out his little chest in pride.

"And it's also a good thing you're only twelve inches tall. Yes, we all know how fast you are, Flix. You are the fastest brownie in the lands," said Mirial in amusement. "But don't linger, Flix; dragons can sense magical creatures," Mirial cautioned.

"Yes, ma'am," said Flix, saluting. And without further ado, Flix blasted off in such a dazzling display of speed, he could have been a lightning bolt.

Vicinia stood on the balcony of her tree palace. She was basking in the anticipation of her consolidated power with Ushativa. In contrast to her ebony skin, her long white hair wafted in the light breeze. "Only a couple more years, and I will be unstoppable," she said to herself. "I will rule all the surface elves and the dark elves will fall in under me." She laughed maliciously.

A dark shadow suddenly cast overhead. A shadow that every living thing ran from, except Vicinia. The source of that shadow was an exceptionally large inky-black dragon, and it landed in front of Vicinia, face-to-face.

"Ah, Cinder, and how was your patrol run, my magnificent dark ally?" Vicinia cooed.

"It was boringly uneventful," Cinder said in his low, booming voice. "Nothing challenges me. All quiver or flee before me."

"That is because you are unchallengeable, my great champion. But do not worry, I believe there is going to be opposing forces at work on my rule. I feel you may find a bit of sporting action soon enough. In the meantime, patrolling is the only option for now," Vicinia explained.

Cinder nodded in compliance to the powerful Vicinia.

"You must be hungry, Cinder. There is a group of wood elves who had recently stood against me. I had them rounded up. They are in the back plaza, and you may have your fill of them," Vicinia said.

Cinder nodded, and with a wicked smile, he took his leave to feed. Vicinia went back into her throne room and focused intently on an object floating atop a pedestal that was covered by a clear glass cover. It was the Winter Rose.

Flix speedily made his way to the central city of Elendar and came upon the House of Elendar, which had been occupied by Vicinia for almost one hundred years. There were dark elf guards mixed with dragon men, known as drake men, all black as coal. They surrounded the giant tree palace and plaza. Most of the wood elves were tucked away in their dwellings, controlled by Vicinia, and were rather unhealthy—save for a couple dozen wood elves grouped together, all trussed up, in the plaza, next to a very large dragon as dark as night. And to Flix's horror, the dragon was feeding on them, one by one. Flix could sense the vileness of this giant creature which likely matched that of Vicinia's heart.

Cinder lifted his head and paused as if he sensed a presence. He turned his head in the direction of this presence, though saw nothing there. Nevertheless, he knew what it was!

Flix dashed out of there the moment the dragon turned its head his way. "Time to go!" he said to himself frantically. In record time, Flix was suddenly back at Mirial's side, all wide eyed and looking a little pale.

"Whatever is the matter, Flix? What did you see?" asked Mirial.

"A very big nasty black dragon of enormous proportions," Flix said in a breaking voice. Then he rambled on, avoiding the rest.

"FLIX!" shouted Mirial, interrupting Flix's rambling. "What else did you see?" asked Mirial slowly.

Flix got hold of himself and explained all he saw, including the disturbing scene of Cinder dining on wood elves. Mirial turned pale herself and sat down to think over what Flix had described.

Vicinia heard Cinder's telepathic message to meet with her. "What is this about, Cinder?" asked the dark elf queen as she came out onto the balcony to meet with Cinder.

"I have sensed a spy," said the giant dragon.

"A spy? What kind of spy?" asked Vicinia, intrigued.

"A sprite—some little brownie fellow," responded Cinder.

"Did you get a look at him?" asked Vicinia.

"No, he was amazingly fast. He was there and then gone instantly. But I have his magical scent," the dragon said with a wicked grin.

"Very good, my magnificent champion," Vicinia cooed. "Find him and bring me the nosy little busybody, plus any companions he has as well! And once I am through with him, you can eat him." Vicinia shrugged absently.

Cinder laughed evilly and took his leave, looking forward to chasing down the nosy sprite. Vicinia felt there was more to this little encounter than just the spy. She cast an ancient spell that revealed the truth of her suspicions: Mirial, the daughter of her daughter, Ellen-Row, was with him.

"I know about this dragon. He's familiar to me," said Mirial. "We have to find more about this beast, and I know someone who will know about such a monster." Mirial picked up her bow and headed off.

"Who might that be?" asked Flix curiously.

"Her name is Lady Sylriena, and she's a powerful enchantress of the high elf kin. She resides in a magical castle of sorts northeast of here. She can help us," explained Mirial.

"Well, let's go. I've never met a powerful enchanting wizard before," said Flix, forgetting all about the giant evil dragon.

Mirial and Flix headed off northeast to the palace of Sylriena. The snow was deep, the forest was thick, and the way was long. Mirial summoned a giant brown bear friend called Brawn to ride as a mount.

They were not more than a day on their trip when they ran into trouble.

A sudden shadow appeared from something large flying overhead. The trees wilted and the animals fled in terror as it swooped down. Mirial, Flix, and Brawn could feel the vitality drain from them as they fought off despair from the shadow passing over them. Cinder had come to claim them! They tried to outrun the dragon, but they were not as swift as him; only Flix could but he did not want to abandon his friends. Mirial fired some arrows at Cinder, but they only bounced off the beast. The dragon circled above them, savouring the anticipation of his capture. His quarry had nowhere to run and nowhere to hide, so he thought!

Mirial looked at Flix and desperately said, "Get Brawn out of here. I'll hold off the dragon as best I can."

"You won't stand a chance, Mirial. You will perish," Flix argued.

"Perishing is not what I have in mind," responded Mirial.

"You mean to be captured?" asked Flix in wide-eyed surprise.

"Why else would Vicinia send this beast after us? And he hasn't even roasted us yet," Mirial reasoned. "NOW GO!"

Flix nodded. "I'm coming back for you, my friend."

With his fiery breath, Cinder set the forest ablaze around his quarry. The dragon landed within his ring of fire. Crushing and cracking trees like match sticks, he busted through the woods to his victims. When he cast his eyes upon them, he roared in victory. At that moment, Flix hopped onto Brawn's back and they were gone. Cinder let out a terrifying screech and blasted the spot where Flix and Brawn were only a moment before. His fiery, raging breath melted all within its wake. His main quarry had gotten away. Then he set his eyes on Mirial, who stared right back at him. This wood elf was unknown to Cinder, and he would have eaten her without question, but something about her caused him to pause.

"You're a skilled and strong one, little elf, full of will and purpose," said Cinder. "What's your name?" asked the dragon while his saliva sizzled as it hit the ground.

"My, my name is Mirial," she said, a little afraid but feeling brave.

"Mirial?" the dragon said while coming almost nose-to-nose with her. The dragon saw who she really was now. "Not just Mirial, but Mirial Takauri—you are part dark elf and the granddaughter of Vicinia," said Cinder, chuckling.

Surprised, Mirial angrily said, "How-how do you know that?"

"Oh, my poor little elf, I'm a dragon, and not your average dragon. I see things most creatures don't see." The dragon laughed in length. "I know someone who would just love to meet you." And without any more discussion, Cinder grabbed Mirial in one of his giant claws and took to the air, back to Vicinia's palace.

Mirial sat on the floor of a cage, all shackled up. She was a little down and feeling quite angry at her predicament. Vicinia approached Mirial in total satisfaction of her captive.

"Mirial Takauri, the daughter of my daughter, Ellen-Row. There could be no better captive in my cell than who is shackled before me," Vicinia cackled.

"Go to hell, witch," Mirial shot back in anger while standing up.

Vicinia heartedly laughed at her good fortune. "I'm sorry, my granddaughter, Vicinia cooed, but you were the only one who could have undone the power of the Rose. And now you're all locked up in my cage," Vicinia taunted amusingly.

"You evil queen, you killed my mother," Mirial yelled at her.

"Now, now, Mirial, such anger. It will do you no good, my dear. But, before you meet your end, I want to see what my poor granddaughter is made of." Vicinia smirked. "Open the gate and unshackle her, then give her a sword," Vicinia instructed the guard.

The guard obeyed the powerful queen without question. Mirial just glared at Vicinia. She was now Mirial's most hated enemy.

Mirial and Vicinia squared off. The first couple of blows they traded, clearly established that Mirial was sadly outmatched, and Mirial was no novice with a blade either.

"I should tell you, Mirial, that I bested the city of Elendar's most masterful swordsman when I took the crown," Vicinia bragged tauntingly. "Shall we have some fun, my dear?" She grinned at Mirial.

Mirial mustered her courage and attacked Vicinia with the best of her ability, but Vicinia easily countered.

"Pathetic!" Vicinia chuckled as they clashed swords. "So pathetic," she reiterated before disarming Mirial and tripping her to the ground. Mirial groaned as she fell to the floor with a thump. Vicinia's sword point was at Mirial's neck while Mirial glared back at her queenly assailant.

"It appears that you are no match for me, Mirial," said Vicinia. "Such a pity; you could have been a worthy opponent, but you are not!" she said flatly. Then Vicinia said some strange words that made Mirial not able to move nor speak; the dark elf queen levitated her in the air by some unseen force.

There, she floated helplessly at Vicinia's mercy. To add to Mirial's humiliation, Vicinia made a gesture with her hand that made Mirial float back into the cage. Then with another wave of her hand, Vicinia made the door slam shut and lock. At the same time, Mirial came crashing to the ground. Mirial could move again but was at a loss for words, and she felt a little broken. She looked up at Vicinia, who approached the cage.

"I could have killed you so easily. But I may have use of you yet, my granddaughter," Vicinia said. The dark queen turned and left the room, leaving Mirial to her humiliation and misery.

Some time went by; Mirial didn't rightly know how long. One loses track of time when locked up in a cage. It was completely dismal. Suddenly, Flix turned up out of thin air.

"Hi, Mirial, good to see you again," Flix greeted her in a cheery mood.

"Flix, what in the nine hells are you doing here?" whispered Mirial in utter surprise and joy at seeing her little friend again.

"I came to rescue you!" said Flix flatly.

"Rescue me?" said Mirial, a bit amused and flattered all at once.

"Yes, the same way I took Brawn away from that big nasty dragon," said Flix seriously.

"Where did you go?" asked Mirial, remembering his sudden little disappearing act.

"I went to fey land with Brawn," said Flix cheerily.

"You can do that?" asked Mirial, impressed by her little friend.

"Yes, I can, but not all the time. You see, some of us fairy folk can enter our heritage Spirit Realm, and some cannot. We can even take folk with us, like I did with Brawn. And Brawn had a wonderful time," said Flix with enthusiasm. Then Flix rambled on about the whole experience.

Mirial cut him short. "Yes, yes, Flix, it sounds amazing. I'm sure I will get to see it, but we have got to get out of here," she pressed.

"Oh yes, you're right. Sorry, Mirial, I just get so excited sometimes about doing important stuff. Here, grab my hand," Flix instructed.

Mirial held Flix's little hand and both disappeared out of the cage. They reappeared outside Elendar city, in the snowy forest right beside Brawn the bear. Flix knew that time was of the essence, and bypassed fey land altogether. After a happy little reunion with Brawn, Mirial mounted the big bear, as she would a horse, and they quickly left.

"I know the way to Lady Sylriena's castle, so follow me," said Flix cheerfully, and off they went northeast, into the wintery landscape.

It was not until next morning that Mirial's disappearance was discovered. Vicinia flew into a fit of rage and punished her guards harshly for not being more vigilant. Cinder had an extra snack that morning, along with his breakfast. After feeding on incompetent guards, Cinder met with Vicinia.

"My winter queen, what is it you ask of me?" asked the big dragon.

"My champion, you know how disappointed I am at Mirial's escape. I should have taken extra measures to ensure her incarceration," said Vicinia with a sneer. "Hunt them down and bring them both back to me," she instructed. "I have a feeling that they may become very dangerous."

"Very well, my queen, it shall be done," said Cinder in his rumbling tone.

Then he took his leave, to the sky, to begin his hunt for a quarry he underestimated the first time. It would not happen again. He sensed around, and after a while, he picked up the magic of Flix in the northeast. "There you are, my little friends," Cinder said to himself, then headed off to the northeast, with everything wilting from the wake of his shadow.

Mirial, Flix, and Brawn were making good time but had a long way to go. The unending winter wilderness seemed daunting, but Brawn was a large cave bear and could carve his way through the snow quickly. It was not that challenging for Flix either. After a few days, they came to the fringes of Elendar's lands, and the snowy landscape gave way to green forests and low mountains. It was a pleasant transition, but their satisfying feelings were short lived. An ominous, familiar presence hit them and was getting stronger.

"Cinder!" Mirial said as her heart sank. "Now what do we do about him?" she asked in a fed up and angry tone.

"No worries, I have a plan," Flix said with enthusiasm.

"Of course, you do," responded Mirial, not at all surprised.

"I will use my lightning speed to throw him off since I'm the one he can detect," Flix reasoned.

"Flix, that's a great idea. If I could hug you right now, I would, but we don't have the time for that," Mirial said, breathing relief.

Flix simply smiled and bowed; then in a whiz, he was gone. He was gone so fast, Mirial and Brawn didn't even see him go.

Cinder was zeroing in on his quarry's location. But his satisfaction was short lived when there was a sudden change in direction. Not only was the direction suddenly straight north, but also much further away. Grumbling to himself, Cinder followed. When he got closer again, there was another sudden change in direction and distance. Cinder cursed at this foolishness, but then he realized something. "You little devil sprite, your comrades are making for the castle of the enchantress, and you're steering me away. Very clever, but you must join back up with them before you reach your destination. Now that I know what your little game is and where you are going, lead on, little brownie, lead on," Cinder said to himself with an evil grin.

After a couple more days of playing cat and mouse with a dangerous dragon, Flix suddenly arrived back with Mirial and Brawn. "I tricked him; I tricked the big nasty dragon," Flix said, all proud of himself.

"Well, I hope you tricked him enough that gives us adequate time to reach

Sylriena's castle," Mirial responded hopefully. "But we are getting close. Less than a day's ride."

In most of the time it took to get to Sylriena's Castle, Cinder had almost caught up with them. Cinder laughed to himself heartily. "There's no hiding from me," he rumbled with evil glee. "I can sense you, you little nosy sprite," he spat.

It was a long tense journey with a large menacing dragon on their tail. It felt much longer to travel to their destination than it would have otherwise.

Suddenly, Mirial, Brawn, and Flix came over a rise and upon the majestic view of Sylriena's enchanting castle. Thick mist surrounded the area, and the castle was in the middle of a mountain lake, surrounded by sparsely spaced pine trees and alpine meadows. The castle rose out of the cloud of mist, like it seemed to be floating there. They could hear soft melodic harp music drifting from somewhere close to the shoreline. Mirial and her companions approached the shore cautiously. They felt enchanted by the melodic sound.

When they got closer, a beautiful elf lady sat on a large rock, just offshore. She had waist-long, straight silver hair and was dressed in a light lavender gown. She was playing a large harp, made of some ornately crafted exotic wood. She was playing a melody that calmed the soul. Mirial, Flix, and Brawn were mesmerized. The elf turned her head and looked at them with green almond-shaped eyes and smiled.

"Welcome, Mirial, Flix, and Brawn. I have been expecting you," she said in a kind and welcoming voice. "You must be hungry and in need of rest."

Suddenly that familiar dreadful feeling of the approaching dragon washed over them—it changed the mood quickly!

"Cinder's coming," Mirial said, concerned.

"I will deal with the dragon," Sylriena said with surety.

Suddenly, Cinder was upon them! As he swooped in, Cinder could see his quarry, but the trees around the lake did not wither from his shadow. Sylriena outstretched her arms and began to chant. A wind came along that quickly got stronger. Cinder shrugged it off at first as a minor nuisance, but when he positioned himself to exhale a devastating fire attack, a gust of wind threw him off. He muttered a magic power that would cancel Sylriena's spell, but nothing happened. Her spell was beyond his capability of power. Suddenly, the wind gusts turned into a vortex surrounding Cinder as he got closer. The swirling dark clouds above Cinder, released continuous lightning bolts that only hit the dragon. As a result, Cinder was rendered helpless.

Mirial and Flix watched in awe at the scene before them. Sylriena was still concentrating on her magic power. Her robes and long hair were waving in the wind, and the words of her incantation echoed through the air. Then not too far off, the mighty dragon Cinder was unable to concentrate or fly, and he came crashing down to the ground with a mighty thump. Slowly, the vortex and lightning subsided.

When Cinder awoke, he was in pain. He hurt in every corner of his bulking self. His ego was also bruised, and he was furious. When he gathered himself together to go looking for his dangerous assailant, she was gone as well as his quarry. The castle was also gone, obscured by the mystical fog that hung around the area. All Cinder could do was limp back home confused, battered, and bruised.

The inside of Sylriena's castle was beautiful. Mirial and her troop looked around in awe. Elven craftsmanship and tapestries ordained the banquet hall. The place was lit with candles that burned faerie fire, which never went out. A soft blue glow filled the room. A measure of calmness washed over them. The place felt warm, and Brawn the bear had already found a cozy rug to fall asleep on. Flix laid on top of him to get some rest as well.

"It is so beautiful here. Thank you for helping us," Mirial said to Sylriena.

Sylriena chuckled. "It is my pleasure, no need to thank me," she responded. "I've been watching Vicinia and you for some time. And I have been waiting for you to grow up."

"You've been watching me all this time?" Mirial said, astonished.

"Yes, you're Vicinia's bloodline and the only one who can undo the spell of the Winter Rose. I will help you further. In a few days, I will take you to Eldarra, home of the high elves. If you are to stop Vicinia, you are in much need of training. I have a guest room prepared for you. Now rest, Mirial," said Sylriena in a serious but gentle tone.

Mirial nodded her head a little dazed, not knowing how to respond. Then she asked, "What can you tell me about the big dark dragon operating under Vicinia?"

"The dragon is a very dangerous foe! His name is Cinder, and he is a dragon of a rare bloodline, known as Paragon. Cinder's bloodline is straight from the spawn of Lavaithyon. And Lavaithyon is lord of all dark drakes from the depths of the abyss. Cinder holds some of Lavaithyon's powers, and he's very ancient as dragons go," she explained to Mirial. "Somehow, Vicinia made a sweet deal with him to gain him as an ally for her own goals."

"I see," responded Mirial. "How do we kill him?"

"We will discuss that soon enough, but rest for now," said Sylriena.

Cinder finally made it back to the winter palace of Vicinia. He was all banged up and bruised, but the one thing that was bruised the most was his ego. Nevertheless, he reported to Vicinia, who did not take the news well. Her fury was so great and frightening, even Cinder took a step back.

"Mirial and her friends will pay when the time comes, and when that time comes, we will be ready," Vicinia said in counsel with Cinder, who looked forward to his ultimate revenge.

The following morning, the sun rose over Sylriena's castle. Its bright rays glowed through the morning fog that blanketed the area. The morning dew shined like little sparkling crystals. Mirial and her company took in the breathtaking scene as they prepared to go.

"Simply enchanting," Flix said with an appreciative smile.

Mirial said a quick goodbye to Flix and Brawn since she would be going to Eldarra without them. Although unhappy about their separation, Flix and Brawn knew they would see Mirial again. "Keep watch over Vicinia's actions. I will be gone for a while," Mirial said to Flix.

"Yes, ma'am!" said Flix with a smile. Flix already missed her.

Then Sylriena voiced some strange words and waved her hand, and in an instant, Sylriena and Mirial were gone.

Suddenly, Sylriena and Mirial came to in a place surrounded by tall ornately crafted crystal towers, mixed with giant trees. There was aspen, elm, and pine trees of various sizes that complemented the towers in perfect harmony. Mirial's breath was taken away by it all. High elves walked about doing their various tasks.

"Welcome to Eldarra; come," Sylriena said to Mirial, whose mouth was still agape. Sylriena took Mirial to meet Galindril, King-Priest of Eldarra, who had been waiting for them. They walked up the large pillared steps and into the council chamber. The chamber was ordained with art and tapestries. At the far end, Galindril sat on his throne with a silvery wooden crown on his golden-haired head. He smiled as they approached him.

"Mirial Takauri, much I have heard about you from Sylriena," he said warmly. "Welcome to Eldarra."

"Thank you, Your Majesty," Mirial said bowing, but feeling uncomfortable from the council clergy staring in judgment of her.

Sylriena stepped forward and spoke. "I have come to seek the council's support in training Mirial to save Elendar from Vicinia, Queen of Winter. We all know the legend of the Winter Rose, and Mirial is the only one who can break its spell," Lady Sylriena campaigned to the king-priest and the council.

"But this girl before us is part dark elf," said one council member in disapproval.

"We don't deal with dark elves; they are evil," chimed another.

The council erupted in agreement, but the king-priest sat calmly through the negative berating.

"Not all dark elves are evil!" Sylriena yelled at the council, but the council was too lost in their own prejudice of dark elves. Finally, the king-priest stood up off his throne, and the council drew quiet. Mirial held her head low; she was almost in tears.

Sylriena's anger grew towards the council. "Vicinia's power is growing, and in two years, she will be unstoppable in her quest to conquer all the elven kingdoms. Mirial is the only one who can stop her, and you won't help her because she's part dark elf?" she screamed. "You all don't deserve to be part of this council," she said flatly. Then Sylriena turned to face Galindril. "I am Sylriena, high arcane enchantress of the high elves, and I have made my point clear."

Galindril paused, and with a sigh, he said calmly to Sylriena, "Please take Mirial with you and wait outside—we must deliberate!"

Sylriena snorted in disgust and turned to walk out. "Come on, Mirial, let us leave this council of idiocy so they can... *deliberate*!" she said with sarcasm.

After waiting outside the council chamber for a while, the king-priest came out to meet with them. "The council has agreed to help you, Mirial, through my convincing, of course. But you must remain as my personal guest. I see the very importance of your mission; I always have," he said in acceptance of her.

"Thank you, Your Majesty," Mirial said, smiling and fighting back tears. But it did make her feel a little bit better.

Galindril looked at Sylriena, who was still miffed and ready to bring down the stars on Eldarra. He nodded to her sheepishly, then walked back into the council chamber.

Soon after Mirial had settled in, she began her training. Galindril set Mirial up with the best weapon and combat instructors that Eldarra had to offer. They quickly realized how natural Mirial was at fighting. Although her training was going well over time, the council still shunned her.

As word got around Eldarra about Mirial, many elven residents acted cold around her, though not all. Many of the high elves didn't like the idea of someone who was part dark elf being such an important guest in the city. But Mirial took the unacceptance stoically and poured all her focus and efforts into her training. For two years, this went on. Galindril looked on in amazement as Mirial grew more in skill from her instructions. However, Mirial's best efforts to make any friends outside the king-priest's palace tower were washed. Although some began to accept her, many did not.

One day, out in the garden of the palace, Mirial broke down and started to cry. Out of nowhere, Sylriena suddenly appeared beside her.

"It's been two years, and I have barely any friends, other than you and Galindril, and I miss my forest friends," Mirial cried to Sylriena. "Even my instructors scorn me. Nobody likes me." She sniffled.

Sylriena hugged Mirial close to comfort her. "Listen, Mirial, everyone is the same inside and made of the same material and energy—no matter how they look or where they come from. It is just how they were programmed; that is what really determines how someone believes and acts out of either wickedness or kindness. Most of these high elves don't see that. I don't think they get out that much to see the world. Sometimes, it can be a simple matter of conscience or lack of conscience," Sylriena explained.

"I wish I was a powerful arcane caster like you so I could just disappear to some pristine place for a while. Maybe that is why I enjoy my forest walks outside of Eldarra so much," Mirial said to Sylriena, her head bowed low.

"Your heart is strong, Mirial, and your purpose drives you towards victory over a tyrannical ruler called Vicinia. Do not lose your focus. You're the only one who can save the elven kingdoms," said Sylriena.

"Why me?" Mirial asked, frustrated.

"Because you were born to! Although most of us can choose our own destiny, sometimes, it's chosen for us," Sylriena explained.

"I guess I'm just lucky," Mirial said, forcing a smile.

"You have a rare talent of which you have flowered into a skill beyond that attained by any elf. Your instructors are jealous of that, I think," said Sylriena, a little amused. "It will serve everyone well."

Mirial and Sylriena shared a chuckle. Mirial was feeling better, and she talked with Sylriena a little more before retiring for the day. The next day was going to be a big day. It would be two years to the day that she had arrived in Eldarra. Galindril had asked Mirial to meet with him and the council.

From atop a hill, Vicinia looked out over her vast, built-up army. Two years had passed since she last saw Mirial, and now the time had come. Immortality was in her grasp. In just a couple of weeks, it will be the winter solstice. It has been one hundred years since she picked the Winter Rose.

Her vast army of dark elves have gathered under gloomy skies, alongside the drake men under Cinder's command. Cinder was looking forward to his revenge.

"Our forces are strong; we must march at once," Vicinia said to Cinder, who was sitting next to her.

"All the drake men from the Animus Mountains in the North have come to me. We will be unstoppable," Cinder replied wickedly.

"Are all the preparations ready?" Vicinia asked Zaire, her dark elf general, who was also standing by.

"Very close to being ready. A day or two perhaps, Your Majesty," her general replied.

"Good, make it sooner; we march tomorrow," Vicinia instructed with an acid tone.

General Zaire dropped to his knee while bowing his head, and replied with respect, "Yes, Your Highness."

Mirial walked into the council chamber with her head held high. She felt different than when she had first come to Eldarra, and she made a promise to herself the night before to not worry about what anyone thinks of her. She had accomplished great skill and would carry herself with pride.

The council finally had warmed up to her over the last two years, but some were still just as judgmental. Mirial did not care—she stood proudly in front of Galindril.

"You have changed a great deal, Mirial. When you first arrived, you were so timid and out of place. Now you stand in front of us a warrior of great potential—a warrior we have not seen since the days of our forbearers," expressed Galindril proudly.

"Thank you, Your Majesty, you have trained me for a great purpose against a tyrannical threat that puts all of us in danger," said Mirial.

"Yes, and I cannot express enough about the titanic measure of your importance," replied Galindril. "After years of Vicinia's tyrannical rule, the wood elves of Elendar have suffered. They are sick and drained of health and controlled as slaves. They are locked within the main city to supply Vicinia with vitality from their life force dew to the symbiont connection between Vicinia and the Winter Rose. We could be next? You must go and help your kin Mirial. But before you go, I have something for you. Come!"

Mirial followed Galindril out of the council chamber and into the garden, where they met up with Sylriena. Sylriena was holding a mighty bow and a sword. Galindril said to Mirial warmly, "I present to you Aumistral, the sky fire bow—a mighty bow given at the beginning of our time to the lord of the high elves by Shellna Calista, Goddess of the Hunt. The strike of this bow is thunderous, and its aim is true. I also give to you this long sword. Its name is Lummestar, sister sword of Elmmestar and Ammestar. They were forged by the forbearers of our kin. It can devour spells, cut deep, and eradicate evil."

Speechless, Mirial took the mighty weapons with honour. Then she said, "Thank you, I-I don't know what to say. Words fail me."

Galindril and Sylriena only smiled. Then Galindril put his hand on Mirial's shoulder and said, "Use them well and they will carry you to victory. They are guardian spirits of the elven fey."

"I will use them to honour all the elves who stand to be free," Mirial said.

"And I thought you could use a little help," said Galindril with a big grin. Suddenly a large winged unicorn like creature landed in front of them. The hooved creature was dark brown with large white wings. The bold animal seemed to be crossed between a unicorn and a Pegasus, and from the brow of its horse like head, a long green horn protruded from its forehead. The creature was majestic, and Mirial was enchanted by the mighty beast.

"This is Albion, and Albion is an alicorn. He is strong and swift, and he is a champion among his kind," said Galindril proudly.

Mirial approached Albion and touched his forehead. "Hello, Albion, I'm Mirial and I will be your friend," she said. There was an instant connection she felt with him. Mirial turned to Galindril and Sylriena to say her goodbyes. "I thank you both for everything, but the time has come to deal with Vicinia. And we don't have very long to do it."

Galindril and Sylriena both embraced her. Sylriena said while smirking, "I will be around to lend a hand."

"I know you will," Mirial responded, smirking back. Mirial then mounted Albion. "Well, my friend, this is it," Mirial said to Albion. "May your kind, pure heart, stout strength, and swift wings guide us to victory."

Then the mighty alicorn jumped into the air and flew off with Mirial waving a goodbye to her friends of Eldarra.

Vicinia's army moved through the elven countryside unchecked, ravaging small elven communities in their path. The dark elf General Zaire rode the mighty dragon Cinder to view the army's advance. Cinder rained terror and fire on any unsuspecting victims along the way. He was enjoying their suffering!

Meanwhile, Vicinia sat in her giant frozen tree palace of ice in Elendar, viewing her army through a scrying mirror. Due to the power of Sylriena, she had been unable to view Mirial and Eldarra, her priority, until now.

"There you are, Mirial, my unworthy opponent," Vicinia said to herself while she watched Mirial, riding Albion, land in a forest glade. Vicinia scoffed and chuckled as she watched Mirial happily reunite with her friends Flix and Brawn. What Vicinia did not like was Mirial's transformation and her new alicorn friend. Vicinia dispatched the mirror image and had a tantrum that shook the walls. "We will see about you and your friends, Mirial," Vicinia screeched. "I've only just begun to unleash my potential!" she spat with a clenched fist.

Albion had the ability to do many magical things, and teleporting was one of them. Albion and Mirial arrived quickly to lands just north of Sylriena's castle. Plumes of smoke could be seen on the southern horizon, from Vicinia's advancing army. Time was getting short. Mirial was happy to see Flix and Brawn again, and her friends felt the same, but there was no time to really celebrate.

"This is Albion, a new friend," Mirial introduced the alicorn.

Flix's eyes went wide with wonder. "Wow, he's majestic. And you, Mirial, you have changed. You are much healthier, and confident," Flix said impressed.

Mirial smiled. "We are all changing, Flix, but right now, we have got to change a bleak situation. Are you up for a little recon, Flix?" Mirial asked her little brownie friend.

"Am I up for a little recon?" asked Flix. "I am Flix Dazzle-Dew. Recon is my middle name," he said excitedly.

Mirial chuckled to herself. "I knew I could count on you, little buddy. Scope ahead and make note of what we are dealing with. Albion and I are going to drum up some help." Then Mirial and the alicorn jumped back into the air and were swiftly gone.

Vicinia pulled a scroll out from under her robe. She rolled out the scroll, unveiling a written text of an ancient, powerful dark magic spell. It was written from the blood of demon victims. Vicinia started to recite the demonic words out loud. Arcane words of demon speech rolled off Vicinia's tongue as she built the power from the page. Reaching into the dark dominion, she connected with the lower planes of the underworld and opened a portal. Vicinia's eyes went demonic black. With a crescendo, she ended the spell: "Children of Ushativa, come to me now!"

A moment later, an army of man-sized winged demons came through the portal in a constant stream. They were dark in colour, each with a bony body and vile visage. Vicinia laughed evilly at her success. Then, through using telepathy, she connected with Cinder and General Zaire and said, "Champions of the sky, slay Mirial and this alicorn and be done with her, once and for all."

"Yes, my queen," Cinder and Zaire both replied obediently before immediately starting the hunt.

Mirial and Albion travelled far north. They landed on the high point of a hill. Albion pranced wildly and let out a loud neigh. The clouds gathered and rumbled with lightning flashing here and there. Albion had put out a call throughout the north lands, to all the great beasts of the natural world.

The beasts came in droves. Oversized bears, mountain lions, wolverines, and stags of tremendous strength and power gathered before Mirial and Albion. A host of alicorns also arrived, who bowed before Albion. Thousands of beasts had gathered before the day was done. Mirial capitalized on her ability to communicate with animals—what she said, they understood.

Mirial stood on a big rock and put out a fiery speech. She spoke with vigour. "You are the mightiest of the natural world. The Queen of Winter has pushed most of you north. We summoned you to join us and take back what was stolen from all of us. I am Mirial Takauri, granddaughter of Vicinia Takauri, Queen of Winter. I am the only one who can restore the land's back to how they once were. But I need your help. So, join us and we shall be the Hammer of the North that drives Vicinia back to the deep caverns beneath the world."

There was a giant roar from the mass of large animals joined in the common cause. As Mirial stood there, caught up in the camaraderie of the moment, a voice spoke to her from behind. "We will join you!"

Mirial spun to look upon a male wood elf. He was leading a force of wood elves who had fled Vicinia's advancing army and had banded together.

"My name is Gillis, and we have lost our homes and most of our families. We have much to pay Vicinia back for," Gillis said evenly.

Mirial clasped Gillis on the shoulder and said, "You are most welcome to join us, my friend. It is time to act, and we have got to move fast."

Flix Dazzle-Dew must have circled Vicinia's army half a dozen times before meeting back up with Mirial. He had to keep moving to not gain the attention from Cinder, up in the sky.

"Hi, Mirial, Flix Dazzle-Dew reporting back," he said in speedy speech after he suddenly appeared.

"What did you see, my little friend?" Mirial asked Flix.

"It was nasty! There are dark elves and drake men cutting a swath through the land, laying waste to any who oppose them. Cinder is also creating his own personal path of destruction."

"I will deal with Cinder," said Mirial. "We must stop them, here and now!" Then she leaped back up into the sky with Albion.

Flix jumped on the back of Brawn the bear and joined with the giant animal army next to Gillis and his wood elves. Flix unsheathed one of his two little swords, which were no more than light, thin daggers to a full-grown elf, but he was fast and deadly with them. Gillis nodded to an elf who held an air horn, and the elf blew it loudly. The army moved to meet with Vicinia's dark forces. Once they contacted the winter queen's army, they figured out key tactical strategies and positioned themselves accordingly. Then, they charged!

Vicinia viewed the animal and elf army through her scrying mirror and chuckled to herself. "What a pathetic little gathering," she said. Vicinia then sent out a command to her giant demon force currently circling in the air, "After battle has joined, attack and leave no one alive," she ordered.

Mirial and Albion caught sight of Cinder, and he was closing fast. Cinder had seen them first. Mirial's heart was racing as she readied her bow. "Be ready and steady, my friend," Mirial yelled. But before she could let a shot fly, Cinder blasted a ball of searing flame towards her, which caused Albion to turn sharp and dodge the attack. Mirial almost fell off as both combatants passed each other by.

On the ground, the two armies met in a titanic and violent clash. It was total chaos. Gillis held back a portion of his force so he could fire volleys of arrows down on Vicinia's troops. The large animals plowed into the surprised dark elves and drake men, over running the front lines. Momentum was in their favour. Brawn the bear led the way, for he was one of the mightiest beasts of the wilds of the natural world.

Coming over the southern horizon loomed another threat. A mass of dark winged creatures approached quickly. *"Minor demons! Lots of them,"* Albion said to Mirial telepathically.

The gathered alicorns mustered themselves behind Albion to meet the demon creatures head on, but there were too many. Without hesitation, Mirial brought her bow up and fired a shot that cracked like a straight lightning bolt. It blasted one of the demon creatures to ash. She kept firing, round after round, and downed several, but there were too many and Cinder was still her priority. The mass of demon spawn descended on Mirial's army and wreaked havoc. Mirial had to focus on Cinder; her army was going to be in trouble very soon.

A voice suddenly entered Mirial's head; it was Sylriena! *"You deal with Cinder and Vicinia, I will deal with the demon spawn. Don't lose your focus, Mirial."*

Mirial moved to re-engage with Cinder as storm clouds started to converse overhead. It was a familiar spell Mirial had seen from Sylriena before.

The battle on the ground was ferocious and now fully engaged. Mirial and Albion combated with Cinder and Zaire. They stayed close to Mirial so she couldn't use her bow against them. Mirial only saw this as an opportunity to change tactics. Albion moved in close before Mirial jumped off him and onto the back of Cinder to face off with Zaire, sword-to-sword. Mirial's sword grew bright and kept Cinder's darkness at bay. It also thirsted for Zaire. Very few taunting words were exchanged between them, mostly just sword blows. Zaire was the finest sword fighter in the dark elf army and was personally trained by Vicinia. But now he found himself out matched.

Sylriena's spell had now taken hold. Lightning bolts blasted around the combatants in the air, frying the winged demons with every strike. In the chaos around them, Zaire fought Mirial ferociously. But then Mirial dispatched Zaire after a few quick deceptive moves. Mirial's sword, Lummestar, had revealed its strength when her final blow cut the dark elf general in half. Then Zaire fell off Cinder and far to the ground. Mirial jumped off Cinder onto Albion, who was close by, taunting Cinder.

"Fancy sword moves won't do much against me, little elf," roared the big dragon. "I will turn you to ash with one breath." Cinder snapped his head to face Mirial and Albion. Then he breathed a searing hot stream of dragon fire. But Albion was quick and Cinder's fire missed its mark.

Vicinia looked on feverously at the battle as it unfolded—especially Mirial's conflict with her champion and general. She did not like what she saw!

Cinder gained the upper hand in his goal to fry Mirial and her alicorn. But after an intense chase around the battle area, Mirial finally got a lucky break. She fired a clear shot with her bow that landed on the dragon's underbelly. It charred a big hole in the beast. Cinder groaned with the unexpected hit.

"Nebulus Virulent, that's your real name," yelled Mirial. "Let me introduce you to Aumistral, the sky fire bow."

Cinder roared in rage, which cost him careful vigilance against his dangerous enemy. "And now elf, you die!" he bellowed.

As Cinder swooped around for a breath attack, Albion positioned himself for Mirial to make the perfect shot. Cinder closed in hard and fast, fixed on Mirial and Albion. He opened his mouth wide to roast them with a blast of searing dragon fire. As Cinder was just about to let loose his deathly fire breath, he realized his mistake. In that critical moment, Mirial fired her bow. The lightning strike from her shot went straight into Cinder's mouth and blasted the inside of his head. The mighty invincible Cinder went limp and fell to the ground with a mighty crunch. The once feared and powerful Cinder was dead!

Vicinia, viewing the conflict through her mirror, fell into silent shock. Her general and champion had both been bested, and she knew where Mirial was headed—straight for her.

Mirial and Albion wasted little time celebrating their victory and headed straight for Elendar's winter palace of Vicinia, Queen of Winter.

Mirial's friends and those on the ground who witnessed the slaying of Cinder and Zaire cheered Mirial on. They started calling her Mirial the Hammer Star of the North. But the battle was far from victory. It raged in full, and there were heavy casualties on both sides. The elves, led by Gillis, we're running out of arrows from shooting at the winged demons. And Sylriena was soon losing strength upholding such a powerful spell. Many of the alicorn forces had been brought down. The battle scene on the outlying area of Elendar had turned from a snowy winter white to a splatter of red. Vicinia's demon force had taken its toll on Mirial's tiring army.

As Mirial and Albion got closer to Vicinia's palace, they fell out of Vicinia's viewing. Albion had a magical stealth ability that came in handy, disrupting Vicinia's preparations, magical or otherwise, for Mirial's imminent arrival. Vicinia could only sit on her throne, armed and waiting.

Mirial patted Albion's head and whispered to him, "We are getting close, old friend. Land as close to Vicinia as possible."

When the palace tree came into view, Mirial saw a heavily guarded balcony. "Land there; might as well go right through the front door," she said. Albion landed on the balcony. Mirial jumped off Albion, sword drawn. She dispatched the dark elf guards with ease, then marched right on in. She made her way into Vicinia's throne room.

There sat Vicinia on her throne, a cocky grin on her face. Mirial was ready to knock that grin right off Vicinia's face and then destroy her, but she kept herself calm. Her sword Lummestar, however, illuminated bright, hungry for Vicinia's blood.

"That's a cute name they call you, Mirial. The Hammer Star? Mirial, Hammer Star of the North. It's rather amusing," Vicinia mocked.

"I'm glad you find it amusing, Vicinia, but I'm no star. I am just an elf trying to free the elven kingdoms from a tyrannical dark elf bitch called Vicinia, my own grandmother," Mirial shot back angrily.

Vicinia chuckled. "Well, you bested my general Zaire at swordplay and defeated my mightiest of all champions with that fancy bow of yours. But do you really think you could just march into my own throne room and best me?" Vicinia said while she laughed an evil cackle. "Your army is in peril. And while my heart beats, my army follows my every whim," Vicinia said while she gestured to the Winter Rose beside her, set in its glass case.

The frosty sparkling lavender petals of the rose were radiant. It looked innocent but enchanting at the same time. Mirial set her eyes on the Rose and thought to herself on how she might get it. "You might find I've learned a few new tricks since our last party," Mirial said sarcastically.

Vicinia laughed. "But it will do you no good, Miss Hammer Star, because now, my granddaughter,"—Vicinia quickly stretched out her hand—"YOU DIE!" Suddenly, she blasted Mirial with a life draining spell, which had no effect. Mirial just grinned. Vicinia tried another spell, and it also fizzled.

Mirial chuckled. "Got any more to share with me?" she goaded.

Vicinia growled and tried a third spell, which, unknowingly to Vicinia, was being absorbed by Lummestar. "So, that's how it's going to be, is it? Royalty-to-royalty, toe-to-toe, blade-to-blade," growled Vicinia.

"Grandmother-to-granddaughter," Mirial finished with a snarl.

The two combatants met in a titanic clash of swordsmanship. Mirial and Vicinia traded strikes, counterstrikes, faints, and parries with vicious determination. Though equal in the skill of swordplay, Vicinia still had the edge.

On the battlefield to the north, things looked grim. Vicinia's army had gained the upper hand. Gillis had run out of arrows and was now involved in heavy melee combat. To make matters worse, Lady Sylriena was running out of power. Vicinia's army was too big and too strong. Only one alicorn remained, due to the massive demon force.

Flix had been busy carving up dark elves and drake men with his deadly little blades while looking out for Brawn as well. Then out of concern with the situation, he broke away from the battleground to meet with Sylriena.

"Sylriena, what do we do? Things do not look good," said Flix hastily.

Fatigued from casting powerful spells, she looked at Flix and said, "Go help Mirial, Flix. I'm sure she could benefit from your abilities. It might help us all."

"You really think so?" asked Flix, excited with hope once again.

"Yes, I really think so," responded Sylriena.

Flix looked to the south and said, "I'm off!" He was gone in a flash.

Flix whizzed through the wintery forest and arrived at the palace of Vicinia, a few minutes later. He saw Albion up on the high balcony. Flix new Mirial was near, which meant Vicinia was also.

Mirial and Vicinia's duel had reached a stalemate. Taunts were traded as much as sword blows. Then Vicinia got the upper hand and forced Mirial on the defensive. She found an opening in Mirial's defence, putting her off balance. Vicinia disarmed the Hammer Star of the North. Mirial stumbled to the ground; her sword, Lummestar, clattered across the floor.

"I see you're still pathetic," Vicinia sneered with pleasure. Savouring the moment in anticipation of her soon-to-be victory, Vicinia laughed. "And so you fail, my granddaughter. I'm so close to being immortal, standing beside Ushativa, as the shadow queen of all fey. This moment I will remember—the day I spilled your blood."

Mirial looked around. She viewed the Winter Rose beside the throne. Her sword lay by a tapestry on the other side of the room. The situation did not look promising. Then she heard a whisper from behind the tapestry call her name.

"Pssst, Mirial, it's me Flix," Flix said, as he poked out his head from behind the tapestry for just a second.

Excited, surprised, and glad to see Flix, Mirial gestured to him to get Lummestar to her.

Vicinia moved towards Mirial. "Goodbye, Mirial, I wish this contest between us could have gone on a little longer. I have to say, though, I am a little bit disappointed."

Then in a flash, like it appeared in her hands, Mirial had her sword back. "Well, I wouldn't want to disappoint you, Grandmother," Mirial responded back with an icy tone.

Mirial and Vicinia were off again—except Mirial changed her tactics.

She fought with a calculated, defensive routine. She had one thing in mind, getting the Rose! Vicinia's demeanour had deteriorated, and she fought wilder while, in contrast, Mirial stayed calm. Lummestar was hungry for Vicinia's blood but could not get to her yet.

Then Mirial had an idea. She yelled, "FLIX, GET THE ROSE!"

"OK, I'm on it, Mirial," responded Flix.

Mirial suddenly broke from Vicinia and tumbled towards the Rose. She knocked the glass covering protecting the Rose off its pedestal, and it fell to the floor. As the glass shattered on the floor, Flix whizzed in and snagged the Rose.

Vicinia lost it! "NOOOOOOOO!" she screeched. Her attention was split between the meddlesome brownie and her biggest adversary, Mirial. Vicinia's anger channelled towards Mirial, and she let fly a lightning spell. The spell had no effect as Lummestar absorbed the magical energy. In desperation, Vicinia turned to look for the Rose and the little blighter who stole it.

Mirial seized the advantage and threw her sword at Vicinia. When the Queen of Winter turned back towards Mirial, Lummestar struck her and buried itself deep into her chest, right up to the hilt. No words were exchanged. At that moment, the moment before death, the only thing Mirial saw in Vicinia's eyes was the look of denial. Then, Vicinia fell dead to the floor.

On the battlefield to the north, there was a sudden shift of circumstance. All the minor demons Vicinia had summoned fell out of the sky and turned into dark vapour. The dark elves and drake men felt the sudden lack of power from their winter queen and paused—something had changed.

Gillis didn't argue with the sudden fortunate change in the air and situation. He rallied what was left of his elven and animal force and charged. Vicinia's once mighty army was routed. Mirial and her friends were victorious.

Flix and Mirial went back out onto the balcony to meet up with Albion. Flix gave the Winter Rose to Mirial. "I believe this belongs to you," he said, grinning.

"Thank you, Flix, you were a great help. If it wasn't for you, things might not have turned out well." Mirial embraced her little friend in a well-deserved hug.

"Awwwww, shucks, Mirial, it was nothing. Those were some pretty fancy sword moves, princess. And what you pulled off on Cinder was mighty impressive, Miss Hammer Star," Flix teased.

"Yeah, but what would I do without the fastest brownie in the land?" said Mirial as she mounted back up onto Albion.

"Yeah, you're right, I am the fastest, you know," responded Flix proudly.

Mirial laughed. "And the most modest brownie, too, I see."

Flix hopped on to Albion with Mirial, and Albion took to the air. They flew back to meet up with Sylriena and Gillis. Being reunited and relieved, they embraced each other in their victory over Vicinia and her dark rule. Mirial's friends were exhausted from the battle. Their victory was bittersweet, though, because, sadly, the battle had been costly. Brawn the bear was wounded, but he had made it through.

After a short recuperation, Mirial and Sylriena travelled to Elendar's sacred garden and Silver Oak, where the Winter Rose had been picked. Mirial set the Rose back to its original stem. It was an emotional experience for her. So much had happened because of this rose. It was a moment she never thought she would ever experience. Sylriena had came with her for support through it all.

In the coming few months, winter loosened its grip on the lands of Elendar and a vibrant life began to return. Mirial was given praise by all the high elves and the wood elves. The King-Priest Galindril said for all to hear, "It matters not what one's origin is, or what they look like—it is what's in their soul that matters."

The new King-Priest of Elendar gave Mirial a golden tiara with an emerald jewel set in its central apex. But Mirial was far too wild for royalty; her place was out in the wilderness. Celebrations were had on Mirial's victory, but after several months of hanging around the renewed palace in Elendar, Mirial was getting bored.

Flix, standing beside her, asked, "What should we do, Mirial?"

"I don't know. I was thinking of heading north," Mirial responded.

"Not without saying goodbye," a familiar voice said from behind.

Mirial and Flix spun around to see Sylriena standing there. "You're quite right, Sylriena." Mirial smiled. "There is a wide world to explore."

Sylriena nodded. "Well, come by and visit me anytime at my castle. You're both always welcome, Brawn as well," she said to Mirial and Flix.

"We will," said Mirial. Then Mirial collected her things. With her sword, Lummestar, and Aumistral, the sky fire bow, Mirial and Flix hopped on Albion and flew off into the setting sun, looking for new adventures.

Deep within the Woodland Realm
where the fey folk dwell and roam,
the elves prevailed for ages old
tied to their forest home.

Their soul was braided with nature's land,
linked to the spirit world.
Like chiming bells, they wove their spells
from mortal beings, far and furled.

In the northern reach of Rithanon
among the frosty silver glades,
a hero rose from the land
from a promise she had made.

To free her home and the elven lands
from the grip of winter's throes;
put an end to the evil dark elf queen
and the power of the Winter Rose.

The Jewel of Fortune

In a dark alley beside a rowdy tavern, lurked the two most prominent thieves in all of Terrence, the capital city of Edingal. Heklar and Toral were waiting for a rich merchant within the tavern to finish his evening of bingeing. This fancy dandy looked like he carried a heavy and fat purse, ripe for the plucking. Toral, the thinner and smaller of the two, was keeping watch when the merchant exited the tavern.

"He's coming out," Toral whispered to Heklar. "Be ready," he motioned.

Big Heklar nodded as he readied his stout cudgel. When the merchant reached the two thieves, they grabbed him and pulled him into the alley. Then with little effort, they quickly beat the poor man with the cudgel. Upon searching their unconscious victim, they found the pouch of gold and silver coins, with the odd juicy gem.

"Not bad," Heklar remarked in his deep voice. "These baubles will fetch a fine price." He grinned evilly.

As they chuckled in pride of their handiwork, another dark cloaked figure revealed himself from the shadows nearby. Heklar and Toral ceased their activity and drew blades, arming themselves.

"Who approaches?" Toral demanded in his gravelly tone.

The stranger held up his hands to show that he was not a threat. "Whoa there," the stranger remarked. "I'm nothing more than a messenger."

"Does this messenger have a name?" asked Toral threateningly.

"The name's Brost, John Brost. At my master's will, I have come to inform you, the finest thieves in the land, that my master has a proposition for you."

"A proposition?" Toral stepped forward. "Oh, I do hope it pays," Toral said, half-mockingly but serious.

"It-it does," stuttered John. "He'll pay handsomely. My master is very rich and influential," John confessed diplomatically, trying to not get maimed.

"Who's your master and how much will he pay?" asked Heklar in his low, intimidating voice.

"My master is Mitric Cornell, also known as Mitric the man. He is the branch leader of the handler's thieves guild here in Terrence," John stated with more confidence. Then John pulled out a fat pouch of coins and tossed it to Toral, which Toral caught in one hand. "Like I said, handsomely. That is payment of one hundred gold pieces, just for your time to meet with him. That should do to start with, wouldn't you agree?" John said.

Not to long after, Heklar and Toral stood in front of Mitric the man in a hidden backroom of the Grey Goose Tavern. The Grey Goose was situated in the city's southwest end. It was a tavern amongst many taverns, brothels, and gambling dens in the Coterie Court, which was a crossroads plaza of many streets. The Grey Goose stood as neutral ground for underworld business, settlements, and shady deals. It was where all the action was. Every night, and all night long, the court was a circus of plotting, backstabbing, and debauchery. But, when Heklar and Toral arrived to meet with Mitric, they were well received in the court, and with great respect.

John stood beside Mitric as they shared a stare down with Heklar and Toral. A table stood between them with a leather bag on it, in front of Mitric. John nervously rubbed his bald head while Mitric stroked his neatly trimmed black goatee in thought of the whole meeting. Heklar and Toral stood side by side, still cowled but unblinking. Silent minutes went by before Mitric finally broke the icy tension.

"Heklar the Horrid, and Toral the Grim," said Mitric in an impressive tone. "I have heard much of your exploits, which are many. It's too bad you didn't join us when the offer was made, but of course, it still stands."

"Is this an ass-kissing party or are we making some kind of deal?" asked Toral, not yet impressed but cautious.

John shifted nervously from Toral's brazen comment, but after a few seconds of tension, Mitric broke out in laughter. "Yes, we're making a deal, a deal that will benefit all of us," Mitric stated with a wide grin.

Heklar and Toral looked at each other with raised eyebrows.

"I'm sure that you're aware of, or heard of, Magantai the wizard in the Royal Palace, have you not?" asked Mitric.

"Yes, he is King Darien's royal advisor, and a rather powerful archimage. What about him?" asked Heklar.

"Well, in his tower, he holds a large jewel—a jewel with magical powers that can give you fortune," Mitric explained excitedly.

"Or misfortune, depending on how it's used," John interjected.

"Yes, but the wealth you gain is enormous," Mitric bellowed, slamming his fist into the table.

"And you want us to go and steal this jewel from an archimage who has attained the greater path of arcane magic," Heklar nervously pointed out.

"That's right," Mitric said calmly. "And for your efforts, I'm willing to offer you this bag of gems, which is worth ten thousand gold pieces in value," Mitric said before he slid the bag across the table in front of Heklar and Toral. "Consider this as half payment."

Heklar and Toral were stunned at the large offer of such wealth, but they accepted hesitantly. They couldn't help but feel there was a catch. In the shady underworld, such deals with great sums of money always had a catch.

After Heklar and Toral had taken their leave with the big bag of gems in hand, John looked at Mitric in concern. "What makes you think they'll succeed," he asked Mitric discreetly.

"Oh, they will," said Mitric. "They are the finest thieves and street fighters in all the land." He chuckled. "But I don't think they're quite as smart as I am," boasted Mitric. "I'm going to set a trap."

John looked at Mitric confused and said, "I don't understand; what do you mean? What kind of trap?"

"You see, my friend, when Heklar and Toral deliver the jewel, I will have them disposed of. This way I get the jewel, keep the gold, and have no witnesses," he said with a grin. Then Mitric started laughing. When John understood his master's plan, he joined in the laughter.

Heklar the Horrid and Toral the Grim moved down the streets of Terrence, going from shadow to shadow. Silent and unseen, they moved down into the dark and dingy ancient catacombs of the city. Under the sewers, the catacombs sprawled far and wide, which Heklar and Toral knew well. They made their way quickly towards the Royal Palace of King Darien. But as they did so, movement in the dark followed. The rat men were stalking them.

Heklar and Toral drew their weapons as the cloaked rat men moved in. Brandishing wicked blades, the rat men closed in fast on the two thieves, and so began the clash of steel. In the mesmerized dance of blades, the thieves were slaying the rat men who had surrounded them. Many there were, and as they came, Heklar and Toral dispatched them quickly. Even though the thieves' skill largely outmatched the rat men, their numbers made up for it. The situation soon became tense. Heklar and Toral were becoming worried until the rat men broke off the attack when they realized they were outmatched. They slinked off back into the darkness of the shadows, hissing as they went. Toral quickly threw his dagger into the leg of a lagging rat man to stop his retreat.

"Your buddies can go but you cannot," Toral demanded with a grimace. He looked at Heklar and said, "We need information."

Heklar grabbed the rat man and held him up by the throat with one hand. He had him pressed against the wall with his feet dangling down. "Why did you attack us?" Heklar growled.

"You're in our territory and not welcome," the rat man squeaked.

"That matters little to us. But you know these catacombs better than anyone," said Toral. "We seek an entrance into the wizard's tower at the palace. Do you know the way?" asked Toral.

The rat man nodded and croaked out a "yes" as best he could. Heklar put him down and let him go so he could speak. The rat man gathered himself as he traded a scowl with Heklar. He then gave detailed directions to a place under the tower, an entrance guarded by traps and magical wards.

"Thank you." Toral grinned, revealing his silver tooth. "Now, scurry off to your dirty pack before I decide to carve the pelt off your filthy hide," threatened Toral as he booted the rat man in his butt to help him along.

In haste, the rat man scurried off into the gloom of the catacombs.

"We let him go?" asked Heklar.

"It matters little, my big friend, and we must hurry," said Toral.

So, Heklar and Toral sped off, following the directions the rat man had given them.

Heklar and Toral arrived at the entrance location. It was an old spiral stairwell blocked off at the top. It had not been disturbed for many years, and with good reason. Toral studied the blocked passage with a well-practised eye.

"Careful," cautioned Heklar. "The wizard's wards are old, but..."

"They are still potent and dangerous," Toral interjected. "Yes, I know. And you cannot see them," he added. Toral pulled out a special gem, one that when you looked through it, it would reveal secret hidden things. With careful precision, he rubbed the hidden wards away with a cloth. In the process, he discovered a rather nasty, hidden mechanical trap, made to neatly behead someone. Toral took care of it as well.

Before long, the two thieves were through the entrance and stood in an old square chamber with various hallways leading off it. One was a stairway heading upward.

"That's the way," Toral presumed seriously. "But I have a bit of a bad feeling about all of this," he muttered.

"Yes, me too; that was way to easy," said Heklar.

Heklar and Toral carefully started to make their way up the dark, unlit stairwell to the wizard's tower. They moved carefully, floor by floor, diligently checking each room. They found the wizard's bedroom, and he was fortunately sleeping. Without disturbing him, they moved on. Disturbing Magantai did not sit well with the two burglars. On the next floor up, they came into a fancy study chamber. There were bookshelves, a desk with a window behind it, and a pedestal in the centre of the room. The pedestal had a large red jewel on top covered by a glass case.

"That's got to be it," Toral whispered to Heklar.

Heklar nodded to Toral and checked around to make sure there were no unexpected guardians or unwanted surprises. Carefully, they approached the pedestal. Toral put his revealing gem to his eye to examine the glass cover. The gem revealed nothing, which worried him.

"Not a damn thing," Toral whispered, gritting his teeth. "Damn it, it had to be a glass case. Glass cases make me nervous."

"I don't like it; it's just too easy," said Heklar, shaking his head. "Let's just grab the thing and get the hell out of here," Heklar suggested, in a harsh whisper.

"Are you crazy. You sound like a rookie thief. It's not that simple," Toral responded. "If we just lift the case and grab it, some hidden spell could go off," Toral explained, raising his voice unintentionally.

"Hush, quiet," Heklar said, cringing. "You'll wake up the wizard and that's the last thing we want. And you call me a rookie?" Heklar jabbed back at Toral.

Heklar and Toral argued a little bit longer, but dawn was approaching and time was running out. So, the two thieves refocused themselves and devised a quick grab-and-go plan. Then, Heklar boldly lifted the glass case and Toral grabbed the jewel.

The first moment was tense, as they expected something bad to happen. But just as they felt relieved that nothing went boom, the pedestal instantly turned into a big multi-headed serpent. Surprised, but not surprised that something happened, the two thieves drew weapons. The serpent was fast. One head coiled around Heklar's leg, and another head wrapped around Toral's waist. The fight was on.

"Throw me the damn jewel," shouted Heklar, who was closer to the window.

"I'm not really in a position to do so," Toral pointed out, as he cut one head off with his sabre.

Serpent heads gnashed their teeth and jousted with sabres and daggers. Heklar and Toral were trying to gain the upper hand. Fighting some strange beast, they have never encountered before was bad enough, but worst of all—it was noisy!

Magantai the wizard woke up from a loud ruckus that was coming from his study. He went upstairs to inquire as to what had so rudely awakened him. To his surprise, he got there just in time to see the two burglars in his study finish off the serpent. Magantai cast the first spell that came to his mind. It was a concussive force of air that blasted Heklar and Toral, and many other things, to the floor.

"The wizard—he's awake!" shouted Heklar.

"Get to the window, quick!" shouted Toral in response.

Magantai was preparing another spell, and they did not have much time to act. As Toral went out the window, Heklar dumped a bag of marbles down the stairs towards the wizard. Magantai stumbled on the marbles and fell, thumping down the stairs, which disrupted his spell. Heklar did not stop to ponder his good fortune. He quickly followed Toral out the window. The two thieves found themselves in bushes on the ground below the window.

"We must move fast," said Toral. "The wizard will raise the alarm."

"Lead the way," replied Heklar.

Heklar and Toral evaded the palace guards and went over the wall and into the streets of the city.

Magantai was furious. He yelled, "GUARDS," at the top of his lungs as he stumbled to his feet. The wizard muttered to himself, "Two street rats in my study, huh? By my brown beard, I'll find them," he said while gritting his teeth. Magantai went into a room next to his study and uncovered a crystal ball sitting on a table. He looked intently into it. "I'll find you." He grinned, determined to catch the two rogues.

Heklar and Toral quickly moved from shadow to shadow in the city streets. Besides the activity of a city that was waking up and stirring in the early morning, the two rogues were unheard and unseen. The two thieves could hear sounds of shouts and the clinking of armour coming from outside the palace gates. Heklar and Toral paused for a minute to reorient themselves.

"You hear that?" Toral pointed out.

Heklar nodded. "Sounds like our wizard friend has alerted the guards," said Heklar, amused.

Toral chuckled with Heklar. "I'll bet he's tracking us, so we best get moving," reasoned Toral. "We must meet with Mitric at the agreed location before sunrise."

Heklar and Toral sped off to the Grey Goose Tavern, with a pack of palace guards hot on their heels.

Once more, Heklar and Toral stood in front of Mitric the man in the same backroom of the Grey Goose Tavern as they did before. This time, the table between them was empty. John stood beside Mitric as last time, and he looked a bit nervous. Mitric looked pleased to see them—almost too pleased, thought Toral.

"I trust it wasn't too difficult," said Mitric. "Do you have the jewel?"

"Yes, we have it," said Toral flatly. "And yes, it was risky, even for us. It wasn't just a casual smash-and-grab or walk down the street," he added.

"Good." Mitric smiled. "Let's see it!" he demanded.

"Gold first," said Heklar. "I don't see the other half of payment on the table."

The smile left Mitric's face as he motioned to Johnny. John stepped forward and put the bag on the table. The bag clattered as the first bag did during their first meeting. Heklar and Toral exchanged nods with silent common understanding. They did not trust Mitric and Johnny one little bit.

"Ahem," Mitric coughed. "The jewel please, if you will." He drew out.

Toral gently pulled the enchanted jewel out from his cloak, and he slowly put it on the table. He never took his eyes off Mitric.

Both Mitric and Johnny's eyes lit up at the sight of the jewel.

"Slide the gem bag this way, and the jewel is yours," said Heklar.

"Yes, yes, I will," stalled Mitric. "But first, I have a bonus payment for successful service." He smiled.

When Mitric said *bonus*, Johnny knocked hard on the door behind him. In a sudden burst of activity, several armed and cloaked men entered the room, some from hidden doors in the walls. A dozen or so crowded around Heklar and Toral, pointing their swords and crossbows at them. The two legendary thieves, still staring at Mitric and Johnny, did not even flinch.

"I knew I couldn't trust you," Toral said to Mitric with a smirk. "I should have just kept it for myself," he scowled. "Maybe we will keep it."

"Yes, you could, but you are not really in a position to bargain," Mitric pointed out as he picked up the big brilliant-red jewel.

"Is that so," said Toral, smirking. "You forget who we are."

"You have only twelve men, and not twelve men of the best," added Heklar.

"I know who I'm dealing with," Mitric scowled back.

The stare-down between Mitric and the two thieves was intense, and it went on for several moments. The hedge of weapons from the twelve men rounding Heklar and Toral tightened. Mitric broke the tension first when he said, "Dispose of them!" in a calm manner.

The room exploded into a fury of action when Heklar and Toral drew weapons. The twelve men did not expect such speed of swordplay. Mitric and Johnny went for the door for a quick exit. But when Johnny opened the door, guards from the palace pushed their way in. It was utter chaos! The din of clashing steel mixed with shouts and thumps was deafening. Mitric was no novice with a blade either, and he held the guards at bay easily. The fight turned into an all-out brawl of Mitric's men fighting the guards as well.

Amid the battle, Johnny was dragged off by the guards. Mitric unfortunately slipped and fell to the floor. Many palace guards where upon him quickly. As they wrestled with him, the jewel fell out of his pocket and clattered across the floor. Toral turned when he heard the jewel hit the floor, and he saw it lying under the table.

"I see it," said Toral to Heklar. "Be ready to go!"

"We better be quick," Heklar shouted, as he dispatched his last opponent. "The guards will be on us next, and soon," Heklar warned.

Toral rolled underneath the table and nabbed the jewel as the room was still in total chaos. He came out of the other side and jumped back over the table.

"THIEVES," Mitric yelled when he saw Toral grab the jewel; he was still in the arms of the guards and being dragged off.

Toral grabbed Heklar by the sleeve. "Come on, time to go, my big friend," he said out loud.

Heklar hesitated for just a couple seconds before following Toral out the hidden door. Something caught his eye. The bag of gems was still sitting on top of the table. Without missing a beat, Heklar grabbed the bag before leaving the room.

Mitric and Johnny were dragged off to prison. The palace guards, plus what was left of Mitric's men, separately searched the surrounding streets for Heklar and Toral. Both parties wanted their hides, but it was to no avail.

Back in the wizard's tower, Magantai the wizard was looking through his crystal ball across the room in frustration. Something unexplained had blocked his scrying.

In a cold dark alley, somewhere in the city, Heklar the Horrid and Toral the Grim admired their spoils. They chuckled at their handiwork as they peered into the so-called Jewel of Fortune.

"That would fetch a juicy price, my friend," Heklar said to Toral.

"That it would." Toral smirked back. "But I think we will hang onto it for a little while," he reasoned.

Nodding with mutual understanding, Heklar and Toral sped off silently and unseen into the shadowed alleys and streets of the city, off to find another lucrative venture.

Heklar the Horrid and Toral the Grim,
one was large and the other thin,
cloaked in shadows, silent and shrewd,
daggers in hand with masks skewed;
in alleys, elusive cowled and cold,
depriving victims of silver and gold,
in the chill of night that hides their sin
lurk Heklar the Horrid and Toral the Grim.

The Tragic Tale of Uthgrail, the Mad

Lord Lorne Uthgrail was a rich, handsome, and talented musician. He lived in a fancy manner keep just outside the town of Boon, in the Kingdom of Caldona. He often held lavish parties and entertained his guests with his classical organ music. He schmoozed with the rich elite and, on occasion, even rubbed shoulders with royalty.

At one such party, there was a beautiful young lady by the name of Celeste. She was well sought after by many a man and lord. Uthgrail was captivated by her grace and beauty, so he felt he had to ask her for a dance. He elevated his courage and approached her.

"Hello, my lady, and welcome to my manor," he said to her. "It is a wonderful night, wouldn't you agree?"

"Yes, my lord, thank you for your hospitality. You are a charming host," she responded happily.

"May I have the honour of this dance?" Uthgrail asked, bowing to her.

"Why of course, my lord," answered Celeste, accepting his offer.

As they danced, Uthgrail was swept away by her charm and beauty. He was so taken by her, he fell madly in love with her that very evening. After the party, he kept thinking of her for days. He could not shake the vision of her from his mind, so Lorne Uthgrail decided to try and win her hand.

Lorne sent Celeste a bouquet of lush red roses. Within the bouquet was an invitation to dine with him on his deck by the light of the moon on the following evening.

In a short note, Celeste replied to Lorne's invitation. It read:

> *I am so deeply sorry, my lord, but I cannot accompany you. I am betrothed to the town baker, Mr. Matthew Sims, but thank you,*

Lord Uthgrail, for your kind invitation. Please accept my decision with dignity. — *Lady Celeste*

Lorne Uthgrail was heartbroken! He was disgusted that a lady of such status as Celeste could be betrothed to a lowly baker. He fell into his organ music to cheer himself up. Sweet classical verses could be heard on the wind. But instead of quenching his sadness, it only enhanced his feelings for Celeste. He could not get the thought of her out of his mind. Growing even more madly in love with her, he decided on an attempt to try and win her hand again. But this time, he would use his music to win her heart.

On a moonlit night, Uthgrail went forth to Celeste's house. He set up outside her window with a lute and the agenda to impress her. And so Uthgrail called up to her, "Celeste, my dear Celeste, are you in?"

The window opened. "Who, is out there this night?" Celeste asked as she peered out of the window.

"For it is I, Lord Lorne Uthgrail, my dearest," said Lorne. "Now let me serenade you with a song I have written for you, and I will show you my talents." His manner held a needy vibe.

"You already revealed your talents to everyone at your party, but if you must." She sighed irritably.

So, Lorne Uthgrail played his song with passion, and he went overboard in his musical accompaniment. Celeste felt he was showing off too much, and she just sighed and rolled her eyes as Lorne brought his song to a close with a bombastic crescendo. Through Lorne's eyes, he thought he had impressed Lady Celeste greatly, but he had not.

"Goodnight, Lord Uthgrail," Celeste said in a short tone. Then she waved him off and slammed the window shut.

Poor Lorne sadly went home and, in his grief, fell into his music again with wild abandon. The organ music grew more depressing. He did not venture from his manner for weeks. He still could not get the vision of the Lady Celeste out of his mind. She was haunting his every dream.

A couple days later, Lorne went to the weekend market and met up with Celeste, quite by chance. Losing all pride, he approached her and fell to his knees, pleading and begging.

"Oh, my treasured and dearest Lady Celeste, for you are in my heart day and night. You haunt my very dreams," Uthgrail chimed. "I can give you a life of lavishness, luxury, and plenty. Why, oh why, must you settle for just a baker such as Matthew Sims. Please consider me, Lady Celeste, I beg of you," Uthgrail said, while clawing at her feet.

"NO, I cannot! Now leave me alone!" Celeste yelled at Uthgrail with disgust.

"Please, please, please, Celeste, you are in my soul," Lorne pleaded in absolute desperation while clutching her ankles.

"GET AWAY!" she said, desperately kicking Uthgrail off. When Celeste finally broke away from Lorne's grasping, she ran off through the gathering crowd.

Lorne flew home and attacked his organ music with ferocity, falling deep into obsession, for he worshipped the Lady Celeste and needed her. The music was wild and even more depressing than ever. It sent chills through any who listened. The organ verses weaved with his obsession for Celeste. He would do anything for her, and he would do anything to get her. Then Lorne realized there was one major obstacle in his way—Celeste's fiancé, the town baker, Mr. Matthew Sims. With a pleasurable little cackle to himself, a vile plan formulated in the mind of Lord Lorne Uthgrail. A plan that would remove Mr. Matthew Sims out of the way and open the door for himself to Lady Celeste.

Secretly, one early morning, Lord Uthgrail carried out his wicked plan. On that fateful morning, Mr. Matthew Sims was opening his shop. Bakers usually start in the early hours of the morning, and it was still dark. Lord Uthgrail was sitting and waiting for him in the shadows nearby. Without warning, Uthgrail sprung upon Matthew and clubbed him unconscious. There were no witnesses to view his dirty deed. Quickly, Uthgrail tightly tied up Matthew in a big blanket, then loaded the baker into his carriage.

As fast as his horse carriage could go, Uthgrail thundered back to his manner. He unloaded Matthew Sims, untied him, and then locked him up, deep down in the darkest dungeon Lorne had under his manor house.

"There you will stay, Matthew Sims, never to see the light of day again," Lorne Uthgrail declared with fanatical pleasure. Lorne laughed wildly as he went back upstairs. He was proud of himself, pulling off his vile plan, and now focused on winning over the Lady Celeste.

In mad hope, Lorne reached out to Celeste once again, but she did not reach back. Celeste was grieving over Matthew's mysterious disappearance, and she somehow knew in her heart who was responsible for his abduction, even though the constable's investigation turned up no evidence. Celeste's suspicion of Lord Uthgrail could not be proven.

In a shaking state of obsession, Lorne stalked Celeste and watched her every movement. On one occasion, he got far too bold in his creeping and friends of Celeste chased him away. Uthgrail's reputation was falling. He was slowly shunned by all. Growing to a mad state, Lorne Uthgrail gave in to the darkness that twisted his heart.

"If I cannot have Celeste, then Celeste cannot have Mr. Matthew Sims," Uthgrail yelled out to the howling wind. "And all that shun me shall know that I shall haunt their every dream if they are to hear my verses," he declared. Then Lord Uthgrail locked himself in his manor house, with Matthew Sims deep down in his darkest dungeon.

Lorne played the most heart-wrenching music. He played for days and he played for nights—without food, drink, or sleep. The musical verses were so depressing and dark, it aged him into a twisted state of horror. Then Lord Lorne Uthgrail suddenly died!

That was the day the horrific music stopped, and in its place, an eerie presence filled the air.

Though Uthgrail had died, Mr. Matthew Simms was still alive. He was still locked up, deep down in Uthgrail's dark dungeon. The darkness had permeated him, and under Uthgrail's manor, he developed into a clawing wretch.

A foulness took to the air surrounding the keep of Uthgrail's manor, especially at night when the wind blew strong. From then on, nobody went near the manor house, as mysterious, haunting sounds could be heard coming from it. No one dared to venture within—and still don't to this day.

In the dark, after midnight, a faint sound can still be heard on the wind—the sound of an organ playing classical music. And, if one dares to stop and listen, the music grows and grows and grows more depressing and sadder, sadder and madder, until, finally, it ends in a crescendo of unspeakable horror. If you are foolish enough to listen, you, too, just might fall into a trance and go mad.

*In the dark of night,
when the wind blows cold,
you can hear the voices calling.*

*Trapped unseen,
in a fearful hold,
are the sounds of wretched clawing.*

*In the night's chill air
is the mad despair
of an organ's growing sound.*

*If you dare to stay,
you might fall prey
to madness or not be found.*

The Gold and the Dragon

A long time ago, in the Grey Mountains, just southeast of Edingal, there lived a dragon who had the largest treasure of any dragon. His name was Profusus Luxuriance. Now Profusus was not a cruel dragon, and he did not gain his wealth by heinous means. It was just a simple matter of luck that he had chosen his lair in a cave that was laden with gold. Profusus loved gold, as all dragons do, and proceeded to excavate all the gold out of his lair's cavern walls. This made his home a bit more spacious and provided him with an enormous pile of gold, more than he could ever use. So, he decided to share it with those who would do good things with it.

To protect his gold, the dragon put a powerful spell on it. Anyone who stole any of his gold or gained it for wicked intent would turn into gold. Profusus hated scandalous thieves and rotten no-gooders who harmed innocent people, so he had to make sure his shiny golden treasure was secure.

"That should do it," Profusus said, incredibly pleased with himself. "Now I can carry on with my tasks without worry."

And so Profusus proceeded to go about his business and tasks every day, as dragons normally do.

One day, he was busy napping in his lair when he heard a noise within the cavern. Profusus snapped his eyes open and smelled the scent of a human intruder. He lifted his head and looked around the cavern, keenly sensing the intruder.

"Come out and show yourself, thief," the dragon rumbled. "I can smell your odour and sense your presence. I can feel your stench of character. Reveal yourself or I will devour you before you ever attempt to exit my lair," Profusus warned.

The man showed himself willingly so as not to provoke the dragon.

"Who are you, mister, and why have you come?" the dragon said, narrowing his eyes.

"I-I am no one of consequence, O mighty dragon." The man stumbled over his words. "I only wish to ask a favour of thee, O Profusus," the man stated cautiously.

"Why do you come to ask a favour of me so readily armed?" Profusus asked.

"News of your wealth has travelled far and wide, Mr. Dragon, and I only seek but to claim a bit of it," the man said while gaining his courage.

"News? What news? I have told no one yet," the dragon rumbled angrily.

"Men can smell and desire gold. We can find it and hoard it as well as dragons can, and it haunts our very dreams," the man explained, wild-eyed. "We will do anything to gain it."

"I can sense your greediness, little man," the dragon said. "You will get no gold from me. Now leave before I make you my next appetizer. I was just contemplating dinner," Profusus warned with a wicked grin.

The man could not control his greed. He drew his big sword, which was laced with a substance poisonous to dragons, and he lunged at Profusus. "I will have your gold now!" the man yelled. But he made it only three steps before Profusus snatched him up and casually but quickly munched him down.

"Mmmm, a bit tart," Profusus said to himself while licking his fingers. "I should really roast thief first in the future before devouring them," he stated flatly. Then with a sigh, he went back to his mid-afternoon nap.

When Profusus awoke, he noticed a new addition to his lair. Profusus missed nothing in his warm cavern, and standing near the exit was a brand-new golden statue. He narrowed his eyes, viewing the second unwise thief attempting to steal from him. But he grinned in satisfaction, seeing that the enchantment on his gold had worked wonders.

"You're a little smarter than the first burglar who tried to steal gold from me, but not the wiser," Profusus said. "I think I will keep you here as a warning to those who dare to attempt the same folly."

The following day, a third man had entered the dragon's big cavern, and he approached Profusus cautiously. The dragon brought his big head to bare and viewed the man with skepticism.

"Who are you and what do you want?" Profusus rumbled. "Are you looking to be lunch as well, or to become a permanent addition to my home?" the dragon asked dangerously.

"I-I'm just a man in search of charity, O mighty dragon," he said, stuttering.

"Indeed!" the dragon responded, narrowing his eyes.

"No, its not for me, but for others who are less fortunate, for I am successful and in no need of such riches," the man explained. "I have brought you a gift from my craft in exchange." The man presented a magnificent sword, forged by his own hands.

Profusus considered the man and sensed generosity. He was indeed authentic and spoke truthfully, so he relaxed his demeanour. "You are smarter and wiser than the first two men," Profusus stated. "That is a fine gift you bring, sword maker, and you shall be rewarded with charity," the dragon said heartedly. Profusus gave him a healthy sack of gold, far more than the sword's worth. Then Profusus bid him a farewell with good tidings.

Over time, the dragon Profusus Luxuriance and his gold became well known beyond measure. Folks from far and wide travelled to the dragon's lair seeking riches. The honest and generous ones returned wealthy, while the greedy, dishonest ones became statues of gold, adding to the dragon's growing golden statue collection. Then one day, two men came and approached Profusus. Each man had a different nature and different agenda from the other.

"Who are you two and what do you want?" the dragon asked in his thundering voice, as he always did.

"Hello, mighty dragon," the first man said. "I am a generous man who helps the weak and the poor, and guides those less fortunate than I am. I seek only your wisdom and not gold to aid in my own purpose, O Profusus the magnificently wise."

The dragon was struck by this man's kind heart and was pleased with him. Besides the sword maker, no other man such as him had ever before graced his lair. "You shall have all the gold you want, my friend," the dragon said. "Share the treasure as you will to those who need it most and leave no man poor."

The first man bowed. "Thank you, Profusus. Your immense generosity proceeds itself and will not go unnoticed, my friend," he declared.

The second man was so greedy and so vile, he had planned to slay Profusus and take all the treasure for himself. He drew an enchanted magical sword for dragonslaying and confronted Profusus. "The golden hoard will be mine," he screamed and advanced forward in attack.

Profusus sensed his greedy and evil nature and moved to breathe fire on him, then devour him. But the wicked man was faster, moving quicker than Profusus. The man plunged his sword into the dragon, and Profusus Luxuriance died. The evil man gloated in glee at his triumph, then turned to kill the kind man. But before he could slay the kind man and enjoy the riches of the gold he would claim, the evil man turned into a golden statue.

The first man was relieved at the evil wicked man's untimely demise but was also saddened by the dragon's death. With help from those he trusted, the kind man took the gold to be shared and left the collection of golden statues, except for one. Then they sealed off the lair and hid the entrance so it could not be found.

When all was done, the kind and generous man and his friends took the golden statue of the evil man who slayed Profusus and put it on display. It was displayed in the kind man's hometown square of Gild so that greedy men would learn from their folly.

For ages old, it was told
about the coveted treasure found;
men would search for the precious gold
in the endless wilds abound.

It drove men on, twisting their souls
and making them go mad
because once gold fever takes its hold,
it can turn good men to bad.

Clovis and the Village of Sword Makers

In the fourth century of the current age, out of the dust of the second darkness that was widely known as the destructive Chaos War, a proud and noble stock of humans settled in the fertile land just east of the Cambrian Mountains. These human people were made of strength and will and were quite accustomed to battle. They were the Edinglees, a small group compared to other peoples, and to them, fighting for survival was commonplace.

Once the Edinglees had settled in their chosen land to which they called home, they grew prosperous. Years went by, and they had built towns in various areas of the land. Farming, mining, foresting, and various other business endeavours had grown lucrative. The Edinglees had begun trading in commerce with other kingdoms but were still far too scattered a people to form a nation.

One day, just before the yearly harvest, raiding parties from a strong human stock known as the Abinglees started plundering farms and villages. From the North, they came, and they were many in number. Their lands covered a vast area from north to east, but they were always looking for more.

Two strong Edinglees warriors, known as Clovis and Sigrem, held the Abinglees back with the help of a large mustered band of fighters. Clovis was strong, with an average build. He had shoulder-length black hair, with a short well-kept beard and clear blue eyes. He bore a birthmark of a single spiral on his right forearm. Sigrem was large and muscular. He was clean shaven, with long brown hair and grey eyes. Clovis and Sigrem were both stoic, experienced warriors of much skill, and fighting was their business.

"They are too many, and they strike before we can stop them," complained

Sigrem. "We have been battling them for two months, and yet they still persist. We have lost much."

"Worry not, friend Sigrem. Winter will be here soon, and they will be forced to head back north before the snows settle in the mountain pass."

The snows soon came, and the Abinglees raiding bands started to head back north. The head Abinglees band, led by Hutha the Champion, approached Clovis and Sigrem before they departed. With long blonde hair, typical of the Abinglees, and a beard, Hutha was a strong and large man; he had words for Clovis and Sigrem.

"We have shared many blows on the field of battle, and yet we stand before each other," Hutha said. "But know that our contest will continue in the spring, when I return with King Ulseth at the head of his great army," Hutha added ominously. "You Edinglees will not last, and your resourceful lands will be ours. I suggest you submit to King Ulseth when winter breaks and save your people."

"Do not think we will submit so easily. We Edinglees have a strength and will beyond measure," Clovis growled.

"Then, you will perish!" Hutha said stoically before he departed.

Clovis and Sigrem stood before a council in a central village in their land. The news Clovis brought of the Abinglees returning in the spring had troubled the council greatly.

"This is news of grave tidings, brave warriors," the spokesman answered. "How are we to prepare for such a dire threat?"

A volley of suggestions flew around the room, which escalated into debate and soon, argument. Ideas such as moving, arming up, fortifying, or just plain giving up were hotly contested. When the verbal brawl reached a crescendo of shouting, finger pointing, fist slamming, and shaking, Clovis and Sigrem looked on in frustration. It all suddenly ended when Sigrem slammed his big axe down into the table with a great cracking thud.

"You sound like bickering children instead of council men," Clovis pointed out irritably. "You're Edinglees!" he shouted. "All of you have fought many battles against our rival kin and against the goblin, troll, and ogre hordes. We are warriors!" he passionately pressed.

There was a calm in the room before one councilman spoke up. "Then what do you suggest, brave Clovis?"

"I have thought of a way that may help us. The mountain dwarves of

Cambria might be able to aid us," disclosed Clovis.

"The mountain dwarfs of Cambria? How can they help us?" asked another councilman.

"Why not the elves of Elendar too?" another added sarcastically.

"They have secrets and knowledge that we can learn, and I will go to learn them. Then, I will use what I have learned to save our people, instead of sitting here and debating the fate of the Edinglees people in a damn committee," Clovis roared.

Before the council could respond, Clovis stormed out. Sigrem looked at them with a wry grin and said while nodding his head, "Gentlemen." Then he followed Clovis out the door.

"Who appointed those idiots?" Clovis asked Sigrem in irritation.

"Um, well we the people did," Sigrem responded.

Ignoring his friend's answer, Clovis turned to Sigrem. "Stay here and look after things, Sigrem. I am off to Cambria at first light."

"How long will you be gone, friend Clovis?" Sigrem asked.

"I don't know, a month perhaps? It is about a week there and a week back. I just hope we have enough time," Clovis answered.

"May the high gods protect us," said Sigrem.

"Yes, and it's the high gods who only know our fate," Clovis responded.

The next morning, Clovis was off at first light. In the gloom of the late fall season, he headed west to Cambria, the kingdom of the mountain dwarves. It was a cold and wet eight slow days, but he was welcomed warmly into the dwarven kingdom city of Rack-Hagen, which was located under the silver Spire Mountain. Clovis was brought to the dwarven king, Thane Dawlin.

"Welcome, Edinglees warrior, what brings you to our mountain halls?" asked the dwarven king.

"O mighty King Dawlin of Cambria, I have come for aid and for knowledge. My people are under grave threat from the Abinglees. They will invade at winter's thaw, and I fear we will not be victorious," Clovis explained.

"I thought the Edinglees were a proud and noble warrior people, capable of fighting any enemy that threatens them. How is this so different?" asked King Dawlin.

"We have fought them, but they are too many. And their King Ulseth will bring a great army against us come spring," Clovis responded. "Word says, you hold powers and secrets of weapons and battle. I hope to learn from you so I may defend my people."

The dwarven king sat back, pondering the request of Clovis for a moment. A small council around King Dawlin ensued. When the council resolved, the dwarf king looked at Clovis. There was a tense few seconds that felt more like minutes before Dawlin spoke. "We shall help you," the dwarven king declared.

In delight, Clovis was overjoyed and thanked King Dawlin wholeheartedly. The dwarves showed Clovis the great forge and anvil, then gave him instruction in both forging and battle. But in the short time he had, Clovis new there was not enough time to learn all the dwarven crafts and knowledge. Clovis, however, underestimated the dwarven connection to divine power.

The dwarves lead Clovis to the temple of the dwarven gods to undergo a sacred ceremony. Within the temple, Clovis was given instruction by the high priest of the ritual before the priest began the ceremony. It was a three-days and three-nights affair of gruelling prayer, seeking any kind of divine intervention. Clovis had many visions of his life, past and future. It was filled with love, passion, war, and peace. Then he envisioned a village of great importance and a crown. He saw his people united and strong. Then without warning, all this knowledge with a sense of divine peaceful feeling, came flooding into him; then a voice entered his mind.

"*Clovis, mighty warrior of the Edinglees, I am Ratulga, dwarven Goddess of Spirit, Kinship, and Unity.*"

Clovis stuttered and could not speak. He was too overwhelmed.

"*Me and my fellow immortals of the dwarven gods have given you a great gift. You will unravel this gift in fourteen days time under the tutelage of master smiths and warriors of Cambria. The skills and knowledge we bestowed you are transferable to those you wish to share them with. But only three tradesmen can be instructed: one alchemy metallurgist, an arms man, and a smithy. Along with the three tradesmen, twenty-one metalwork smiths of regular folk may be chosen to be instructed as well. You will have fourteen days to instruct the tradesman and to train your chosen twenty-one smithies; then fourteen days to forge the weapons needed, with another two weeks or more to train your army with them—only then will you be ready to defend your kingdom,*" Ratulga explained.

"Thank-thank you," Clovis muttered; that was all he could say.

"*Farewell, brave Clovis, and know that the Protector of the World is watching you. Take comfort in that and go with faith and trust,*" Ratulga concluded, then left the strong Edinglees warrior's mind.

An exhausted Clovis collapsed to the ground. The dwarven priests let him rest awhile. The ritual was over, but now the training was to begin. Clovis finally woke up after a well-needed rest but awoke changed. He was determined and ready to begin the training period. Over the next fourteen days, it was a whirlwind of learning what would have normally taken many years; it was nothing short of a miracle.

Clovis learned the secrets of forging arms and armour that only the dwarves and the elves knew. He also learned various combat styles and battle tactics unknown to any of his human counterparts. At the end of an exhausting and exhilarating fourteen days, Clovis was transformed into a divine saviour of the Edinglees people.

After a day or two of rest, Clovis was ready to depart back home. "Thank you, King Dawlin," Clovis said warmly to the Thane of Rack-Hagen. "Just know that our kingdoms will always be friends and allies."

"We have forged an unbreakable bond that will last as long as the gods look down upon us," responded King Dawlin. "Now, go put your skill to use and defend your people."

Clovis and Dawlin clasped shoulders before Clovis took his leave. Clovis, with all haste, headed back to his homeland and a particular central village. It was difficult riding, as the snow had started to settle in as the grip of winter was taking hold over the lands. But Clovis only made it back in five days. He put himself up at an inn for the night, where he met up with his friend Sigrem. They shared a pint of ale, for their spirits were high.

"Send word to the council leader that I have arrived back. I wish to speak with him in the morning. It is of grave importance," Clovis said.

"As you want, friend Clovis. You have changed much, and I am curious to see what you have learned," Sigrem responded.

In the morning, the council leader met with Clovis. "You are back, brave Clovis, our saviour, and what is it you will save us with?" asked the councilman with a mocking undertone.

Clovis met the councilman squarely and said, "Send for three tradesmen: the master of arms, the master alchemist, and the master smithy."

"Why on earth do you need them? I thought you were…"

Clovis cut him off. "NOW!" he shouted in the councilman's face. Clovis was not in the mood to argue.

The councilman was a bit taken back. "As you wish, Clovis," he responded, a bit stunned.

Before long, the three tradesmen Clovis had demanded showed up. He began to instruct them of what the dwarves had taught him, and he led them to the village centre. There he prepared the open site for a ritual to pray to the high gods—a dwarven ritual he modified for sharing his knowledge and skill with the three tradesmen. They prayed for seven whole days to gain the high gods' blessing.

At the end of the seventh day, a storm cloud formed, followed by a tremendous crack of lightning and thunder. It continued for a time until the clouds broke. A calm ray of sun shined down onto the four praying men. Then High Goddess Tyra Traviena, the Watcher and Protector of the World, smiled down upon them. She reached down with her hand and touched the earth. In the centre of the four praying men, where she touched, a rumbling thump pulsed outward, empowering the entire village. Then everything went silent. Only the blowing wind could be heard. The village was divinely empowered, and the three tradesmen were forever changed. The high gods had spoken to them, and the tradesman now understood what Clovis had learned.

The four men opened their eyes and looked at each other with a common understanding.

"We must round up all the smithies in the area," Clovis said.

The other three nodded in unison, then went about gathering as many smiths as they could muster. There were twenty-one in total.

The centre of the village became a court of forges. The smithies began a marathon of learning from Clovis and the three craftsmen for fourteen days and fourteen nights. As the master tutor, Clovis watched over their learning. At the end of the two-week marathon, the smithies were each given a ring. The rings were blessed by Umitar, God of Crafts and Skill—divine rings to pass down their skill and knowledge as master swordsmiths, weaponsmiths, and armour makers for generations to come.

"You have done well, my friend," Sigrem said to Clovis while clasping his shoulder. "The support of your cause has reached far and wide, to all our people. Many have come to join you as our leader in your fight."

"Many thanks, my good friend, but it's not just my fight—it's ours, the Edinglees peoples', and I'm afraid it's just the beginning," Clovis said in a serious tone to his friend Sigrem. "I think you know what must be done."

Sigrem knew what Clovis was getting at. "Armour and weapons, then training," he guessed.

"That's right," Clovis responded. "We have lots of armour, shields, and weapons made, with more to come. These arms are of great quality, which will match the quality of training you and I will enforce on those we arm," Clovis explained.

"Well, then, it's early winter and we have not much time to be ready before spring. Let the forging and drilling begin," Sigrem said with a smile and a bow.

The twenty-one smithies, plus the three tradesmen, began making arms and armour of high-quality dwarven steel. Clovis and Sigrem began training those equipped by the arms and armour. The smithies worked quickly and steadily while Clovis and Sigrem trained and drilled relentlessly. As more and more people came to the village area, their forces grew until they had a substantial army. At mid-wintertime, before the spring, the Edinglees people were well on their way to becoming able and ready to meet the threatening Abinglees' armies from the North. It was the year's end turning, and Clovis was made leader of the Edinglees people by all the region's council leaders.

At a celebration feast, a young innocent girl, no more than eight years old, approached Clovis and offered him a gift. It was a gift of virtue and strength, a sacred thing that only the innocent could acquire, then give away. It was a winter rose—a mystical lavender flower of life that grew under a mystical Silver Oak, known as the Tree of Life. But the winter rose only blossomed at the midwinter's turning and were extremely rare. It held special mysterious powers and secrets that most did not understand. It was widely known for its positive powers, but it had a hidden dark side. In a dark soul's hands, it could be used for ill will!

"Thank you, little one." Clovis smiled as he accepted the rose from the young child. "This will indeed ensure us victory." He tucked the rose in his vest and the celebrating went on.

After the year's turning celebration, the training and smithing resumed. It was getting close to spring, but winter would not let up. It had extended beyond expectation. This was good as well as bad. It held the Abinglees back from marching south, but crops also needed planting. Either way, it gave borrowed time for preparation for the Edinglees. Finally, there was a break in the weather patterns.

Hutha and King Ulseth of the Abinglees finally marched south, with their massive army. Their druidic order worked wonders with allowing a break in the winter they thought was over. But the magic of a mystical power held firm, and it was only temporary. King Ulseth was feeling high and mighty in his vanguard at the front of the procession of his grand army. His blonde braided hair fit well with his braided beard and gilded crown, set in his steel helm. He sent Hutha ahead through the pass to address the terms of surrender from the Edinglees.

Hutha arrived in two days time at the village of sword makers. "Who is in charge?" he asked, as he noticed the growing flock of armed and armoured confident men-at-arms.

"I am," answered Clovis while pushing his way through the crowd. "We finally meet again, Hutha," added Clovis with a dangerous undertone.

"Yes, and I see you've been busy," Hutha sneered.

"We have been very busy of late, Hutha, and I think the odds are heavily in my favour at this time, wouldn't you agree?" Clovis said.

"It matters not, Clovis. I come with terms from King Ulseth," Hutha said, matching Clovis's undertone.

"And what terms does the greedy King Ulseth demand?" asked Clovis.

"Terms of your unconditional surrender, of course, before he grinds your little gathering into the frozen ground," Hutha boldly explained.

Clovis smiled and looked around at his chuckling men. He stepped forward to Hutha and looked up to him on his horse. "You tell your king that he's not welcome here. He has worse manners than a dirty alley rat. Tell your king that I will see you and him on the field of battle."

Before a stunned Hutha could respond, Clovis spun Hutha's horse around and slapped its rump. The horse kicked off at a dead run through the parting and laughing crowd. A surprised Hutha hung on tight as his horse was helped out of town by an amused throng of well-armed men. When Hutha was sent well on his way, Clovis turned to Sigrem and said, "It's time; give the order."

"Saddle up! We head north to meet the Abinglees," Sigrem yelled. "It's time to show them the warriors we are made of," he added, heightening the moral.

When Hutha got back to King Ulseth with the answer from the Edinglees and the little message from Clovis, Ulseth almost fell off his horse from rage.

"That insolent Edinglees filth. I will show those dogs who holds sway over these lands. Forward to victory!" the King shouted.

The massive Abinglees army started moving south, out of the mountain pass towards Antwan Trading Post. Clovis and his army moved north quickly and got to Antwan Trading Post many hours before King Ulseth. He knew the enraged king would not be thinking straight, and he chose his strategic ground wisely. He set his army on open, high ground, with a river to their left, a bog on their right, and forest land to the rear. Then he sent scouts ahead to observe and bait the enemy. Clovis placed his archers to the front and his cavalry on both flanks. But most of his cavalry was hidden back in the trees.

Before long, the Abinglees' force approached and faced the ready Edinglees' army. A seething, moody King Ulseth was at their head, and he set his army in a similar formation, given the terrain.

"Clovis has chosen his ground well," King Ulseth said to Hutha. "But we have a much superior force and numbers. Be ready for my command," he advised Hutha.

Hutha just nodded and said nothing. He was having second thoughts. Judging by what he observed and had seen, Hutha was not so sure about the superiority part. The Edinglees had changed since his raids before winter. They were better equipped, and they looked more organised and confident—those changes concerned him.

Meanwhile, Clovis looked out at the Abinglees' army and was satisfied by what he saw. His men were confident and ready. Morale was high. Everything he so passionately prepared for over the last five months had come to this moment. He knew his people's strength and will. He knew the conditions and the terrain. He knew himself and his enemy. He knew the weakness of King Ulseth. He knew his man!

"They look pretty sure of themselves, Clovis," Sigrem remarked.

"We will see how sure of themselves they feel when battle closes. Remember, Sigrem, wait for my signal and lead the cavalry from the forest to outflank them in a pincer movement," said Clovis. "Hit them from behind if you can."

"I will do so, friend Clovis." With a grim look, Sigrem nodded.

Clovis calmly observed the enemy forces and understood what was about to happen. "Let them have the first move," Clovis muttered to himself.

The two armies faced off for a time, like a calm before the storm. Finally, King Ulseth got impatient and ordered his archers to open fire. Clovis retaliated in kind, then ordered his cavalry to charge the Abinglees' flanks. The Battle of Antwan had begun.

The Edinglees' cavalry met the Abinglees' cavalry on their slightly higher ground position. The snowy ground was not too deep, and it alone unhindered movement. Then Ulseth rallied his main force and charged the Edinglees' force up the centre, in attempt to deliver a knockout blow and win a quick victory.

Clovis allowed Ulseth to come in towards them and had moved his force part of the way down the hill to meet him. At the same time, Clovis moved his archers to the back on top of the hill. The cavalry units were still locked in a bitter struggle when the main bodies of both armies met in a violent and sudden collision. The two main bodies of infantry locked against each other tightly in a contest of wills and grit. Outnumbered but not outmatched, Clovis fought at the head of his men with the winter rose still tucked in his armoured chest plate. The power of that rose seemed to drive his men wildly with deadly efficiency.

Hutha and Ulseth were hailing victory cries as the battle went on. Both believing victory was at hand when their enemies central forces began receding back up the hill, in the shape of a bow. But there is one thing Hutha and Ulseth did not miss. The fact that the skill of the Edinglees' soldiers outmatched their own.

Clovis and Hutha met in the heat of battle and squared off with each other. "I was wondering when you'd find the balls to face me," Hutha taunted Clovis.

"I was just waiting for you to finally stop cowering behind your men," Clovis retorted. And with that, both men crossed swords in a personal duel that had been festering for far too long. During that duel, Clovis yelled to one of his captains, "Give the signal!"

An archer let fly a fiery arrow into the air. Then the whole Edinglees' archer force dropped their bows, drew their swords with shields, and charged in to reinforce the centre ranks.

Sigrem saw the arrow go up, and he gave the order. The first cavalry regiment of the rear cavalry force went around the high ground by the riverside while Sigrem lead the second cavalry regiment around the bog area. Before King Ulseth realized it, the Edinglees' cavalry hammered into both sides and behind his main force.

"We are outflanked," he yelled, as he signalled his reserve force to charge in. It did not help much. Then he was suddenly face-to-face with Sigrem.

"You look worried, King Ulseth," Sigrem remarked without hesitation. "How about I take that dirty head from your shoulders for you, and save you from further worries," he said while gritting his teeth.

"You dog," Ulseth responded. But that was all he could say before Sigrem took the initiative and attacked King Ulseth.

As the battle raged in violent and horrible bloody combat, the Abinglees realized that they were in trouble. They were hemmed in on three sides, their rear soon to follow; it would not be long before the Edinglees closed the gap. Their soldiers were not as strong and skilled as their enemy, and their forces were falling in far greater numbers.

"You look tired, Hutha. You can surrender anytime," Clovis remarked.

"I will not let you defeat me," Hutha growled as he pressed the attack. "These lands are rightfully ours, and you have no place within them. Go back to where you came from," he said maliciously while trading blows with Clovis.

"You are misguided, Hutha. We've always been here," Clovis responded. And finding an opening in Hutha's defences, Clovis seized the moment and cleanly removed Hutha's head from his shoulders.

Sigrem and the Abinglees' king were also locked in bitter single combat. Both combatants were determined to end each other. The Abinglees' army began crumbling apart with Hutha's demise, but they still barely held on. Their king was still going strong.

"I will kill you and enslave your people. They will be lower than dogs," King Ulseth spat at Sigrem.

Sigrem said nothing and let Ulseth spout off. With measured precision, he found an opening that his kingly opponent could have easily guarded. His rage and ego had cost him his defence and, ultimately, his life. He was paying more attention to his bravado than his sword and, suddenly, felt Sigrem's sword in his side, buried to the hilt. His eyes went wide and he gasped.

Sigrem looked King Ulseth in his eyes and said, "May the high gods have mercy on your soul." Then Sigrem pulled his sword out of Ulseth with a jerk and the king of the Abinglees fell to the ground—he was dead.

Seeing their king fall broke the will of the Abinglees' army to fight on, and they fled the field of battle. The Edinglees were victorious. The Battle of Antwan was over. They pushed the Abinglees back through the North Mountain pass, driving them from the Edinglees' settled lands.

The Edinglees people were saved, and they made Clovis their king. Clovis put back the winter rose from where it was plucked, as was stated by legend, and winter gave way to spring. He made Sigrem the new master tutor of arms in the village of sword makers, an honorary title that would last through the ages. The Abinglees never attacked the new Kingdom of Edingal again. Over time, the Abinglees became friends with their southern neighbour. Old hatreds faded away and became no more as they formed a mutual bond shared between the elves, dwarves, and men—a bond that would once again one day save the world from a dark time.

The Crown of Clovis would be passed down from ruler to ruler. Each ruler's spirit would be imbued in the Crown until one day a powerful charming warrior queen would unite all the free kingdoms of Rithanon. She would unite them in a common cause against a dark apocalypse prophesised as the Third Darkness, which would threaten the entire world. She would be of the true bloodline of Clovis and bare his features, including the birthmark of the single spiral on her right forearm. Her roll as ruler would be pivotal in helping to bring an end to the darkness.

From the dark grip of winter's hand,
a people merge to make a stand;
a battle raged and a king was made
to rule a victorious united land.

As the line of Clovis was handed down,
each ruler's soul imbued with his crown;
it forged a utopian kingdom strong
to the warrior nation of renowned.

In contrast was a north domain,
where evil was rising once again;
a kingdom of darkness slowly rose
to enslave the whole world in pain.

Then a warrior queen came along
in the land that Clovis had made so strong.
The Kingdom of Light it had become,
prophesized through ancient song.

*Under the queen, all lands would unite
against the north dark land and fight.
And so, foreseen through ancient runes,
the Kingdom of Dark faced the Kingdom of light.*

*The power of the dark was soon unveiled;
the Kingdom of Dark had lastly failed.
Through blood and toil, the lands had fought;
and the Kingdom of Light prevailed.*

A Hero's Tale

Once upon a time, in the county of Ballind, within the Kingdom of Absania, lived a lovely fair lady named Liella Apple-Tane. She lived in a fair castle with her mother and with her father, who was a lord with rich estates. It was also largely spoken that Liella was the fairest lady in the land.

Liella was in good health and good shape. She had long, straight blonde hair down to her waist and sparkling green eyes. Many a noble duke and lord from afar sought Liella's fair hand. But the lovely Lady Liella was not swayed by riches nor by royalty; it was brave humility she treasured. Two particular brave, charming, and handsome knights sought Liella's hand. Though they had similar qualities that gained any lady's attention, they also dramatically stood apart from each other.

The first knight was Lord Wulf Montague. He had blue eyes, short, wavy dark hair, and stood tall. He lived across town in a fancy castle, which stood on breathtaking estate grounds. The grounds were garnished with fabulous gardens. He lived in lavish luxury, with servants and many commoners that towed his line. Even though he was charming and handsome, Montague was also arrogant and conceited. He was masterful with a sword and lance and had bested many a knight at many jousting tournaments.

The other knight was Valedin Clavendane. He was not rich at all but had station as knight, like his father before him. Valedin had sandy-coloured hair and hazel eyes. He was humble, compassionate, and had an innocent way about him. He was proud and chivalrous. Valedin wished to follow in his father's footsteps as a Knight of Traviena, also known as the Knights of Carnebour. The only problem was he was just far too clumsy. In fact, he was such a master at being clumsy, he just bumbled his way along through life. Most wondered how Valedin ever became a knight at all.

The truth was, most of Valedin's past knightly accomplishments—maybe all—were due to his magnificent horse, Talibar! Because Talibar was no ordinary horse. Talibar was large, majestic, strong, and agile. In fact, he was so agile and quick, he stood out from all other horses. His dark brown shiny coat glistened in the sunshine. Talibar was smart and confident for a horse. One could say, that in every way, shape, and form, Talibar was magnificent. But the best thing that Talibar was good at was keeping Valedin out of trouble and saving him from magnificent blunders.

One fine, summer day, Sir Valedin was lounging under a tree with his horse, Talibar. He was trying to compose a romantic poem, in attempt to charm Lady Liella. Valedin recited the first few lines to Talibar. "What do you think, Talibar? Do you think it needs a little more flair to get her attention?"

Talibar rolled his eyes and snorted in disgust. The poem was so lame, it hurt Talibar's ears, and he was tired of hearing it.

"Maybe you are right, Talibar. I've been trying to make this good, but I'm just not a poet. I should just be myself," Valedin declared as he stood up proudly.

Talibar was relieved, and he also stood up. He positioned himself so Valedin could mount the saddle on his back. Valedin leapt up to the saddle, but then he just kept going, crashing to the ground on the other side. Talibar snorted and shook his head. He had seen this far too many times.

Before long, Valedin and Talibar were trotting down the road to the Apple-Tane estate. Valedin sat tall in his saddle. He was unaware that his helmet was cockeyed on his head, but it seemed to always be that way. When Valedin arrived at the Apple-Tane estate, Lady Liella was being led down the steps of the gatehouse by a tall, handsome man: Lord Montague. Valedin's heart sank in his chest. Liella waved to him and approached Valedin while holding Montague's arm.

"Lord Montague, have you met my friend Valedin?" Liella asked cheerfully.

"Why, not personally," Montague responded amused. "Aren't you that clumsy knight I've heard so much about?"

Valedin replied to Montague, "Well, my lord, I don't know about clumsy, but I have my challenges, as everyone does. I came to say hello to Lady Liella and to see how she was doing. It's been some time, my lord."

Lady Liella smiled. "That was kind of you, Valedin; yes, it has been some time. We should catch up after my dinner with Lord Montague. Tomorrow, perhaps?"

"Tomorrow would be fine, my lady," responded Valedin.

Montague smirked. "As you can see, Valedin, Lady Liella is doing just fine." Montague then turned to Liella and said, "I will see you tonight, my lady." Montague mounted his horse to leave. As he departed, Montague commented, "Magnificent horse, by the way. He looks better than you. And hey, you might want to fix your helmet, Valedin; it looks a little cockeyed."

Everyone present laughed and snickered, including Liella but to a lesser degree. Valedin felt humiliated. Without a word, he turned and left.

Montague trotted down the road with his henchman. He felt rather smug.

"My lord, do you think Lady Liella's parents will accept your proposal of marriage to her?" asked Lambert, one of Montague's three hench men.

Montague laughed. "Why, of course. I will just wine and dine the lovely Lady Liella and show off my assets to her; then once her parents see my importance and immense riches, they will beg me to take her hand. After that, I can consolidate the Apple-Tane lands and expand my wealth and prestige," he explained. "Besides, there's no worry, especially from that fool Valedin. It will all go to plan."

Montague and his henchman laughed in satisfaction as they headed across town, back to Lord Montague's grand castle.

That evening, the Apple-Tane family arrived at Montague's grand castle. Lord Montague gave them a tour of his fabulous estate grounds, then put on a lavish feast for his guests. It was all to impress the Apple-Tane clan.

Everything seemed to be going well, right up until the climax of dinner, when Lord Wulf Montague stood up to make a toast and pitch his proposal. "To my friends and guests, thank you for honouring my formal invitation. I have an important proposal to make that will benefit all in Ballind County. I would propose to ask for the union between my lordship self and the lovely Lady Liella—a bond that shall benefit both our two great families and the people of the county," Montague announced with dash and flair.

The only reaction Lord Montague received from the Apple-Tane's was one of shock and awe. Liella's face went red, and her father stood up, pent with rage and disgust.

"You seek my daughter's hand in marriage?" Lord Apple-Tane replied.

"Why, yes, Lord Apple-Tane, just a minor formality is all. But worry not, my lord, all will be fine when your daughter's hand and mine are joined in union," Montague said, smiling from ear to ear.

"It is not a minor formality, you self-important lord of grandship—this is outrageous. You're not marrying my daughter," Lord Apple-Tane declared.

The lady of the Apple-Tane house stood up and looked at Montague, "I'm sorry, my lord, but there won't be any weddings set up today, and I must take my leave."

"Or anytime soon. Come on, Liella, we are leaving," added Lord Apple-Tane.

Then the whole Apple-Tane family got up and left. Montague was still holding his toasting goblet, wondering what went wrong. But the only thing that Montague was concerned about was being turned down by the Apple-Tanes and he was furious. So, to get hold of the Apple-Tane lands, he hatched a wicked plan.

Montague put together a gift bundle of rare goods, which included exotic fruit. Then he sent the bundle with a trusted servant to the Apple-Tane estate with instruction.

"Gareth Butler, my most trusted servant, give this bundle to Lady Liella's parents with apology from me, then come straight back," instructed Montague.

"Right away, my lord," Butler responded. Then the servant Gareth Butler delivered the package the next day and did as he was instructed.

Not long after, Lord Apple-Tane and his wife had both mysteriously passed away. Lady Liella was heartbroken. The other strange thing that happened was that Lord Montague's servant, Gareth Butler, was never seen again after he delivered the bundle to the Apple-Tane estate. Just before the Apple-Tanes deaths, Butler had supposably moved away. This was what Montague claimed to Sheriff Roderick, who was investigating the whole affair.

Some days later, Valedin and Talibar found Gareth Butler's body. He was found in the river, several miles downstream from where Valedin had set up a temporary camp. He reported the body to the sheriff, who was also his friend. They also found a strange little vial tucked away in a hidden pocket in Butler's coat and a stab wound in the servant's back. It all started coming together, but nothing could be proven.

Valedin had paid his respects to Lady Liella earlier in his usual clumsy awkward way, but everything was now looking like foul play. "Liella must be made aware," Valedin claimed to his sheriff friend.

So, Valedin jumped in the saddle on Talibar and was off. He was so fixed on his duty, he did not see the low tree branch when waving back to his friend Roderick. The amused sheriff helped Valedin remount before he carried on with his duties.

When Valedin showed up at the Apple-Tane estate, he was not admitted or allowed to see Lady Liella. She was getting ready to attend a grand ball that evening. All the local lords, ladies, and well-to-do were going to be in attendance; and lovely Lady Liella was the guest of honour.

"So, who is hosting this grand ball?" Valedin had to ask.

The servant at the gate looked at Valedin and said, "Who else would put on such an event of grandeur but the Lord Wulf Montague?"

"Lord Montague, of course," responded Valedin with a forced smile. Valedin knew exactly what he was going to do, but it was a foolish move. "Well, you don't get things done when sitting on your ass," Valedin said to himself. He then looked at Talibar while smiling and said, "Talibar, my old friend, we are going to attend a fancy ball."

Talibar snorted and raised an eyebrow in response because he knew how this evening was going to turn out. It was going turn out to be a disaster!

That evening, all the rich lordly upper crust of society were filing into the big fancy ballroom at Montague's grand castle. Every manner of lavish display was put on. Montague welcomed his guests with charming flair. Many of the young ladies put an eye on him, even some of the married ones.

While grinning, Lord Montague said to his henchman in a low tone, "Every lady wants to be with me it seems. When Lady Liella arrives and sees this, she will not be able to resist my charm or my offer." His henchman laughed with him in response.

Soon enough, Lady Liella arrived, and she looked radiant. Now it was all the men's turn to stare. Montague didn't waste anytime greeting her. "You look lovely, my dear. Welcome to my grand ballroom," said Montague proudly with as much charm and dash as he could muster.

"Why, thank you, my Lord Montague," responded Liella. Liella was still shaken by the loss of her parents and had barely been out since. She felt a bit uncomfortable. She couldn't help but feel there was something off and not quite right about the whole affair.

Soon, the talented bards hired for the ball started playing, and the ballroom became more festive. As the dancing got underway, Montague approached Liella. In courtly manner, he said, "Lady Liella, with you being the guest of honour, it is my duty as the host to ask you for this first dance?" Montague vowed.

"Why, yes, of course, my Lord," she responded.

Montague led Lady Liella onto the dance floor, with all the other dancers. The festive party was growing more electric, and Montague could not be happier with the way the evening was shaping out. Lady Liella started having fun, and everything seemed to be falling into place.

Sir Valedin Clavendane arrived at Montague's grand hall. Festive music and chatting mixed with laughter could be heard from the bottom of the hall's wide steps. Everyone hanging about put an eye on Valedin and his horse, Talibar.

"He's rather finely dressed for a knight," said one.

"Quite the magnificent horse he's riding," said another.

Valedin didn't pay any attention and passed Talibar off to a stable hand after dismounting. "I shall not be too long, my friend," Valedin said, patting Talibar's head.

Talibar snorted and whinnied in concern for Valedin's safety.

Valedin then headed up the steps. He tripped on the way up but quickly caught himself and straightened his composure.

An onlookers commented, "Hmmm, I see he's clumsy too!"

Valedin entered the grand ballroom of the hall. He felt good and was beaming with positiveness. Ladies eyed him up, and he nodded to them in respect. But Valedin didn't come for pleasantries; he had his duty to perform. He looked around the room and took in the festive atmosphere. He grabbed a goblet off a passing drinks tray held by a servant, then made his way to a banquet table. After a few nibbles of the fine display of food, Valedin finally spotted Lady Liella, who was busy dancing with Lord Montague.

As Valedin was watching the couple, a friend of Valedin's attending the party hailed to him. Valedin responded by quickly turning and waving back. But as he did, he unintentionally smacked the fellow next to him with his shoulder, which caused the unfortunate victim of Valedin's clumsiness to knock over a tray of drinks. Being slightly oblivious to the incident, Valedin happily moved on.

Valedin slowly positioned himself, so Lady Liella could see him. Eventually, she did see him, and so did Lord Montague. Liella was happy to see Valedin, but Montague was not. Valedin exchanged pleasant warm smiles with Liella while Montague only glared at him. But Valedin just ignored him. Then a young pretty, redheaded girl, with sparkling blue eyes, approached Valedin and asked him, "May I have this dance, my lord?"

"Why, yes, of course, my lady," responded Valedin, smiling in his ever-so-innocent and charming way. Then Valedin led her to the dance floor.

Montague was less than pleased to see Valedin at his soiree since he seemed to be making headway with Liella. Just as Montague was moving the conversation with Liella from condolences on the loss of her parents to matters of union, Valedin moved up beside them.

"Lovely party, my lord. I can't say I've ever seen it's equal," said Valedin.

"Well, yes, Valedin, a party of the upper class which you are not part of," replied Montague, forcing a smile through his clamped jaw.

Valedin smiled while nodding, then respectfully said, "Well, I didn't really come to talk to you anyway, Lord Montague. My business is with Lady Liella."

"Well, as you can see, she is quite busy at the moment," Montague replied. Then Montague moved away with Liella from Valedin and his dance partner. Montague nodded and motioned to his henchman to throw Valedin out.

Montague's three henchman moved to apprehend Valedin, but Valedin weaved around the dance floor to avoid them. As he moved past Montague and Liella, he said, "My Lady Liella, I must talk with you." At the same time, Valedin was completely unaware that he had caught a woman's dress with his dagger sheath, and her dress started to unravel.

Valedin's pretty dance partner asked, "Are you in trouble, my lord?" when she noticed the three big goons trying to get hold of Valedin.

"No, no, no, my lady, not at all. Not as much trouble as Lord Montague," Valedin wryly responded. "He's in much bigger trouble than me."

The poor woman's dress that Valedin's dagger had caught had now fully unravelled to her waist. Thoroughly embarrassed, she ran out of the ballroom. Valedin, who was completely oblivious to the poor woman's plight, just kept on dancing.

Soon, the three henchmen caught up with Valedin and grabbed him. His dance partner fled off the dance floor, and a scuffle ensued. The scuffle bumped into other dancers and eventually landed onto a table of fine wine and food, creating a big mess. Liella stepped forward and tried to stop it.

"STOP! What are you doing? He didn't do anything," she yelled.

In mid-scuffle, Valedin said to Liella, "Don't trust Montague. The sheriff and I have some evidence of him possibly being responsible for the death of your parents. You see, Montague—"

A fist slammed into Valedin's jaw in midsentence, silencing his speech. Montague's guards stepped in to assist the three big goons.

"I think he's had too much to drink, my lady," said a grinning Montague as he came up to Liella. "Throw him out!" Montague calmly ordered his men.

Liella was stunned at Valedin's words. She was angry with Valedin for bringing up the death of her parents and the possible suspicion of murder by Montague, but deep down, it started to make sense to her.

The party crowd looked on in either horror or amusement as the scuffle made a big mess of everything. Then finally the henchman and guards dragged a stubborn Valedin towards the main entrance. Valedin was yelling and protesting along the way. "Liella, Liella, it's vital we talk. Montague, your villainy will be revealed, mark my words," he declared.

Then the big henchman and guards threw Valedin, with a big heave, down the front steps. He bounced and rolled nicely before coming to a stop near the bottom. "AND STAY OUT!" one of the guards yelled at him.

Soon Talibar showed up to meet a battered Valedin at the bottom of the steps. Talibar shook his head and snorted in disgust. He nudged Valedin with his nose to see if he was all right. Valedin only groaned.

Back inside the hall, Liella was not happy at all and prepared to leave. "I have had enough; I'm going home," she said bluntly. She looked at Montague and saw him as completely rotten. "You did not need to do that."

"He was way out of line, my lady," responded Montague. "Let's not worry about the interrupting ruckus. What about my offer of union?" asked Montague. "You will be well looked after, my lady," he added convincingly.

"I'm so very sorry, my Lord, but a union of marriage between us is simply out of the question. Good night, my lord." And with that, Lady Liella left the ballroom in disgust.

Talibar trotted along, with a bruised Valedin on his back. It was late, and the air was cool. It had been quite the evening.

"Well, that didn't go quite as smoothly as I thought it would, my old friend," said Valedin. "I say, we call it a night."

Talibar snorted and whinnied in response; he knew it had turned out the way he had expected all along—in disaster!

The big party was winding down. Lord Montague, in all his arrogant pride, was seething with rage. "How dare she turn me down—me, Lord Wulf Montague. Can't she not see what greatness was offered to her?" he raged to Lambert, his top henchmen.

"Maybe she's not ready for such a joining yet, my lord," said Lambert

Montague scoffed. "Oh, Lady Liella's ready because I say she is, and I will have her family's lands." Then Montague stormed out.

Lambert timidly responded, "Yes, my lord!"

The next morning, Valedin felt stiff. His unfortunate evening at Montague's had left him with a nice little collection of bruises. But nevertheless, he felt compelled to seek an audience with Lady Liella.

When Valedin arrived at Liella's family estate, he discovered that she was not at home. One of Lady Liella's worried servants informed him that she was missing.

"When Lady Liella was late to awake in the morning, I checked to see if all was well with her, but she was not there," explained the servant with concern. "I have looked everywhere for her but to no avail."

Valedin pondered the mystery of Lady Liella's disappearance and had his suspicions. It was time for a little meeting with Sheriff Roderick.

Montague sat at his table, which was set for a fine dinner for two. His top henchman, Lambert, addressed Montague, "Is everything set, my lord?"

Montague grinned. "Yes, Lambert, bring her in," he said with flare and glee.

Lambert went to the open door and yelled out, "BRING HER IN!"

Montague's guards escorted a struggling Lady Liella, both gagged and tied up, into the room. They sat her in the chair opposite of Lord Montague before they untied and ungagged a very angry and unhappy Lady Liella.

Lord Montague smiled. "Nice of you to join me for dinner," said Montague to Liella over-politely. His tone suggested that he was mocking her. Then he poured two glasses of wine and handed one to Lady Liella. "So, my fine lady, what shall we talk about?" asked Montague, still grinning.

"I told you, I am not marrying you, Lord Montague," said Liella.

Montague laughed. "Oh, I think we've covered that part, but that's OK; that's not why you're here," he responded sarcastically. "The time for pleasantries is over, Lady Liella. You see, I only wanted to marry you to gain your lands. But since I can't do that, I'm just going to force your hand. You're going to sign them over to me," explained Montague.

Lady Liella scoffed at Montague. "You're dreaming. I will never sign, even if you threaten to take my head. Let me ask you, did you murder my parents for those lands, Montague?" asked Liella with an icy inflection.

"Now, now, I'm not a monster," cooed Montague. "I'm not going to take your pretty head, Lady Liella. You see, I know this wizard who is going to provide me with a little potion. When it's ready and when you drink it, my lady, you will feel absolutely obligated to sign over your family's lands to me. And on the side, marry me of course," Montague explained, grinning wickedly.

Lady Liella lost her self-control and threw her wine glass at Lord Montague, plus a few other things off the table. "I knew it: you are a monster," she yelled with anger.

Montague only laughed at his victory and easily dodged the objects Liella flung at him. His guards were quick to subdue Liella, and she sat back in her chair and said nothing more. She felt defeated.

Lord Montague looked at Liella in amusement. "My lady, such table manners. Just enjoy the dinner and relax. But I must say, I do look forward to our time together." Then Montague laughed wickedly.

Valedin and Sheriff Roderick found no trace of Lady Liella's possible abduction. Valedin knew she wouldn't just leave without any notice, and he had a strong hunch as to where she could possibly be.

Valedin looked at Roderick and said, "I think I know where Lady Liella is, and I have an idea." Then Valedin leaped onto the saddle on Talibar's back, almost falling off in the process, and rode straight to Lord Montague's castle. He demanded an audience with him.

Montague accepted the demanded from Valedin with amusement. He met Valedin out in the courtyard. "Why, what a surprise; you have big balls to show back up here after last night, I must say," said Montague mockingly.

But Valedin was serious business. "Shut up, you overinflated windbag of self-importance. When the wind is blowing, I don't know if it's either the weather or just you flapping those big conceited lips of yours. I know you have Lady Liella, Montague; don't deny it," he said with a stern straight face.

Montague was surprised and instantly enraged. "What proof do you have, Valedin? You don't have any," said Montague with rage.

"It matters not, Montague, you inbred, mutated nutsack. I have come to issue a challenge. In one week's hence, a county jousting tournament is being held outside of town. I challenge you in that tournament. The prize will be for Lady Liella's hand," Valedin determined.

Talibar went wide-eyed with surprise at Valedin's declaration of challenge. Valedin straightened up on his horse, Talibar, his face serious and his hand on his hip. He looked unwaveringly at Lord Montague.

Montague wanted to kill him so bad. "Never has anyone spoken to me in such fashion and lived to talk about it. I accept your challenge, Valedin. Now leave my courtyard, you little worm."

"Very well, lord wind sack. I will see you in one week's time at the tournament," Valedin declared.

Montague scoffed. "It will be no contest. You are no match for me, Valedin, or anybody. I will be making a fool out of you, a big fool. Most people become has-beens, but you will never even be that, Valedin."

"You can say what you want, Montague, but both of us know you will never be the man your mother was." And with that said, Valedin and Talibar calmly trotted out of Montague's castle courtyard.

"You should have killed him when you had the chance, my Lord Montague," said one of Montague's henchmen.

"No, no, he is no match for me, or for anyone, for that matter. He's just a bumbling idiot. Besides, it will be fun to humiliate the dumb knight in front of a crowd, and then I will kill him," said Lord Montague with a smile.

Valedin felt quite pleased with himself. "I'm going to show that villain Montague a thing or two, Talibar, and save Lady Liella from him," he boasted proudly.

Talibar snorted. He was pretty sure that Valedin was going to need a lot of help.

As they pulled up beside the stable of Valedin's cottage, Valedin caught his foot in the saddle as he dismounted and came crashing to the ground. Talibar just shook his head and whinnied a bit. Valedin was not just going to need a lot of help, he was going to need help of epic proportions.

The next day, Valedin was explaining his plan to his sheriff friend, Roderick. "Valedin, what are you doing? We have almost enough evidence to arrest Montague. You do not need to enter in this jousting tournament against him," Roderick voiced with concern.

"Well, you see, it's a matter of honour and chivalry, Roderick. I don't expect you to really understand. You're a sheriff, not a knight," replied Valedin.

Roderick rolled his eyes and sighed heavily. "Oh, I understand perfectly well, but I hate to break this to you, my friend, but…" Roderick hesitated.

"But what, Roderick? C'mon, tell me," asked Valedin.

"Well, Valedin, you just… cannot joust, my friend," said Roderick.

"Can't joust? Of course, I can joust! I am a knight," said Valedin proudly.

"Yes, you're a knight, Valedin, just not as skilled a knight as Lord Montague. You're not going to win," Roderick pointed out as gently as he could.

"Well, thank you for your counsel, Mr. Sheriff, but I am going to enter the tournament. And I am going to practise for the tournament. And then, I am going to win that tournament. Plus, in the process, I am going to beat Lord Montague," said Valedin stubbornly. Valedin left the sheriff's office in a huff and Roderick in a state of anxiety. Of course, it didn't really help matters when Valedin tripped and fell face-first to the ground on his way out the door.

Valedin spent the next few days leading up to the jousting tournament hard at practice. He trained on what was known as a quintain, a kind of swivelling dummy post with arms. One arm had a shield fastened to it, which he attempted to hit with the lance tip as he charged by on horseback. The other arm had a heavy bag hanging from its end, as a counterweight for resistance. The bag could also swing around and hit the jouster if they were not charging by fast enough, nor paying attention. And other than Valedin falling off his horse, Talibar, more times than Roderick and Talibar could count, Valedin got smacked by that heavy bag far too often. This was due to Talibar's unmitigated strength.

Valedin was getting a little better, though, but most of Valedin's success in avoiding the bag and not falling off was really attributed to Talibar. Talibar tweaked his movements so Valedin could hit on target fast enough to avoid the bag and not fall out of the saddle. Through it all, Talibar had figured out how they were going to beat Montague.

Talibar's obvious display of prowess did not go unnoticed to Sheriff Roderick. By week's end, practice started paying off.

"Bravo Valedin, besides having the most magnificent horse in the land, I believe I do see some improvement," said Roderick.

"Why, thank you, Roderick. I do believe I know what I'm doing," Valedin proudly responded.

Roderick left it at that. They packed up and went home to rest up for the upcoming tournament the next day.

Lady Liella was looking out the window from her fancy room—a gilded cage, it was. Being held hostage for her own lands by a nasty lord was getting her down. Suddenly, the door opened and Montague walked into the room.

"My lovely Lady Liella, would you like to join me for dinner. At least we can act civil, don't you agree?" asked Lord Montague.

Lady Liella lunged forward and slapped Montague in the face, then spat at his feet. "I would rather kiss a troll than spend any time with you," responded Liella in disgust.

Montague composed himself. "It matters not, my lady. Soon my potion will arrive on the day of the jousting tournament, which is tomorrow, and then you will have no choice. Stay in here if you wish; you cannot go anywhere and you're being watched," explained Montague.

"I'm going to take pleasure in disappointing you, Lord Montague," raged Lady Liella.

Montague laughed. "Try as you may, my lady, but fighting against that potion's effects will serve you none. Goodnight, my lady!" Montague left the fancy chamber and locked the door, leaving a brooding Lady Liella throwing things around the room.

The day of the jousting tournament had arrived. The trumpets sounded, the horns blared, and the crowd cheered as the knights came into the jousting arena. Single file they came in, displaying their impressive banners and arms in parade. At the head of the procession was Lord Montague. As each knight passed the duke's balcony, they left their ceremonial shield to be set on a display rack known as the Tree of Shields. As the knights lined up in front of the duke's balcony, there was all but one: Valedin was not present! Montague smirked at his easy victory, thanks to Valedin not showing up after he so brazenly made the challenge a week before.

After waiting a few moments for the missing contestant, the duke stood up and started to speak. "My people of Ballind County, what a great honour it will be to witness our local brave knights compete in—"

A loud crash outside the arena entrance cut the duke's words short. Then Sir Valedin entered the arena. Valedin hailed the duke. As he did so, the tip of his banner lance caught a string of flag pendants, which he dragged along with him. The crowd responded in a mixture of gasps, murmurs, and laughter. But besides Valedin's clumsiness and awkwardness, the other thing that stood out was his horse.

Talibar pranced proud and tall. He stood out from all the other horses, looking strong and confident. "What a magnificent-looking horse," people were saying. "A mighty and kingly horse," was another abundant comment from the crowd.

Valedin and Talibar joined the line of knights, who were muttering similar words as the crowd. But one knight was disappointed at the site of Valedin showing up, and that was Lord Montague.

The duke finally gave his speech, and the challenge terms were set between knights. The terms for Lady Liella's hand between Valedin and Montague were finalized.

As the knights headed to their prep stables, Montague passed Valedin and said, "I'm going to be keeping Lady Liella warm at night, every night, Valedin, just so you know."

"Yes, warm with your blustery hot air, Montague," responded Valedin.

"You are nothing but a clumsy clown, Valedin. You will be first out of the contest," Montague retorted confidently with a sneer.

"Montague, even if you were twice as smart, you'd still be stupid," Valedin retorted back.

"I'm going to impale you and cut you to pieces, Valedin," snarled Montague.

Valedin only smiled and responded back, "You know, Montague, you're a poster boy for birth control, or troll-rearing. Let me ask you, do you still like nature despite what it did to you?"

Valedin and Montague were the last two knights to leave the arena, due to their little verbal jousting match. Finally, the arena judge moved them along. As they parted, they got a few more minor jabs in at each other.

"Idiot," said Montague.

"Pig," responded Valedin.

"Stupid," said Montague.

"Evolutionary throwback," responded Valedin with the last words.

When Valedin got to his prepping stable, Roderick was there to greet him. "So, you're seriously going through with this, huh, Valedin? Even if you lose, which you probably will, I have collected enough evidence to arrest Lord Montague. Plus, I have secretly placed men where they might be needed best."

Valedin smirked while dismounting, getting his foot caught in the stirrup in the process. "My dear sheriff, what makes you think I'm going to lose? Besides, it is a matter of honour," Valedin remarked with pride.

Sheriff Roderick shook his head in disbelief and gave up. "Well, I might as well be your prep team and help you lose," said the sheriff.

"That's the spirit, but losing is not my plan," responded Valedin, smiling.

The trumpets and horns blared, and the jousting tournament had begun. Talibar was primed and had sized up the other horse competitors. Beating them was going to be easy, but the hard part would be making Valedin win in the process. Talibar had his work cut out for him.

The tourney was well underway before Valedin got to joust. Montague had already racked up a series of wins, and he was gaining momentum.

The joust was to gain as many points as possible against an opponent in three passes. It was one point for contact on a shield with a broken lance. It was two points for contact on breastplate with a broken lance; and three points for knocking your opponent off his horse. In the event of a tie, either combatants would keep jousting, or they'd settle matters by sword in one minute of time. A similar point structure was used, and any ties were broken by an extra minute of combatting.

Montague was fast becoming the crowd favourite because he was unhorsing most of his opponents on the first or second pass out of three passes. Then, finally, it was Valedin's turn. Valedin didn't put in for a lot of challenges because Montague was his focus and saving Lady Liella was his priority. But he did need to warm up his self-perceived jousting skills. Roderick made sure Valedin was well seated on Talibar before he handed Valedin his lance.

"Well, here we go, Roderick," said Valedin, grinning.

Talibar was primed and ready to charge. The trumpets sounded, and the two contesting knights set off. Valedin's first joust was on!

"I can't watch," Roderick commented. Then he averted his eyes.

Valedin was flopping in the saddle and leaning to one side during the charge. But just as the knights were about to connect and share lance blows,

Talibar shifted himself to put Valedin's lance on target. There was a mighty crash. The crowd gasped and cheered as Valedin's opponent fell to the ground, unhorsed. When Roderick finally looked, he was happily shocked. But Montague was disappointed and had expected epic buffoonery—he and his prep team were utterly speechless. The horns sounded, and Valedin was declared the victor.

Valedin won the match and, miraculously, a few more after. He even made it into the top rating, alongside Montague, who was still racking up wins. The crowd marvelled at Talibar's prowess and movement. He never winded or wavered, like the other horses. And Valedin went from crowd fool to crowd favourite. Even Roderick was getting caught up in the cheering for Valedin. The clumsy knight had surpassed Montague as most popular knight, and Montague was not happy about it at all.

The match between Montague and Valedin was coming up, and Montague felt he had to do something about it. Valedin and Roderick were passing by, heading to their prep stable after another unlikely spectacular win. Montague intercepted their path. "From clown to crown, huh, Valedin? What kind of sorcery are you using? I'm crying foul due to your seemingly enchanted horse," said Montague angrily.

"Step aside, Montague; it's not our fault that Talibar makes your horse look like an old nag," responded Roderick. "Why don't you feed him better oats, instead of the scraps from your table, Montague."

Valedin smirked at Montague. "We don't have time to argue with the shallow end of the gene pool that is lord windbag. We must get ready for the next joust. I'd love to stay and trade insults, but I do need a worthy opponent. Now, will you excuse us?" Valedin said sharply. Then Valedin, Talibar, and Roderick moved past a raging and seething Montague.

"Oh, we will see who's going to come out on top. I'm going to fix you really good, Valedin," Montague mumbled to himself, seething with hate.

Before long, the match between Valedin and Montague had finally arrived. They were both top of the leaderboard, and the crowd was waiting for this moment. Before the tournament, Montague had designed little harnesses that could quickly connect his armour to his saddle. He was now going to employ their use to ensure a clear victory against Valedin.

In preparation for the final joust, Montague's trickery was unknown to Valedin and Roderick, but it was not lost on Talibar. Talibar snorted and whinnied, making a fuss to draw his comrades' attention towards Montague. They only just calmed him down, thinking he was spooked or upset. Talibar eventually gave up and snorted sharply out of frustration. It was up to him, so Talibar studied the situation carefully.

Finally, the two nights were ready, and the horns blared for the final showdown. The crowd cheered in response. More of the crowd was cheering and chanting for Valedin than Montague, and this infuriated him. Montague's ego was far too big to accept it.

Roderick was grinning. "Hear that, Valedin! The crowd loves you."

Valedin smiled back. "Yes, it feels good, but more importantly, it angers Lord Montague, which makes him focus on his ego more than the tip of his lance. When the match is over, you can arrest him, my friend Roderick."

Valedin and Roderick fist bumped in agreement. Valedin almost slid out of his saddle in the process.

A single horn sounded for the two knights to be ready, and the flag was dropped for the joust to begin. The two knights set off down the guide rail. As they thundered in towards each other, Talibar stared down Montague's horse, who was second best to Talibar in the tournament. But Montague's horse was no match for Talibar. Talibar's intimidating stare down caused Montague's horse to flinch.

When the two knights met, they both collided on point. There was a great crash and both knights' lances shattered on impact upon each other's shields. Valedin was almost knocked to the ground but managed to barely stay on, thanks to Talibar. Montague was stern and unmoved. He felt confident for his upcoming win.

The horn blared. "One point for each knight," the field judge declared.

Valedin reset himself to focus. The crowd was cheering with vigour. Valedin and Roderick strategized for the second pass, but Talibar already knew what had to be done. He had a good look at Montague's saddle on that first pass.

The horn blared for the knights to be ready. Then the flag was dropped, and the two knights were off on their second joust. As they closed the distance between each other, Talibar stared down Montague's horse again, as he had done the first time. At the last second before contact, Talibar did a slight manoeuvre that made Montague miss his mark and caused Valedin to dip his lance low. While Montague's lance tip just barely glanced off Valedin's shield, Valedin's lance tip caught the little harness on Montague's saddle. One of the two connecting harnesses that fastened together Montague's saddle and armour had broke.

The horn blared. "No points scored," yelled the jousting judge. The crowd was in confusion about the outcome. They were in a mixed state of cheer, laughter, and outrage of the second joust.

"What happened there?" asked Roderick, a little confused.

Valedin was a bit confused himself on the outcome. "I'm not sure, Roderick. But I think Talibar had something to do with it."

Meanwhile, Montague cussed away. "Damn horse of Valedin's. It's too smart for its own good." Montague looked down at his broken harness.

"We don't have time to fix it, my lord, but you still have the other harness," said one of Montague's many prep teammates, trying always to please him after every joust.

Montague snarled. "It's of little concern. I'm going to win anyway."

The horn sounded to call for the third and possible final joust. The two knights got ready for the third charge. Talibar was primed for the last and final pass. Everything was falling into place the way he had hoped. Now all he needed to do was place Valedin's lance square on target to make Montague sail through the air.

The horn blared, and the flag was dropped. The two knights set off strong. Talibar gave this charge his all. He needed all his strength to accomplish what he intended. As the knights closed in on each other, the crowd cheered in anticipation of the outcome. At the last critical second before contact, Talibar dropped just slightly low. This caused Montague's lance to aim high and Valedin's lance to aim low. There was a mighty crash. Montague's lance hit Valedin's upper shield and shattered. Valedin's lance missed Montague's shield altogether but connected with the lower breastplate of his armour. Valedin's lance shattered as well, but the force was so great, it broke the second harness between Montague's saddle and his armour. Montague violently tumbled off his horse. His face dug a nice little furrow before he came to a full stop.

The crowd went nuts cheering, and so did Roderick. Valedin flopped in his saddle a little dazed, but it did not matter—he had won. The horn blared and the judge declared Valedin as tournament champion.

There was a frenzy of celebration as the crowd flooded the field. They hoisted Valedin up and carried him around. The duke awarded Sir Valedin with the champion title and a healthy sum of gold. He and several others commented on how magnificent Talibar the horse had performed. But, when Valedin searched for Montague to settle their terms for Lady Liella's hand, he was nowhere to be seen.

Valedin and Roderick looked at each other. "Montague has gone back to his castle," they both said in unison.

Valiant Valedin heroically jumped onto Talibar's back before he slid off the other side to the ground with a crash.

Roderick sighed and shook his head while laughing. He muttered to himself, "Nothing changes. Valedin, wait till I get the guard. You cannot do this alone," explained Roderick while he helped Valedin back on his horse.

"There is no time to waste. Lady Liella must be saved," insisted the clumsy but courageous Valedin.

Roderick didn't argue anymore with his friend. He simply helped Valedin get sorted, and then the valiant knight was off to save the day. Roderick had to get his guard together sooner than he had time to do it—not to just arrest Lord Montague but to save Valedin's butt as well. It was a good thing that he had already placed guards in key locations before the tournament.

Montague returned to his castle in record time. He snuck away while all the attention was on Valedin. Upon arrival, his henchman Lambert approached him. "Your potion has finally arrived, my Lord Montague," said Lambert. Then Lambert presented it to him.

Montague snatched it out of Lambert's hand. "Not a moment too soon," grumbled Montague. Then he went straight up to Lady Liella's room, kicked open the door, and stormed in surprising Lady Liella, who was snoozing. He forcibly grabbed her and dragged her off her bed and out the door.

"Montague, what are you doing? Leave me alone! You're hurting me," Lady Liella screamed. She kicked and punched in protest but to little effect.

"Shut up, you wench. Now, you sign your family's land deed. No messing around," Montague explained.

"I'm not signing anything, you cruel, arrogant ass" spat Liella.

"We will see," responded Montague. He pulled her down to the main room and forcibly sat her in a chair. The land document and a feather pen were on the table in front of her.

Lady Liella spat on the document and kicked Montague's leg. "You don't get it! I'd rather die than let you have my lands after what you did," she screeched.

Montague winced in pain, then grabbed Liella's hair and violently pulled her head back. "Such manners for such a pretty noblewoman. You see, I do get it. It is you who does not!" Montague showed Lady Liella the small vial of potion. "Do you see this, my dear? After I make you drink it, you will feel obligated to sign." Montague laughed in his anticipation of final victory. "And oh yes, my lovely Lady Liella, you will also find me irresistible, therefore feeling wooed into marrying me. HAAAA-HA-HA-HA-HAAAA!" He laughed further in evil satisfaction.

Lady Liella fought against Montague's grasp violently. "Force her mouth opened, Lambert," Montague yelled. As Montague was about to pour the potion down Lady Liella's throat, he heard his name being called from outside the main door. Then a guard approached Lord Montague, interrupting him.

"What is it?" he snaped angrily at the guard.

"A knight calls out for you, my lord. It's Valedin, the champion of the tournament, my lord," the guard nervously informed Montague.

"WHAT! You got to be kidding me?" protested Montague. "Watch her. I will deal with him quickly." Lord Montague grabbed his sword. The nervous guard asked Montague what happened to his face, but Montague only responded by punching the guard in his jaw as he stormed past and out the door to meet Sir Valedin the champion.

Valedin was calmly sitting on his horse, Talibar, out in the courtyard when Montague came out to meet him.

Montague chuckled to himself. "Valedin, you really are brave, or stupid, to show up here after the tournament."

"Not stupid at all, Montague. I've come to simply reach a fairly won settlement since you left in such a hurry," chimed Valedin.

"Get off that horse, and we can settle this man-to-man, once and for all. You are in no position to demand settlement, Valedin."

"As you wish, Lord Idiot. But I know you hold Lady Liella inside your keep against her will. I can see it in your well-chafed face, Montague. You'll never get away with it," Valedin responded. Valedin proceeded to dismount, and he got his foot caught in the stirrup while doing so.

Montague and his men all laughed at Valedin's blunder. "You cannot hope to beat me without that stupid horse," Montague said mockingly.

Talibar's ears picked up at that comment, and he was not amused at all.

Inside the main door, Lady Liella could see and hear everything going on.

Valedin collected himself. "Very well, Lord Bigot, then we shall settle this like men," Valedin replied stoically. As Valedin drew his sword, it momentarily got caught in the scabbard. He stumbled as he finally unsheathed it.

Everyone in the courtyard laughed hard at Valedin's embarrassing clumsiness.

"I will make this quick, Valedin, but to be fair, I will let you go first. I don't want to spoil the fun. Ladies and gentlemen, I present to you, Valedin, the tournament champion!" Montague goaded Valedin in mock amusement, humiliating him further as best he could.

Suddenly, Sheriff Roderick and his men came galloping through the gate. "Stand down, Montague. You are under arrest for the kidnapping of Lady Liella and—*for murder*."

"I will not stand down. Close the gate," Montague yelled.

The gate guards did not respond to Montague's command.

Sheriff Roderick smiled. "You see, Montague, those guards are not your guards; they are mine!"

"KILL THEM!" yelled Montague.

The courtyard exploded into combat of arms. The sound of clashing swords and shields mixed with shouts and yells filled the air.

Valedin awkwardly swung his sword at Montague, but Montague dodged it easily. It went on like that for a few moments. Montague was letting Valedin tire himself out before finishing off the bumbling knight. The battle in the courtyard was fierce, and Roderick had very quickly put most of Montague's men to the ground. Even Lambert, Montague's best fighter, was having a hard time battling the talented and skilled sheriff.

As the fight went on, Valedin got smacked a few good times by Montague, who was just toying with him. Then Valedin turned quickly and yelled to his friend, "Lady Liella is inside; we must free her." Montague was not expecting the sudden out of rhythm swing from Valedin. There was a loud ding sound—the flat of Valedin's sword had smacked Montague clearly in the head, adding to his chafing. When Valedin turned back to see why Montague yelped in pain, Valedin's sword smacked him again.

Roderick only smiled out of relief and amusement and shook his head. Then he finally disarmed his opponent, Lambert, knocking his lights out.

Montague stumbled in a daze and tried to come to his senses. His head was rattled, and he completely forgot about Talibar, who had ideally positioned himself to have his own shot at Montague. In one sudden move, Talibar lifted both of his hind hooves and, with a mighty kick, booted Lord Montague, who flew fifty feet across the courtyard. He landed, tumbling ass over teakettle, into a collection of rather sharp and hard metal tools leaning against the stone wall. Talibar snorted in satisfaction. Montague laid in heap, unconscious and unmoving but groaning slightly.

The battle was over quickly as the sheriff's men overwhelmed Montagues guards. Roderick arrested Montague, who was still alive. Meanwhile, Valedin freed Lady Liella, who was very pleased to see him.

Clasped in irons, Montague sat on his own main steps. He glared up at Valedin, Roderick, and Lady Liella. "What proof do you have of such charges against me?" he spat.

"Well, besides the obvious," Roderick said, pointing to Lady Liella. "I will tell you!" Sheriff Roderick thought for a moment, then squarely faced Montague. "Let me see now, a gift of rare fruit that was addressed from you to the Apple-Tanes—fruit that only you would know to export from abroad. Then, the fruit was poisoned by a paid servant who delivered the package of fruit to the Apple-Tanes. And then the would-be servant assassin, Gareth Butler, was never seen nor heard from again. Does that sound rather familiar to you, Lord Montague?" asked Roderick.

"It wasn't my doing. It was the courier who committed the murder. I deny any involvement," stated Montague.

Roderick shrugged in amusement. "Deny away, Montague. That's easy to say when you could have easily disposed of the delivery man to tie up loose ends and any evidence of involvement. But a witness told me he saw the courier leave your place with gift in hand, the same night the courier had disappeared."

Montague squirmed uncomfortably and fumed in anger while the sheriff continued.

"Upon investigation, poison was found on the fruit by process of alchemy. Plus, the courier's body was found downstream on the riverbank by Valedin and was later identified as Mr. Gareth Butler. He still had the vial of poison that matched the poison on the fruit that killed the Apple-Tanes. And everyone in town knows that this delivery man was your servant for years, Lord Montague. Your motive lines up with your actions of kidnapping and potential murder. And now, we found this also in your possession."

Roderick held up the Apple-Tane estate document. Montague only scowled.

"You're not getting away with this, Sheriff Roderick and Valedin Clavendane. My influence and wealth are far too vast to lock me up for long," boasted Montague.

"The odds are stacked against you, Montague. I would not count on any way out of this after the court is through with you. Oh, by the way, I love your new look, my lord. Your complexion is compatible with your nature," said Roderick, referring to Montague's badly chafed face.

"Just you wait and find out, I'll be coming back for you all," threatened Lord Montague.

Roderick smirked and calmly said, "Take them away!"

And so, the sheriff's men loaded Lord Wulf Montague and his henchman into a wagon and carted them off to a dungeon to await trial. Montague's guards were freed. Roderick looked at Valedin and Lady Liella. "Happy trails, my friends. I will see you both soon."

Lady Liella took Valedin's hand and said to him, "It looks like you won my hand after all."

Valedin smiled an awkward utopian smile of bliss. And he was sure he was closer to attaining his goal as a Knight of Traviena, like his father.

After Valedin awkwardly mounted up onto Talibar the Magnificent, almost falling off again, Lady Liella hopped up behind him. Everyone waved as they left. And Valedin and the lovely Lady Liella rode off, thus living happily ever after... well, mostly!

Here comes valiant Valedin.
He's always in a blunder.
With all the success that he has had,
it kind of makes you wonder.
He bumbles along by trick or by stunt;
by luck, he never fails,
but that's because of his magnificent horse
ensuring he prevails.

In the Dark of Shadows

*Made by dark immortal hands
to destroy the newly created lands,
a sword and crown were evilly sown
in the Dark of Shadows, most unknown.*

*The iron crown was forged by fire.
From the spirits, the demon sword expired
to grieve the world and swallow whole
in the Dark of Shadows' true desire.*

*They were placed upon the world with wrath
to consume all life within their path;
to torture souls sadistically
in the Dark of Shadows' mournful grasp.*

*They slew and fed all that was worth;
the seeds of destruction now unearthed
to quench all Light and ravage souls
in the Dark of Shadows' eternal curse.*

Thunder roared, lightning flashed, and the earth trembled. Darkness fell across the lands. Hot gale force winds blew, creating all matter of turmoil. Plague and famine began ravaging the world.

The undead and demon-kind rose, flocking to the banner of the seventh dark lord, Ouglen Angrimar. Ouglen was the true bloodline descendant of the only son spawned by the fallen god Akurus. The power of Akurus flowed through him, and it was strong. The drake and dragon-kind of Lavaithyon and those who supported the will of the fallen god Akurus all joined the growing legions of Angrimar.

Key items tied to the line of the dark lords of which Akurus designed had been found by trusted agent minions of Angrimar: Gramour, a powerful demon sword; the Crown of Quitus, made of twisted iron; and the Dark Stone, pulled from beneath the Tree of Anguish. With the iron crown, Angrimar crowned his champion, Luthier Holmdring. Then he raised a mighty black tower fortress in the northern Broken Lands. When the black tower was complete, he loosened the chains of a dark entity trapped in the lowest bowels of the abyss. The high gods trapped this powerful immortal entity long ago, during the war of the god's, which also became known as the First Darkness.

The dark entity now rose, unloosened, and gave power to the fallen gods who it had created or corrupted by its own design. They were to bring the world to ruin. This dark entity fed on life spirit and light, and it was always hungry. As the darkness spread and grew stronger, the legions of the Dark Lord Angrimar grew more powerful.

The mortal kingdoms banded together in desperation to fight the great dark host that marched under the black banner of Ouglen Angrimar. But the hope for victory looked bleak indeed.

After years of terrorising chaos, slavery, savage war, and death, an unlikely group of heroes banded together. The group was led by a knight of little-known origin. This knight was full of hope. Even though things looked bleak, he believed that all was not lost. The knight's name was Sir Justin Carnebour! And Sir Justin Carnebour's aim was to put an end to the dark rule of Ouglen Angrimar.

Justin was pure at heart, strong in soul, and skilful in war. He prayed to the Watcher and Protector of the World, who had saved the world once before. She was the goddess Tyra Traviena. Mounted on Eau-Darmuk, the Shining Dragon, Traviena led the high gods against the fallen gods during the war of the gods' and was victorious. With her spear, she and the Shining Dragon battled Akurus and his demon lords. She sent them back down to the lower plains of the abyss, and now, Justin needed her strength.

Justin chose a central, remote location high in the Absanian Mountains.

The chosen ground was consecrated by the high gods. Then, Justin sat in prayer to the goddess Tyra Traviena. The Watcher and Protector of the World heard the prayers of Justin Carnebour. The mortal's champion was calling for aid to battle the demonic and dark armies fuelled by the fallen gods—and Tyra Traviena answered. She would help them!

Then came a cacophony of thunder and lightning. Like falling meteors from the sky, seven hundred spears modelling Tyra Traviena's spear, landed on the chosen ground. The high gods had answered him. The spears formed into great lances, and the Dragons of Good Spirit came to Justin with instruction from Eau-Darmuk and Tyra Traviena.

Justin rallied as many good warriors as possible, with heart and faith like his own, to follow him. They mounted the dragons and carried their new thunder lances as they would on horseback and as Traviena had, armed with her spear on the Shining Dragon. Now, it was up to Justin and his force to drive the darkness away.

Word went out to all the empires and kingdoms to rally for the showdown battle against Ouglen Angrimar. At the calm before the storm, the king of the high elves presented Justin with a gift—an ancient sword crafted by the high spirits of the high gods just after the War of the Gods. The sword was called Lambent, and it had the high soul of the High Spirit Endellion within it. Endellion's soul had chosen a mortal champion to end the line of the dark lords and defeat them: That champion was Sir Justin Carnebour. He had gained the trust of the high gods and now all the kingdoms would follow him to save the world from death and ruin.

The Dark Lord sensed the gathering of forces against him, and so he acted. Ouglen attacked from the sky with a mighty force of dark dragons, while his champion, Luthier, attacked on the ground. Luthier was a powerful wizard of note, and he called on all the great necromancers to aid him. They raised legions of undead. And with those legions, they attacked with the goblin armies led by the first goblin, Bulthungril. An immortal captain of the fallen gods and he had led vast goblin legions before, during the War of the Gods. Bulthungril had never been defeated in battle. Now, once again, he was leading a great army horde, but this time, it was under the line of the dark lords. His personal mission was to avenge his army's defeat during the War of the Gods. So, out of the North, the vast armies of the undead, goblinoids, and other foul beasts swept over Rithanon. Their black mass spread over other areas of the world as well, all to crush the gathered resistance of the free peoples, who were under the watch of the high gods.

The kingdoms and empires rallied and united their shattered remaining forces under Justin Carnebour's banner. Then they stood their ground. The great armies met, and so started the great battles of the Chaos War.

As the great battles begun, Justin mustered and organized his personal forces of dragon knights. On dragonback, with their new thunder lances, the knights attacked all foul things in flight. Anything that stood before Justin and his knights perished. Ouglen Angrimar threw all his best demon-kind and dragon-kind against Justin's mighty but small force of seven hundred. But it was to no avail. All were cut down from the sky. The morale of Justin's men grew high, and hope seemed finally at hand.

The news quickly spread amongst the ground armies from those who witnessed the effectiveness of the dragon knights. This made them fight harder and gave them hope.

After a time, Justin rallied his troops and headed north, to the heart of the darkness itself—the black tower of Ouglen Angrimar.

The Dark Lord Angrimar detected the incoming menace. His sub-lord, Luthier Holmdring, had informed him that the high gods had blessed Justin's force of seven hundred and all that stood before them were slain. Angrimar summoned, for the first time, the demon drakes from the darkest bowels of the abyss. Great dark dragons, with black shiny hides and menacingly armed with razor sharp talons and teeth, spawned. Their screech could paralyze their victims, and they could drain life from any being. With acid for blood, they also breathed hellfire, which burned and melted all before it. A few thousand, Angrimar summoned, and he mounted the beasts with demonic riders armed with black iron weapons. But before Angrimar could properly organize his defence force, Justin arrived at the tower.

A desperate battle closed in the air around the tower of Ouglen Angrimar. Justin's force was greatly outnumbered and quickly overwhelmed, but they hung on. Justin met the Dark Lord Angrimar in the air, and they clashed with mighty swords. The light of Lambent clashed with, Gramour, the dark demon sword that swallowed all light and goodness. After a violent exchange of brawling in the air, they both crash landed on the highest parapet of the tower. Justin and Angrimar continued fighting on foot. They fought their way into the room where the Dark Stone was held. In the desperate duel, Justin managed to smash the Dark Stone with his sword, hurling it to somewhere in the lower planes of the underworld.

Ouglen Angrimar roared in defiance at Justin's bold act and immediately started losing power. The tower started to shake, rumble, and crack. In the chaos of the collapsing tower, Justin tried to slay Ouglen, but Ouglen was swallowed up in the collapsing tower. Justin barely escaped alive on his dragon mount.

The dark power shifted dramatically, and Justin Carnebour's force finished off the remaining demon drakes. The great desperate battles that raged many days and many nights began to wane in favour of the united kingdoms.

It was unclear if Ouglen Angrimar was dead, but his power was gone. The powerful archmage Danjable, who was Justin's friend, managed to defeat Luthier Holmdring in a rather close contest of arcane power. Luthier's demon sword had abandoned him and the twisted iron Crown of Quitus swallowed him into the Darkness of Shadow. Forever, he was to be damned to exist in undeath, never to see the light again. Far away, to the north lands, he was taken, to a hidden location only known to the fallen gods.

Bulthungril's forces were defeated by the combined armies of the elves, dwarves, and men. But Bulthungril himself escaped. Although he slayed many, the one goblin still endured; he would not perish, for Bulthungril was the first mighty goblin of goblins and he would serve again under the next of the dark lord line.

Many believed that Ouglen Angrimar had survived the battle and went hiding into exile, perhaps passing his power and genes to another, to carry on the dark lord line.

As the mighty battles ended and the power of the darkness weakened, the high gods chained the dark entity of the Destroyer again. But their efforts to do so created cataclysmic events upon the world. Mighty earthquakes shook the lands. Raging fires and massive vortex storms, rampaged everywhere. Once what was, was no longer. Gone were the civilizations of the ancient times, and a new age had begun. The Second Darkness—the Chaos War—was over. The world had to rebuild from the ashes.

The hero Sir Justin Carnebour and his knights were praised as the protectors of the world and would continue as such under the high gods, till the high gods perished. Justin's line would forever be tied to Lambent. And with Lambent, his line was bound to end the line of the dark lords that Akurus set upon the world.

Heroes

In the night of a full moon's frosty cold,
beneath the light of its brightening fold,
I walk along and sing many a song
from legends of unsung heroes, bold.

The myths of yore hold mighty tales,
from times of magic and kings so hailed,
when villains hired dark things dire,
when men to mighty monsters paled.

From the shadows of the darkened night,
a hope came forth and blazed to light;
by will that poured and might of sword,
heroes rose to stand and fight.

The Dark Lord sought and gained great power.
The kingdoms suffered; their subjects cowered.
The darkness brought the evil rot,
And the people fought in their desperate hours.

The heroes struck down the Dark Lord's hold
and new stories are bred from times of old.
The bards did hail and sing great tails
of unsung heroic tales told.

Brave Knights

It was the early ninth century of the current age, just over fifteen centuries ago. An evil blanket of dark power had fallen over the lands of Rithanon, decaying all the natural world. Danmol Vindiku, the eighth dark lord in the line of the dark lords, reraised the black tower in the North. It was the tower that was wrought by the seventh dark lord, Ouglen Angrimar, who brought about the Second Darkness, widely known as the War of Chaos. Danmol desired to bring about the third and final darkness before its time, for his lust for world domination was strong, as was the power of the fallen god Akurus, which flowed through his veins.

To strengthen his will and rule, Danmol rebuilt the dark tower atop the highest mountain—which he named Mount Ouglen—in the heart of the northern Broken Lands, widely known as the Kingdom of Dark. He set an orb—the Dark Stone—within the black tower. The Dark Stone had been used by Ouglen Angrimar during the Chaos War. Justin Carnebour had cast it off the world and into the outer planes of the underworld when the tower fell, but Danmol sought it out and found it!

Danmol donned the twisted iron crown and rose the demon sword, Gramour, above his head. In completeness of his cause, through the crown and the stone, he released his power, strengthened by the dark god Akurus, and called all dragons of malice to him.

Hearing his call and once in his influence, one thousand dragons submitted to his will and served as mounts for the newly formed Knights of the Dark Order. They would head the procession of the dark army for the shadowy underworld, led by Danmol Vindiku.

Down in the southeast, Belicose, the lord of all good dragons, called the Knights of Carnebour to arms. At hand was the greatest threat Rithanon had ever endured since the time of the Second Darkness, when Sir Justin Carnebour founded the knights order. Four hundred good dragons had come, and the knights mounted them, armed with their mighty thunder lances. Sir Paylion, the commander of the knighthood, mounted Belicose. They got themselves set and ready to meet the dark forces of Danmol Vindiku.

The long arm of Danmol's power and influence reached far indeed. It stretched to the far reaches of South Rithanon, and he rallied all the goblin, troll, and ogre tribes together under one banner—that of Delkron, the mighty goblin war chief, who fortified an ancient plateau known as Tarisar, in the heart of the Southeastern Mountains. Amongst Delkron's growing horde was Bulthungril, the mighty hobgoblin warrior who could not be defeated in battle. He arrived to stand at Delkron's side. Proclaiming himself King of the Southlands, Delkron and his army of two hundred and fifty thousand moved out of Tarisar to conquer the Southlands and please his dark master, Danmol Vindiku.

The Southland kingdoms were under grave threat and panic spread. After learning the southern army, headed by Delkron, allied with the Dark Lord, the Knights of Carnebour rallied the armies of the Southland kingdoms to meet them. Twelve hundred knights from Carnebour rode south to join and lead these armies. The kingdoms of Edingal and Abingale also joined forces with the Knights of Carnebour. Another order of knights known as the Knights of Solar, who were influenced by the Knights of Carnebour, had joined the fight as well.

Commander Ballman of Carnebour stood with King Elbrick of Edingal and King Sullen of Abingale near the town of Canora, south of Edingal. They had a combined army of just over a hundred thousand strong.

Early in the morning, on the day after reaching Canora, scouts had reported that Delkron's army was closer than they had anticipated, only the small town of Lione stood between them. With the townsfolk of Lione still inside their walls, they would be trapped if they were not evacuated.

Commander Ballman dispatched a company of two hundred knights, led by Lord Every Kays, to the town of Lione. Lord Kays mission was to get the townsfolk out before Delkron's horde could reach it. He and his company arrived at the town without incident and began to organize the townsfolk to leave in haste. However, it was too late. The horrible goblinoid mass of Delkron's army flowed around Lione like a giant title wave in a black sea.

Far north, Danmol received word of Delkron's engaging of battle. The Dark Lord rallied his formidable force of one thousand dragons, mounted by the Knights of the Dark Order. Armed with various demonic weapons and defiled iron lances, the dark knights set off to destroy the Knights of Carnebour.

To the southeast, the Carnebour force had already left their home base of Carnebour Castle. Armed with their mighty thunder lances and led by their commander, Paylion, they were ready to meet Danmol's dark host.

Far in the southlands, the town of Lione was surrounded. The evil mass of goblins and beasts overwhelmed Lord Kay and his men. The giant force chanted, growled, and sang in anticipation of slaying innocents. Black-bladed pole arms and black banners spread to the horizon as far as one could see. From the evil of Delkron's horde, Bulthungril, the mighty goblin, stepped forward to lead the siege on the little town of Lione.

Lord Kays and his company of knights were unable to get the townsfolk out through the town's main gates in time. Bulthungril's army was upon them before they could rally the townsfolk for an evacuation. Their were only two hundred knights against thousands, they now faced a siege without end, led by a mighty goblin warrior. Those of the townsfolk who could fight took up arms and stood with the knights, which more than doubled their number.

When Bulthungril gave the order to attack, the black mass swarmed Lione's walls. Then came the sudden and violent clash of arms. Cut off and surrounded, the knights and townsfolk fought fiercely to defend their homes and families. In the opening clash of battle, some of the knights started evacuating the townsfolk who were unable to fight through a hidden tunnel, which led to the west under a river.

As the evacuation was underway, Bulthungril sent wave after wave of goblins and beasts onto the walls of Lione. The knights and townsfolk held fast and fiercely as wave after wave of Delkron's hordes fell under the sword of Lione's defenders. Frustration set in for Bulthungril. Just as the last of the townsfolk were evacuated through the tunnel, the tunnel collapsed, sealing off any escape route. The two hundred knights with some three hundred townsfolk defenders were trapped and cut off from any hope of rescue.

In the North, the two opposing dragon knight forces headed towards each other. Soon night fell, and they flew through the dark sky, descending towards each other and the inevitable clash of battle.

In the South, a lull hit the siege of the town. As night fell, things looked hopeless. The defending knights and townsfolk resolved themselves to a bitter end. With nothing to lose, the bleak situation raised their morale, and side by side, as one force, the knights and townsfolk taunted the massive goblin army. Lord Kays pointed his sword at Bulthungril in silent challenge. Bulthungril smiled evilly, then gave the order to attack and to slay every one of the town's defenders, once and for all. As the first goblin gave the command to attack, he claimed Lord Kays for himself.

Commander Ballman of the main force near Canora tried to organize a rescue mission and cut through the mass of the foul army to Lione. But Delkron's dark forces were too many to punch through. All they could do for the moment was get the evacuated townsfolk from the collapsed tunnel to safety.

Bulthungril unleashed an unrelenting assault on the town's defenders. Mounted upon a great giant beast resembling a demonic, defiled wolf and bear crossbreed, Bulthungril leapt on top of the town wall to face Lord Kays. Kays fought the mighty goblin bravely, but he could not match this goblin warrior in skill.

During the duel, Bulthungril strongly overpowered him and eventually slayed him. With a mighty roar to intimidate the town's defenders, Bulthungril savagely displayed Kay's head on his sword, but it had the opposite effect—it only raised their resolve to destroy as many of the attacking horde as possible.

Long into the night the battle went on. Thousands of goblinoid warriors fell from the town's walls. It was not until many hours later that the knights and townsfolk warriors succumbed to their losses and exhaustion. Unknown and untold—thousands of Delkron's horde had fallen before those brave knights and townsfolk warriors were overtaken.

Long into the night, Lord Ballman and the main force could hear the distant sound of battle subside. With the two thousand evacuated townsfolk of Lione all safely behind the city of Canora's walls, Ballman got his army ready for battle. Early the following morning, Ballman gave his order to engage Delkron's unrelenting black tide of evil. Delkron's forces were still under the power of Danmol, the eighth dark lord, so their morale was high, their purpose was menacing, and their will strong.

Far north, after flying all night, the two dragon-knight forces finally met over the remote and distant plains of Sardass. Their clash was fierce and violent, and dragon fire blasted from both sides as they slammed together. Outnumbering the Carnebour knights by over two to one, Danmol thought he had the upper hand. Then he and his dark knights met the mighty thunder lances from legend. The enchanted lances of Justin Carnebour sliced his forces cleanly like hot knives through butter. As the battle joined, the two forces melded together into a massive chaotic, aerial battle over a remote land.

Delkron confidently moved his army north, towards Canora, to engage the allied armies and he also outnumbered them by two to one. Ballman, however, had set a trap for him. By protecting his flanks, Lord Ballman moved his knights and cavalry up both sides. He let Delkron attack his weak-looking bowed centre. And as the horde pressed in, Ballman relaxed the bowed centre back to a crescent moon, drawing Delkron's horde into his trap. Delkron thought he could smash through their enemy's weak centre, but before Delkron and Bulthungril knew it, they were outflanked on both sides. Then Ballman reinforced his weak centre, and the mighty battle was full on. Delkron's army was hemmed in on three sides.

In the North, the dragon-knight battle grew fiercer, and it was taking its toll on both sides. In the chaos of battle, Carnebour's commander, Paylion, riding Belicose, the lord of good dragons, met Dark Lord Danmol Vindiku. Upon his giant dark Paragon dragon, Kraydon, Danmol wielded Gramour, the big black sword, and a shadowy vapour flowed from it. The vile blade moaned in hunger to eat life. The two commanders violently slammed together. Paylion's thunder lance missed Kraydon and went flying from his hands by the violent clash. He drew his enchanted sword and crossed blades with Danmol's black demon sword. Locked together, both dragons scratched and bit each other while Paylion and Danmol shared blow after blow. Lost in a titanic duel, the battle went on around them like thunder. As many knights and dragons, good or evil, fell from the darkening sky raked by flames of dragon fire.

In the North, as well as the South, the two mighty battles were fought in tandem. In the South, the allied kingdoms, led by the Knights of Carnebour, managed to hold Delkron's massive army. Though outnumbered, they had Delkron's hordes surrounded. But the goblin horde carried on, driven by the will and power of Danmol Vindiku, strengthened by the Dark Stone and the twisted iron crown. All day, the battles raged on.

In the North, it was much the same until Lord Paylion finally rammed his enchanted sword through the Dark Lord's chest. The blow knocked Danmol off his dark shadowy dragon. He fell out of sight to the ground. And as he fell, his power waned. The twisted iron crown flew from Danmol's head, rejecting him, and it became lost.

All Danmol's hopes and visions of bringing about the third and final darkness to the world under his rule were washed. This turned the tide of battle. The dark forces of the eighth dark lord saw that the will and power of the Knights of Carnebour could not be broken, and they fled. Paylion and his knights had won the day, but almost half of his force had been spent, perishing in that remote and distant land.

In the South, the hordes of Delkron also felt the wane of power, and the entire army wavered. Lord Ballman of Carnebour felt the weakening of Delkron's forces and seized the moment to press his attack. Before long, as the day wore on, what was left of Delkron and Bulthungril's army had fled. The great battles of Canora and Sardass were over.

Afterward, an elite band was sent to find the Dark Lord Danmol, but he was never found. Although Danmol Vindiku was only dead in body, his life force remained. Like the lord before him, he could manifest into a different form to carry on the dark lord line. His entity could be hidden from view until he'd make himself known again in another form. The elite band raided Danmol's black tower fortress of Mount Ouglen. But the tower was dormant, empty, and drained of power. The Dark Stone was gone; and the demon sword, along with the twisted iron crown, was believed to be lost with him. Further search ended in vain!

The dark threat to Rithanon was over. Not long after the two great battles, the people and crowns of the Southlands held a candlelight vigil in honour of those soldiers who fought and fell in battle; those townsfolk and knights who had died to protect the innocent folk of Lione; and the Knights of Carnebour who died leading the charge to defeat a great evil threatening all of Rithanon.

For a memorial set up at Lione, a verse was written to honour the Knights of Carnebour. It would become known throughout all the lands for ages to come.

*the knights with armour, sword, and shield
and valour upon the battlefield:
With bravery, they fight and die
to honour freedom with lives they lie.
With strength of arms and hard of soul,
they stand to oppose the tyrant's toll.
In dragon's trust, on wings, they sore,
Are the mighty Knights of Carnebour.*

The Wizard on the Hill

Young Bailen Duval was on his way back home to the town of Ravenwood from a hunting trip when he spotted a strange individual on top of a nearby hill. The hill was in a wide-open field, overlooking a vast lake to the east. The stranger was snoozing under a lone oak. Bailen felt compelled to approach and greet this strange individual dressed in brown clothes and a blueish green cloak. A wide-brimmed, pointy chestnut-brown hat was covering his face, only a long grey beard protruded out from under it. A long, strangely carved staff with a crystal set in its top lay next to him.

Bailen approached him cautiously and said softly to him, "Ahem, um, excuse me, sir."

To Bailen's surprise, the stranger suddenly voiced, "Hello, Bailen, I've been expecting you." The stranger greeted him as if he already knew him, without so much as lifting a finger.

"You-you were waiting for me?" asked Bailen.

"Well, it was only a matter of time before you'd show up," the stranger said as he picked himself up off the ground. "I trust your hunting trip on this fine day was a pleasant one, was it not?"

"Who-who are you?" asked Bailen. "You seem to know me," he responded, feeling a little perplexed.

"Oh, I'm sorry." The stranger laughed. "Where are my manners? My name is Dell-Shander," the stranger said joyfully as he reached out to shake Bailen's hand.

"Dell-Shander?" Bailen said in surprise. "You're not the famous wizard from Carnebour Castle, are you?" Bailen felt a little starstruck.

"Um, yes, that's me," Dell said, feeling a little amused, though understanding that Bailen was just a young lad of twelve years and had much to learn.

After Bailen got over his excitement of meeting the famous wizard, he asked," I was wondering, why were you waiting for me, Mr. Dell-Shander?" asked Bailen.

"Well, I thought it was time to have a little chat with you," Dell said in a kind and grandfatherly way.

"A chat? You came all this way from Carnebour Castle just to talk to me?" asked Bailen, puzzled. "Why, and about what?"

"Well, I know your family well, and we can talk about whatever you want to talk about," said Dell, with a smirk. "So, Bailen, what do you want to talk about?"

"I'm not sure what I want to talk about. But really? You know my family?" said Bailen, surprised again.

"Actually, yes, I know your family quite well. You might be surprised how well. But that's a topic for another time. Let us chat about other things for now," Dell-Shander said with a grin.

Bailen accepted his answer and sat there thinking for a minute or two. Finally, he said, "I want to talk about... magic! Can you show me how to cast some spells, Mr. Dell-Shander?" asked Bailen, excited again.

Dell-Shander laughed. "Well, that depends Bailen on if you possess any fey blood or not. Do you have any fey blood, Bailen?

"I'm afraid not," said Bailen with a sigh. "I'm afraid I am quite human." He shrugged. "I guess not everyone is made out to cast magic," Bailen resolved to himself.

Dell patted Bailen on the shoulder, then leaned in, smirking, and with a wink, he said, "the truth is, Bailen, anyone can do arcane magic." Dell-Shander widened his eyes and added, "It's just that they don't know they're doing it."

"Anyone can do magic?" Bailen said, making himself more comfortable under the shade of the tree.

"Yes, anyone," said Dell. "But they must really believe in it. If you have fey blood, magic comes freely and easily in so many different and wonderful ways. Priests cast divine magic, granted to them by the gods they worship," Dell explained.

"Well, if I don't have faerie blood, then how can I cast magic to get what I desire?" asked Bailen, perplexed.

"You don't need to cast it; you just manifest it," said Dell, stretching out his arms.

"You just manifest it?" said Bailen. "How is that possible?" He cocked an eyebrow.

"Well, there is a process you must do," said Dell.

"Kind of like casting a spell?" asked Bailen.

"No, no, no," Dell-Shander insisted. "Like I said before, it's not like casting at all. You see, this process is connected to the whole multiverse. Most people, or all people, do this on a subconscious level. Without realizing it at all, they are manifesting their entire life," Dell explained. "What the process is tapping into, or centred around, is what you intently focus on, you attract into your life," said Dell.

"Wow!" Bailen said in wonder. "So, if I focus on the good things, then the good things come into my life. And dwelling on bad things brings all the bad things into my life, right?"

"Right," said Dell. "But I'm afraid it's a little more complicated than that." He leaned in towards Bailen again, raising his eyebrows.

"How can I do this? Tell me," Bailen replied, getting excited for a third time, which brought some amusement to the wizard.

"OK." Dell laughed. "But you got to listen carefully because this takes practice, all right?" said Dell in a serious tone.

"All right, I'm listening," said Bailen listening intently.

"OK, now, first, you must let go of any need for anything and take a few minutes to bring your whole body, mind, and soul to a completely blissful state. Once you have achieved that, you must visualize and verbally set the intention of what you truly want. But it has got to be something you genuinely want from your heart and the core of your being. Something deep within that you passionately desire, but without having any need for it," Dell explained, accentuating his words with feeling. "Are you with me, Bailen?"

"Uh, yes, I think I'm with you, Mr. Dell," Bailen replied with scepticism.

"Good," said Dell-Shander. "Now, it's very important that when you ask for what you want, you must speak of it using the future tense while being present. Then, create the sense that it is already happening while you feel the feelings of gratitude for already having it. Associate awesome and happy, pleasurable feelings around the actual experience you want. Spend a bit of time getting yourself wrapped around the idea of experiencing it and continue to visualize it. Behave in such a way as if it was here now! After that, go out into the world and let it go. Put yourself in alignment with it, and let it happen. Forget about it and don't go looking for it, just let it come to you and then enjoy it when it happens," Dell-Shander explained matter-of-factly.

"That's it? That's all you have to do?" said Bailen, surprisingly disappointed. "Anyone can do that," Bailen pointed out.

"Well, yes and no." Dell laughed. "It's not as easy as it seems or looks. It comes from a state of absolute belief and a clear soul. Whatever you believe, it will be cast upon you and you will see it. But don't ever question, doubt, analyze, or ever try to figure it out because then you will never see it," Dell said sternly.

"OK," said Bailen, nodding his head in thought. "But what then, after I've manifested something I have wanted?".

"Just simply reset the intention surrounding what you have manifested," said Dell with a jolly laugh.

"Why doesn't everyone do this?" Bailen blurted out, as if everyone was either dumb or stupid.

Dell-Shander laughed and replied, "Well, they do, but most are just unaware of it. It's easier said than done, you know," he said suddenly serious again. "Just remember, my lad, that when you do manifest things, act on them when they happen."

"And so, everyone can do this?" Bailen asked, still a bit perplexed.

"Yes, the multiverse is a powerful and mysterious place, with various planes of existence. We are all connected to it and to each other. Many fools believe this to be uncordial, unnatural, or nonsense," Dell explained, a little disappointed. "Even when it's the most natural of things," he pointed out. "By the gods, some people don't even believe a carrot is a carrot, even if you dangled it in front of their nose." expressed Dell to strengthen his point, then added, "And it's important not to judge them, even yourself."

"Some people don't believe in this?" asked Bailen.

"Oh yeees, most don't, in fact. They think that all magic only comes from pixies and dragons, priests or wizards like old Dell-Shander here," he said sarcastically. "It's just a different kind of magic."

Bailen's face had wrinkled in surprise disgust when Dell-Shander explained the naysayers and unbelievers before he remembered Dell's point on judging.

"But it's far more powerful than you or me," Dell continued. "Only the gods know the true secrets behind the process of manifesting what you desire. Some people call it faith and some call it the law of attraction. But really, you can call it whatever you want." Dell shrugged. "And it's not to be taken lightly," he emphasized seriously.

"It's not?" Bailen said, looking at Dell with concern and confusion.

"No, it's not," Dell-Shander said, leaning in to Bailen. "We can also attract bad things as well. It's all about what kind of energy one projects. The multiverse responds to how we feel for good or ill, no judgments. You see, good energy attracts good energy, and bad energy attracts bad energy. To put it another way, matching energies attract each other."

"I see!" Bailen responded, nodding his head in understanding.

"Now, the most important traits to possess when aligning yourself with what you want are gratitude, honesty, and humility—without fear, shame, guilt, judgment, or doubt. Have no expectation's, conditions, or restrictions and don't focus on the outcome. You really got to believe in it and yourself, or nothing will turn out the way you want. Be very specific about what your heart truly desires and let your instincts guide you," said Dell-Shander with a warm smile.

"Wow," said Bailen in thought. "So, there's a whole way to be, or a state to be in, when consciously manifesting what you desire," Bailen said, fascinated.

"Yes, absolutely," Del said seriously. "And it falls into one of the seven laws of nature, which is why it's so important to be truthful, not only to others but also to yourself. It is in every essence... truth! You see, everyone is a type of magnet attracting the very things they focus on. But if you're angry, deviously dishonest, hurtful, or arrogant, you will attract the bad things. Your heart must be pure with a clear and positive mind."

"Is there a way for evil people to get what they want?" asked Bailen.

"Yes, there is, but we will not speak of it here!" Dell expressed in a grave tone.

The conversation paused as both Dell and Bailen sat in contemplation of the topic. Bailen had to think for a minute and let it all sink in. Dell-Shander gave him the moment he needed. While looking out over the wide lake, they both were enjoying the nice breeze under the shade of the tree on top of the hill. It was a lovely late spring day.

"So, what are the seven laws of nature," asked Bailen, the first to break the silence.

"Well, I will explain them to you, but they are not always heeded," Dell-Shander expressed. "They are as follows: Number one, you and I exist, and we are equally valuable to this world; we are enough as we are and each being has a role to play. Number two, all living things are connected to each other; you and me and even the pleasant tree we sit under. Number three, what you put out, you get back; we attract what we focus on and desire, just like we have been talking about.

"Number four, the present moment of now is all there is; the past is gone, and the future is always in motion—it never really comes and is always a mystery. Number five, everything is in constant change, and motion and always in fluctuation—the law of probability and random outcome in tandem. Number six, nothing is perfect or normal; nature is perfectly imperfect and normally abnormal, and everything is different and unique in its own special way. Finally, number seven, everything has balance, and for every action is an equal reaction.

"You see, things are as they are and supposed to be, even our own destinies. So just because I'm a powerful wizard, does not make me any greater than yourself, Bailen, or anyone else. Accept yourself as you are, Bailen, and know that your path is simply different—that's all," Dell explained. "Refrain from chasing heroic accomplishments for attention, or chasing fame and status because it is already within you. When you truly know who you are, that's when the most comes to you. The attention seeker is always trying to fill an empty void within, which will never get filled. They are status-chasing and being transactional for that attention. So, it's important to only impress yourself and not others, young Bailen. Whatever you mentally attach to, to gain attention will only repulse. Let that attachment go!"

"You have really opened my eyes, Mr. Dell-Shander," Bailen said in wonder. "So those are the seven laws of the multiverse."

"Yes, Bailen, but actually, there are fourteen of them in all if you look harder. Those are the seven laws of the natural world. Even the gods abide by them in many ways that we mortals don't really understand. Some think they do, coming from a place of inflated ego, but they are only subconsciously creating their own negative reality because of that. Any laws or rules made by mortals can only be upheld by the confines of their own limited power and are not static."

"Very interesting," Bailen said in thought. "Is this something to do with the seven holy laws and fourteen virtues written by the gods?"

"In a way it does, Bailen. The high gods' seven laws and fourteen virtues were influenced by those seven laws of the multiverse based on positiveness. But not all the gods saw it that way, unfortunately. Thus, is why there is so much turmoil in the world from conflicting views of negative and positive opinions; or good versus evil ideology, if you will!" Dell explained. "The truth is, that the multiverse does not judge for good or ill. It's all about the vibrational magnetic energy one is tapped into that will rebound back. So, if you judge, you will be judged in return. Be aware of judgmental and negative self-chatter and feeling; it rebounds on oneself. A good rule of thumb is to treat others as you like to be treated, and good things will come to you."

"Holy smokers," Bailen voiced exuberantly. "That just puts a whole new light on things. I suddenly feel a little wiser."

"Good, good, Bailen," said Dell-Shander, laughing joyfully. "I'm all too glad to share my insight with you. You listen and learn fast there, young lad. It shows you possess an open mind."

"So, in a nutshell, I'm guessing that bad people's magnets are negative and good people's magnets are positive," Bailen reasoned.

"That is exactly right, Bailen, but most people have elements of bad and good; it's just a matter of yourself accepting it. True evil focuses on all that is negative, sapping life and joyfulness, and true good focuses on positive things that create happiness and bliss. When one has gone too far into the extreme of negative ways and is unreachable, they want to destroy all that is good. It's because they cannot stand seeing what they themselves are not, and they hate themselves and everything else for it. They are trying to fill an empty vessel that cannot be filled. Unfortunately, it's a disease that's infecting the world," Dell explained sadly.

Bailen and Dell fell silent for a second time momentarily as Bailen took in more of what Dell-Shander had to say.

"Thank you so much, Mr. Dell-Shander, for sharing your insight with me. You have taught me so much about everything. I remember my aunty once told me to listen more than I speak, and I will gain from it," Bailen shared, feeling wiser. "Is this a practice of humility?"

Dell chuckled sheepishly, "Yes, your aunty is right, Bailen, like you're doing now. It is also true that the student can become the teacher. But it has come to that time where I must be going." Dell sighed. "I have a great number of things to do, without trying to do them. You are welcome for the lesson, Bailen, and I'm grateful for your company," Dell added, chuckling.

Bailen looked up at the wizard as they both collected themselves to go. "It was great to hang out with you, Dell-Shander," Bailen said with a warm smile. "I was just wondering, this was not a chance meeting, was it?"

"No, Bailen, it was not by chance," Dell-Shander answered.

"Will we ever meet again?" asked Bailen a second time.

"Oh, I think we will," answered Dell. "Your path is much greater than you realize, so keep practising with that sword and bow you carry around with you all the time. Just remember, accept yourself and accept where you are currently at right now. Stay authentic and honest. Be free spirited and live in the moment while you follow your own path. Don't plan so much and mix up your routine. It doesn't hurt to be a little spontaneous and random while stepping outside your comfort zone, Bailen. Enjoy the journey, not the outcome. Worrying about outcome only ends in disappointment. Visualize what you want and have no attachment to anything, including that fancy sword of yours you so fondly carry with pride," Dell said with a chuckle.

"I will," answered Bailen. "I'm going to save the world from the darkness, and bring it back into the light."

Dell-Shander chuckled to himself. "Best wishes to you, lad. You are wiser beyond your years," he said, still laughing. "You will go far, my young friend, and may the high gods be with you. Be careful of what you intend and wish for—it might come true," Dell said with a grandfatherly smirk and wink.

"Goodbye, Mr. Dell-Shander," Bailen said, feeling a bit different and a little more grown up. He turned away to survey the wide scenery in thought. Dell-Shander patted Bailen on the shoulder, then calmly turned and started walking down the hill. When Bailen turned to look back at Dell and wave goodbye, the wizard was not there anymore—he just simply vanished.

The differences in culture
are never quite the same;
because they are separate realities,
they don't deserve the blame.

Each one is unique
in how they act or what they do;
like individual opinions,
it's the same as me and you.

So, try to understand
and respect your fellow man;
honour other people's ways
and be open if you can.

Epilogue

A late morning of lunch and storytelling turned into an all-afternoon affair. Lounging around under the shade of the gnarly oak tree pub, my friends and I enjoyed the warm and breezy day. Many a laugh and joke had been shared and the odd lesson or two learned as well. We had drunk a few pints of ale in the process, so we all felt a little off-kilter, especially Gerald Wobble-Stick, who had a healthy little stack of empty mugs beside him.

"Well, it's late in the afternoon, and I think I should be on my way. I have told many a tale this afternoon, but that time has come for me to move on," I said.

Quinton and Aveline expressed a chorus of disappointment. "Aww, really? We were having such a good time, listening to your tales from the past, Valdevo," said Quinton.

"Yes, it was so much fun hearing stories of the recent and distant past, Mr. Bard," added Aveline.

"Well, as they say, time flies when things are fun," Denmar the dwarf chimed. "And I think someone has had a little too much to drink and can barely stay awake," Denmar added with a chuckle as he looked over at Gerald.

I chuckled to myself and shook my head in amusement. "Well, halfling's are famous for their love for fine food and fine drink," I pointed out with a smirk.

"You've got that right, Mr. Valdevo. My ale stock is a bit low, and the food pantry shelves are a little bare," replied Denmar, a little annoyed.

Quinton and Aveline snickered and chuckled at poor old Gerald, who was living up to his reputation. "The important thing is he had fun. But it looks like he may be staying the night," said Quinton.

"Don't worry about old Gerald; I'll make sure he gets home later." Denmar sighed.

As everyone began winding down from our afternoon of storytelling, I gathered my things and my lute, and packed it all on my horse.

"Where are you headed, Valdevo?" asked Aveline.

"I'm not sure. I haven't thought about it too much. But now that you ask, I think I will head west. There are lots of friendly towns and taverns along the way. And then we will see after that," I responded with a smile.

"Will we ever get to hear any more of your stories again?" asked Quinton.

"Oh, I think you will. I'm always travelling on the road. I am the wandering minstrel, you know," I said with a smirk.

"He will be around, I promise. He can't stay away from my ale. He has to experience it at least once a year," Denmar piped in, grinning.

"That I do, my friend Denmar, that I do. You have very fine ale. In fact, you have some of the finest dwarven ale I have ever tasted. But it must wait until I return," I explained. Then I mounted my horse once I was all prepared to go.

"Goodbye, Mr. Valdevo Baudelaire," said both Quinton and Aveline.

"Goodbye, my young friends. And a fine goodbye to you too, Mr. Denmar. Thank you for your generous hospitality, my friend. Tell Mr. Gerald Wobble-Stick that I said goodbye to him as well, once he wakes up," I voiced with amusement.

This brought a few chuckles from everyone, save Gerald, who was sound asleep, snoring away, in the late afternoon shade of the gnarly oak pub.

"I will be back; do not grieve. I have much more tales and legends to talk about, trust me on that. There is much more to the world than just the continent of Rithanon. And many more legends, lore, and history to be told. But as I depart, I will leave you with one more verse," I said merrily. Then I picked up my lute and played one more little poetic song after I waved goodbye to my friends, who were waving back at me as I began my slow trot down the road.

A Ray of Hope

When darkness tries to rule,
where there's a will, there is a way—
you'll always find a ray of hope,
of turning dark to light of day.

At times, you have to fight
or view all shades of grey,
but it's the small, kind things that you can do
that really keeps the dark at bay.

A Little Mythology

Immortal Conflict

When the high gods first created the world, their court was strong and all was well. But then a dark entity had permeated its way into the world and corrupted part of the immortal's court. Akurus was the first to fall; then others followed soon after. To the lower planes of the underworld abyss they went, dividing the court. They became servants of the dark unknown entity the high gods called the Destroyer, that destroys all creation and good.

Soon after the division of the court, the fallen gods erupted into conflict with the high gods. There was a mighty clash of power. The fallen gods rose from the lower planes to claim the world for their own demonic vision. They were overpowered by the high gods and were cast back down into the shadows of the lower planes. The immortals who had followed Akurus and the Destroyer were banished to dark realms. The Destroyer was harnessed in chains in the lowest and darkest bowels of the abyss, never to be released again. But the Destroyer endured and could commune with the fallen gods.

And so, ended the war of the Gods, which was later known as the First Darkness. At this time, the Pantheon Age, when the gods roamed the world, ended, and the Age of Empires began, when the mortals built mighty kingdoms and flourished. Now the world was left to the mortals, and they would be guided by the gods who sat in their domains for all time.

The Line of the Dark Lords

At the end of the Pantheon Age, at the close of the war of the Gods, Akurus pulled down the high and pure Spirit Endellion into the lower planes and impregnated her. With her body and soul imprisoned in the lower planes, Endellion gave birth to a child that held the nature of Akurus. Akurus immediately introduced the child to the world and pronounced him as the first lord of darkness. For many centuries, he would live, and his line would be long. By the design of Akurus, the firstborn son of the ninth dark lord would be the one chosen to cover the world in darkness.

But High Spirit Endellion's true spirit could not be owned, and her spirit was saved by the high gods. The spirit of Endellion was put into a vessel to one day put an end to the line of the dark lords. That vessel was a sword, and by the high gods, it was set upon the world to choose a champion that would wield Endellion and destroy the dark lord line forever. Over ages, the sword gained many names, but it would always harness the spirit of Endellion within and aid her chosen champion to seek and sweep darkness from the world.

Heart of the World

In the beginning when Earth Mother Elmathis created the first Tree of Life, known as the Silver Oak, a stone formed beneath its roots. That stone was the heart of the world, or the Mother Stone. The Mother Stone was pulled from the earth when the tree's life was spent. It became the beacon between the high gods and the natural world. It was a form of spirit and soul, connecting all of nature. But if it ever left the world, life would slowly wither. However, there was a hidden danger.

The fallen god Akurus had laid a curse on the Tree of Life. He was jealous of the union between Elmathis, the Earth Mother, and Halios, the Father of Light. And when he laid his curse, it brought anguish to the Earth Mother. This anguish went into the Tree of Life. When the tree's life was spent, its last acorn went black and Akurus claimed it for his own. Akurus planted the acorn in the earth and a black oak grew. It was called the Tree of Anguish, and when its time was done, a stone was pulled from beneath its roots, like the Mother Stone was. But this one was not of life and spirit. It was dark and sickly, full of hate, and the fallen gods relished in it. It was the heart of darkness, the Dark Stone. Akurus claimed it and gave it to the first of his sons—the first in the line of dark lords inhabiting the mortal's world. The Dark Stone would complete a regalia of power with Gramour, a powerful demon sword, and the Crown of Quitus, made of twisted iron. Together, these three items could bring the world to the dark design and vision of Akurus, as once all three aligned, a terrible power would unleash. But, if the regalia were ever to break apart, that power would fade and the light of goodness in the world would triumph over the dark.

Lore

Long ago in the times of old
in far forgotten ages told,
mortal man rose with the land,
along with elves and dwarves of bold.

The goblins came thereafter soon,
then fell into the murky gloom.
The dragons toiled but stood so loyal,
beneath the light of sun and moon.

Kingdoms rose and empires soared,
ruled by kings and many a lord.
Power was wrought and wealth was sought
by clash of arms and might of sword.

Then there fell a shadowed gloom;
the world immersed in pending doom.
The dark one's ire fuelled by fire;
a threat of conquest hung and loomed.

The gods came down with a mighty spell;
the fate of the turmoil world they held.
With dragons aid, the world was saved;
the evil of endless darkness quelled.

The kingdoms flourished again once more.
Although behind the lands closed doors,
whispers talked and, in shadows, walked
to rise again as the dark one's horde.

Special Thanks To...

I would like to thank the following people for there support in making this book possible.

I thank the FriesenPress team for their editing, illustration and design efforts and making my stories a published reality.

I thank Holly Hale and Greg Mantle for their editorial input on a few of my stories.

I thank Catherine Donnelly for the cover art.

I thank my gaming group, Alek Kingsland, Vantha Ung, Max Loran and Scott Filipowski for their input and support.

I thank all my friends and family for their support on this project of publishing the Tales of Rithanon.

Special Dedication

I dedicate the story, Brave Knights, to both of my grandfathers who served in the second world war. My grand father Wilfred Stanley on my mother's side who was in the British home gard and my grandfather Dave Johnson on my fathers side, who served in the royal Winnipeg Rifles of the Canadian army. They served so to go against a tyrannical ideology that can fester any were in the world.

About the Author

Kevin Johnson has been reading fantasy novels since he was a teenager and ran RPG Dungeons and Dragons games for twenty-eight years, though played for thirty-five. *The Tales of Rithanon*, his first book, came out of his love for fantasy, the middle ages, and ancient historical mythology.

Kevin lives on a farm outside of Nelson, BC, in a small community called Harrop-Procter, with his parents. There, he enjoys farm work, writing, and playing music.

Printed in Canada